Memoirs of a Bangkok Warrior

Memoirs
of a
Bangkok Warrior

A Novel

Dean Barrett

VILLAGE EAST BOOKS
NEW YORK

First published by Hong Kong Publishing Company, Ltd. 1983
Reprinted 1985

First trade paperback edition: 1999

Published in the United States by
Village East Books, 129 E. 10th Street, New York, NY 10003

E-mail: Village-East@mindspring.com

Web site: http://www.bookzone.com/asia

Publisher's Cataloging-in-Publication
(Provided by Quality Books, Inc.)

Barrett, Dean
    Memoirs of a Bangkok Warrior : A Novel
    / Dean Barrett — 1st trade pbk edition
    p. cm.
    LCCN: 98-87832
    ISBN: 0-9661899-2-2

    1. Bangkok (Thailand) — Fiction. 2. Americans — Thailand
    — Bangkok — Fiction. 3. Vietnamese conflict, 1961-1975 —
    Fiction. I. Title

    PS3552.A7337M4 1999   813'.54
                   QB198-12270

Printed in USA
Cover Design — Mayapriya Long, Bookwrights Design

This book is dedicated to the late Richard Casner,
one of the finest of the Bangkok Warriors,
and is written especially for those
who have somehow managed to survive
without benefit of
PX PRIVILEGES

". . . In democracies it is the private soldiers who remain most like civilians. . . . It is especially through the soldiers that one may well hope to inspire a democratic army with the same love of liberty and respect for law as has been infused into the nation itself. . . . On the other hand, it often happens in these same democratic armies that the officers contract tastes and desires entirely different from those of the rest of the nation. . . . An officer, having very different needs from those of the country may perhaps eagerly desire war or work for a revolution at the very moment the nation most longs for stability and peace."

—*Democracy in America* 1840, Alexis de Tocqueville

"Enlisted men spent their entire time in the army pissed off at the officers. . . ."

—James Jones to Maxwell Perkins 1946

"Lifers never get wasted. Just the ones I frag, that's all."

—*The Short Timers*, Gustav Hasford 1970

"Let the jury consider their verdict," the King said, for about the twentieth time that day. "No, no!" said the Queen. "Sentence first—verdict afterwards."

—*Alice's Adventures in Wonderland*, Lewis Carroll

1

OUR NATIONAL ANTHEM
12 September 1967

I knew it was going to be a malevolent day as soon as I woke up and saw that my socks were missing again. That meant either one of my roommates borrowed them or else the Thai houseboy left them in my shoes outside the door on the front porch. The Bangkok sun heated the floor all right but still I didn't like walking across the floor in my undershorts and bare feet, especially since my room was visible to our Thai neighbors over the fence. But I did. And, sure enough, there they were stuffed into my shoes on the porch. The houseboy sat hunched over a boot which he was shining meticulously with a toothbrush full of shoe polish. He looked up, brushed his tousled black hair away from his eyes with a shoe-polish-stained brown hand, and saluted: "*Sawasdee krab*," he said with a big Thai grin. He was wearing shorts and a Buddhist amulet around his neck. His T-shirt had a 'Grunt-Power' motto and a multi-colored picture of a GI throwing everybody the bird.

I gave him a quick salute and said good morning to him too. I don't know what the hell he always saluted me for. I was only a Specialist Fourth-Class finance clerk in the Army and about as unmilitary as any other ex-Hawaiian beach boy who joined the goddamned service because he knows wearing costumes and saluting lifers is inevitable anyway.

Taylor always said the houseboy was happy because we were stuck in the Army and he wasn't. But that's bull, because he was only about 17 and a pretty good guy even if he couldn't shine shoes worth a damn. I never did learn much about him because he didn't speak much English and I only learned about a hundred Thai words during my whole 18-month tour of duty in Bangkok. And most of those hundred words were swear words. You know how GIs are. They go to a foreign country and learn about a hundred words and then quit learning. Fifty of those words will be profane curses, and forty will be words to get a girl to bed for almost nothing; so that leaves ten picked up by accident. But I figured if I was going to finish changing this diary into the first memoirs ever written by an enlisted man, I'd better spend a lot of my spare time at it. So I decided the hell with learning Thai.

But I kept my notebook up to date. I can remember our room now as if I were standing in it right this minute waiting for Major Thompson, known as Blinky, and his sidekick, First Sergeant Boogle, known as Bumbles, to inspect us. There were four single bunks, wall lockers, foot lockers, one bookshelf and a small bathroom. Books, magazines, articles of civilian and military clothes and beer cans were scattered about. Several small ant-infested stuffed animals in poor condition (one-eyed rabbit, snake fighting a mongoose, birds with torn wings, etc.) were piled on a cardboard carton next to a floor fan which didn't work for shit.

On the wall were taped hand-written signs in various colors of paper and cardboard. They read: 'Fuck the Army,' 'Happiness is watching a GI who just kicked it for six more years get dicked away by a lifer,' 'Death before Re-enlistment,' and 'The shortest distance between two PXs is a lifer's footprints.' A large banner with a humorous drawing of a Vietcong was affixed to one wall proclaiming: 'Good iron does not become nails and good men do not become soldiers.'

Taylor had hung a large sheet of cardboard above his bunk with a drawing he did of a three-storied outhouse. The waste pipes of the outhouse were so constructed that when the top toilet was flushed, all the shit emptied onto the guy sitting on the seat in the room directly beneath it; and the pipes from the middle toilet bowl emptied all the shit onto the man in the one below. The top outhouse Taylor had labeled 'Congressmen,' the middle one 'officers,' and the bottom outhouse which collected all the shit from the two above he had labeled 'Enlisted Men.'

A large foldout map of Vietnam was on another wall with the printed words, '1967 Foldout Map of Vietnam.' Taylor had crossed out the word 'Foldout' and written in the word 'Pullout.' There were also calendars and movie posters of Chinese sword fighting films on the walls, the kind with sexy young Chinese starlets in tight-fitting silk outfits holding phallic-symbol swords in their hands. And I remember a collection of Chinese and Thai Buddhas was on a table next to a can of Brasso and another stuffed animal that was too ant-eaten to identify. The top of a fake ivory Goddess of Mercy statue usually had somebody's olive-green fatigue hat draped over it.

Besides myself, three GIs shared the room; or, more accurately, slept in the room. The one nearest the door, Eugene Gillis, was nicknamed (by those he didn't owe money to) 'Butterball,' which pretty well described him. He had the distinction of being the only man in the unit to outweigh Hogbody, although Hogbody's appearance was actually more ursine than porcine, and it was all muscle. It was in fact Butterball who deserved a porcine epithet, and the cigarette burns in his fatigue shirts matched his permanently bloodshot eyes so perfectly, he had been voted 'best-dressed man in the unit'. Butterball was the archetypal and rapidly disappearing type of real regular guy without pretensions that you'd like to take home to have dinner with your folks—when he was sober—which wasn't very often.

But it was in the world of the gourmand that Butterball had made his name forever. Rumor-control had it that he would tie three strands of thread around his enormous belly just before he started eating. It was only upon the breaking of the last of the threads that he would finally stop. And although it was a fact that he was always the last to leave any table, except for an occasional burp, a horrific belch and a satiated grin, Butterball himself refused to confirm or deny the charge.

Hogbody, Dick Branch, slept on the bunk nearest the wall, next to Taylor's paintings. Not paintings exactly. Our room was never without massive armies of ants which prowled the walls despite the losses of entire battalions to the waiting tongues and fat bellies of Thai wall lizards, known as *chinchooks*. Taylor regularly stole Scotch tape from the supply room and taped the columns of ants in place as they marched, along with mosquitoes, moths, millers, centipedes, spiders and whatever other living things he wanted to 'collect.' The entire wall looked like a miniature mock-up of the city of Pompeii trapped and frozen in time exactly as it might have appeared on August 24, 79 A. D., except that where, until our era, twelve feet of Vesuvian lava and ash presented problems for group tours, Taylor's transparent strips of Scotch cellophane tape allowed unhindered panoramic views of the incredible variety of anthropod armies which frequented our room.

Hogbody was as tall as Butterball, but surrounded by layers of muscle, not fat. He was the well-built, disgustingly virile, silent type whose masculine physique and obvious strength belied his extremely gentle, pacific nature. And where drink transformed Butterball's joviality into mean-spiritedness, with Hogbody, it could do absolutely nothing.

He had fallen asleep, as he always did, while reading a copy of a body-building magazine. The effort of his exercises, which he performed regularly in the Bangkok humidity, never phased him. But when it came to books and magazines, any page without a picture on it immediately put him to sleep. But from somewhere in his varied life of 28 years, he had gained insights into the fine art of living which is seldom if ever gleaned by a pair of eyeballs skimming over a printed sentence. Hogbody's reputation came from the way in which he would listen to others discuss important aspects of life and then make a comment which showed beyond any shade of doubt that he knew life as did few other men.

The other roommate was Rick Taylor; not tall, not short, not fat, not thin. Just a small unkempt mustache, incredibly hairy arms, legs, chest, and back, contact lenses he was always losing during inspections, and the biggest hate on for the Army that I saw during my entire four-year enlistment. Taylor had been a GI in Asia so long he seemed unaware that a man could meet girls *outside* of bars as well as inside, and that not every girl expected a man to buy her a drink as part of a conversation.

According to Taylor, when he was still quite young he experienced what was for him something of a religious conversion. His apostasy took place not in a cathedral or chapel, but at an American drive-in theater in the back seat of a DeSoto convertible parked in heavy shadows several rows behind the concession stand. While his girlfriend waited for him to change from his missionary position to one of a less conventional nature, he happened to glance toward the screen just as three Thai girls made a brief appearance in *Bridge on the River Kwai*. His mouth fell open and his heart, along with his other

13

functions, came to a sudden halt.

From that moment on, he was never the same. He later ascertained that the girls were 'Siamese,' from a place called 'Siam.' He addressed dozens of envelopes enclosing passionate love letters to the 'Siamese girls in the movie, *Bridge on the River Kwai*,' and sent them to the manager of the drive-in movie to be forwarded. Although he never received a reply, he never forgot them.

And then one day, years later, he learned something so incredible that his life was altered irrevocably. He learned that there were not merely the three Siamese girls whom he had seen in the picture, but literally *millions* of them, and that in a country called 'Thailand' there were cities and towns and villages and streets and lanes and squares and avenues and marketplaces and ricefields and *klongs* (canals) brimmed and glutted and sated and gorged and crammed and cloyed with girls just like them. And it was Taylor's sworn intention to brim and glut and sate and gorge and cram and cloy with them. All of them. And from that moment on, Taylor knew that whoever had said that "beauty is not confined to any one nationality" was a madman.

When I returned from the porch with my socks, Taylor had woken up and he was now searching for *his* socks. In addition to his swearing, the only other sound in the room was the incredibly loud snoring of Butterball.

Taylor was his usual self. "Christ . . . Jesus Christ . . . Damn it to hell!" He finally stopped emptying everything out of Butterball's footlocker and attempted to roll Butterball over. "So help me God, Pineapple, if Butterball took my socks again, I'll kick his ass. So help me God."

I sat on my bunk eating an imported apple stolen from the mess hall and watched him trying to move Butterball. "Saying 'So help me God' with your right hand raised is what got you into the Army, isn't it?"

He thought for a moment before continuing his struggle. "You got a point there, Pineapple. But where the hell are my socks? Butterball: Wake the fuck up!"

Butterball continued to snore. Taylor continued struggling to move his limbs and roll him over to see if his socks were on the bed. "Christ! How much does this clown weigh? If I find my socks his ass is grass and I'm gonna be the mower." Taylor suddenly saw the three broken threads encircling Butterball's waist. He started fingering the threads first in astonishment and then in disgust. "Oh, for Christ's sake! Not again."

"Better be careful," I said. "That's Guinness' *Book of Records* material you're handling."

"Yeah, Pineapple, I know the asshole's a living legend. But if he took my socks he's going off the balcony. I don't give a damn how many threads his fat gut can break."

Taylor finally acknowledged the unyielding, immovable nature of Butterball's corpulence and began searching his own wall lockers. "Damn Butterball. Some hooker on Patpong Road is probably wearing my socks right now. I'll probably find them on the black market." He grew suddenly thoughtful, the germ of an idea arresting his attention so suddenly that, for several moments, it seemed as if he too had been Scotch-taped in place. "Wait one olive-green minute. Where the hell did I find them the last time?"

I decided to be helpful. 'The houseboy put them in your shoes."

He headed for the front door with the focused determination of a lifer who has just learned there's a new PX in town. "Yeah. The houseboy, bless his ass."

I followed him out just to see if the houseboy had struck—like sadistic lightning—twice in the same day. On the porch, in front of the door, boots, shoes and belt buckles were lined up next to cans of shoe polish and cans of Brasso. Taylor stood in front of the houseboy, holding his army belt as if it were a garrote. Taylor was at his patronizing best. "Hi, Somnuck. How's it going today? Everything all right?"

Somnuck again brushed his hair out of his eyes, smiled, and saluted. Taylor returned the salute. "Good. Good. We wouldn't want anything to go wrong for you now, would we?" He sat down beside the houseboy and put his arm around him. "Brown-skinned buddy, you remember last time when I was late to work because I couldn't find my socks?"

Shallow lines of perplexity furrowed Somnuck's forehead bringing his unruly hair even more into his face. "Socks?"

"Yeah. Socks. See, your English isn't bad at all." Taylor jovially patted the houseboy's back and looked to me for confirmation. I nodded. "All right, then. You remember I told you never to put my socks in my shoes again? And you remember what I said I would do if you ever hid my socks like that again?"

Somnuck continued to smile. Taylor walked two fingers across the floor to his shoes and reached in. He hesitated, then slowly pulled out a balled-up pair of socks. He held them up and smiled at Somnuck. "Socks."

Somnuck smiled. Taylor continued to smile but shook his head. Somnuck rose and started to move backward. Taylor grinned. "Always smiling, aren't you? 'Cause I'm in the damn Army and you're not, right?" He jumped up and began moving forward with the belt. "That's why you always salute us, right? Anybody who salutes a Spec-4 is being a wiseass, right?"

Somnuck began laughing and running at the same time. Taylor ran after him. "I'll have your ass for this, mother. Come back and face it." They ran down two flights of stairs and across the second floor landing. Taylor began panting heavily and stopped without catching Somnuck. He began yelling after him. "I'll make you marry my sister for this, you hear? A vanilla-skinned, round-eye! And you're going to have to marry her!"

As Somnuck disappeared I caught up with Taylor. We were both a bit out of breath, and we leaned on the rail and looked below at the activity in the court area. As most of us kept a close countdown on the exact number of months, days and hours left until discharge, we usually referred to the court as Court Countdown. The officers' three-story office building was about 150 yards straight ahead. To our left was a swimming pool and basketball court. To our right was another four-story barracks including on the ground floor—motor pool, laundry, day room, mailroom, and the enlisted men's club, Club Victory. GIs and Thai workers were bustling about in small groups and some were entering Army vans. Thai houseboys were gathered in a circle on the lawn and using their feet, shoulders and heads to keep a rattan *takraw* ball in the air while passing it to one another. On all sides of the court, beyond the wooden fence patrolled by weeds, the wooden roofs of Thai houses and the fronds of palm trees loomed above us.

Army vans, jeeps and buses roared under our building and out of the court, bypassing a Thai guard shack with one sluggish, torpescent Thai guard and a vehicle barrier set permanently in an upright position. The rotund, middle-aged guard's state of alertness was such that he was known as Corporal Comatose, and his only activity seemed to be to smartly salute every moving object that passed his position, and, once or twice a day, to prevent aggrieved, incensed and choleric bargirls from entering the court to seek vengeance on unfaithful GIs whom, they believed, had done them wrong. Beside the seldom-used vehicle barrier was a mess hall—a one-story wooden building from which American GIs stole imported apples to offer to Thai bargirls and mama-sans and taxi drivers in lieu of cash. As Thais loved apples but could not grow them in Thailand's climate, apples surpassed both cash and credit cards in buying power. Directly below our landing was a small grassy area where GIs were playing horseshoes.

Taylor yelled to Warren Freeman, a diminutive, black GI, about to pitch a horseshoe. "Hey, Spearchucker, you gettin' better at horseshoes every day in every way?"

Freeman looked up from his hunched-over position then looked back at the stake and steadied the horseshoe in his hand. "Bite my ass," he yelled.

"Move your nose over," Taylor yelled back.

Freeman yelled again without looking up. "I want that five dollars, Rick. I'm on to something really fine downtown."

"Who's the lucky boy?" Taylor asked.

Freeman threw him the bird. Taylor and Freeman were the kind of friends who are so close they can't say a kind word to each other. But where Hogbody accepted his Army interlude with good grace, Taylor and Freeman fought it every minute of every day. After many unsuccessful ruses, Taylor had finally joined the Army when he realized he was about to be drafted.

Freeman had reported immediately to an Army doctor at a recruiting center and confidently expected his story of a bad trick knee to keep him well clear of military service. The smiling, red-faced, Norman Rockwell physician listened to Freeman's complaint with a sympathetic ear and an understanding nod, and then in a friendly manner asked when the last occasion was on which Freeman had had trouble with his knee. Freeman replied: 'October 1963' and the doctor immediately wrote in large letters across his medical records 'condition terminated October 1963', thereby facilitating Freeman's entrance into the armed services and eventual transfer to

Court Countdown.

Taylor went back upstairs, but I stood for a while leaning over the railing of the landing looking down into the court. It was about five minutes to eleven. I knew that because the chow truck left at eleven to take food out to the old house, known as the 'site,' or 'compound,' where we worked, and the mess hall in the court opened at 11:30. The truck was almost loaded so that meant I had slept about 14 hours but still felt like hell. I waved to Corporal Comatose, blew a kiss to Noy the Laundry Girl, and studied the tall, lanky figure coming in the gate. It was Roy Patterson. His clothes were all wrinkled and as he got nearer I saw the stubble on his lean and sun-burned face. That meant he had shacked with a Thai girl for the night. He looked groady as hell.

At one time, Blinky had actually encouraged his men to 'shack' with a Thai girl as he had felt that men living with the same girl were less likely to catch venereal disease. However, when the number of men present during inspections and other formations dwindled from nearly three hundred down to twenty-three, he reluctantly abandoned his V.D.-prevention policy for his men and ordered everyone to move back to the barracks.

"Hey, Roy, where you been, boy? What's a fine young Christian boy like you doing coming in the court this time of day?" Roy was from Louisiana. I never missed the chance to harass him about his accent. Although he claimed he didn't have much of an accent and that if you're from the South you can tell one southern accent from another right down to which street a person came from. He had just been transferred to Bangkok from 'upcountry' a few weeks earlier but, of the three hundred or so men in our unit, he'd been in Thailand longer than anyone except Taylor. I especially liked to call him 'boy' but he was always pretty good-natured about harassment.

"You did say 'Roy,' didn't you, Pineapple?" he asked with a big grin. He and everybody else called me Pineapple because I'm Hawaiian. "Cause for a minute there I thought you said 'boy,' then I'd have to hit you so hard you'd starve to death from bouncin' and your shirt would run up your back like a window shade. What are you doin' up so early? Hurry up and get dressed and I'll see you in the mess hall."

"Ok, Roy, hang loose. I'll be right down." I put my army belt buckle out for the houseboy to shine, got into some wrinkled civilian clothes and went down to the mess hall. I walked through the chow line, filled my tray with nameless, shapeless, boneless, odorless, tasteless masses which the black market had obviously rejected, and walked over to a table.

Taylor had managed to tear Hogbody away from his body-building magazine, and together they walked through the food line with their trays and over to Patterson's table. The room was about half full. Teenage Thai girls in dainty blue-and-white uniforms were cleaning in both the officers' section and the enlisted men's section. Ceiling fans were spinning noisily. Signs read: 'Officers' Mess' and 'Enlisted Men's Mess'.

Taylor looked at Patterson and smiled knowingly. "Well, Roy, how was she? . . . Now that's a mighty wide grin."

Patterson dangled his long arms by his chair and leaned back. "Son, I can't begin to describe it to you because you probably never had the experience. But if I get a case of the clap off her it will still be worth it."

Freeman slammed his tray on the table and sat down. "Clap? Didn't you take any precautions?"

"Sure, Freeze. I always insist that the girl be extremely beautiful. Otherwise, I keep my pecker right in my pants."

"Sounds like a safe method, all right," Hogbody said. "Where'd you take her, house or hotel?"

Patterson leaned forward again and chased a defiant formation of ants across the table with his fist. "I went to her house figuring to save the price of the hotel. But she didn't even have a mosquito net around the bed. They got me all over."

"Didn't you use Doc Spitz's Kill-the-Clap Techniques?" Taylor asked. " 'A strong rubber, a thorough wash and a good piss'?"

Patterson took a piece of liver out of his mouth, looked at it, and placed it on his tray. "Kill-the-Clap my ass. First the rubber broke. Then there wasn't any damned soap. And third, she was so good I couldn't get up from the bed, let alone walk three blocks to a damned latrine."

Taylor looked at Hogbody and grinned. "Every time I hear the adventures of the Superstud of the South my cheeks ache from laughing."

"It might not be so funny in a few days when he starts dripping pretty green dew off his petal," Hogbody said.

Freeman looked at the food on his tray. "I don't know which is worse. This food or having to listen to you animals talk. Let's get some beer and potato chips in the club."

As we left the mess hall, Taylor grabbed an empty apple carton and carried it in both hands. Patterson turned to him. "Rick, what the hell are you always carrying empty boxes for?"

Taylor gave him a long hard look before answering. "Roy, how long you been in this man's army? If I pass an officer and I've got my arms full I won't have to salute. Whore House Charlie taught me that trick just before he fought the computer. While you were still pissin' Stateside water."

Whore House Charlie was Taylor's hero, his idol, his godhead, his debauched *dingansich* to whom he paid undying homage and about whom he told unending (and unverifiable) tales of virtue and daring. The picture Taylor painted of the theanthropic being known as Whore House Charlie was that of a baby-faced GI who had been stationed many years before in Thailand, and who had used his time and considerable talents to build up and manage the most extensive system of whorehouses in the country, all rated for price, feminine pulchritude, strains of VD available, and the odds on avoiding them. Whore House Charlie, Taylor would inform those who were interested as well as those who were not, had caught the clap 18 times checking out various brothels for his customers while deciding whether or not to incorporate them into his chain.

Charlie was the Colonel Saunders of Kentucky Fried Chicken, the Ray Kroc of McDonald's, the Walt Disney of animated films and a combination Walden Books-B. Dalton chain all rolled into one. Despite vigorous but futile attempts on the part of an equally legendary enlisted man known only as Dirty McCurdy (whose affairs with supple young girls were said to have made even Charlie blush) Charlie's record of 18 cases of gonorrhea was never matched, and he remained the Babe Ruth of whorehouses as well.

Like many successful men of vision, Charlie's genius lay in seeing what was, and of immediately conceiving of what could be. It was the power-of-positive-thinking philosophy taken to its ultimate extreme. Where others saw only broken-down, mosquito-infested, rat-infested, ant-infested, spider-infested wooden houses with holes in the roofs and one or two over-the-hill prostitutes, Charlie saw not whorehouses, not even cleaned-up brothels, but *brothelariums.* Where others saw sunlight streaming through holes in the ceiling as too expensive to repair and completely intolerable even to GI customers, Charlie saw neatly squared-off or feminine-shaped holes with screens, allowing (at no extra charge) the beneficial rays of the sun to warm and caress the two (and often more) bodies writhing in ecstasy on the bed or mattress below. Charlie's redecorated and refurbished solarium-and-brothel houses were converted into a string of modern and healthful *brothelariums* which, combined with his meticulously researched Duncan Hines-type rating system of brothels, employees and diseases obtainable, were an instant success.

Taylor's hero also proved to be a genius in the field of public relations, as far from attempting to conceal his brothels from the police, which would inevitably have kept them safe but sordid, Charlie paid off the police, gave discounts to men in uniform of any kind, and personally officiated at elaborate opening ceremonies of every brothelarium branch, no matter how remote, allowing the 'mama-san of the month' to cut the ribbon. Taylor's was a euhemeristic tale in which not only was the mythological god a deified early hero, but around which a certain unorthodox liturgy had arisen. Whether or not a situation in which each ejaculation could be construed as a libation is a heinous desecration of religion or a desirable purification of iniquity is difficult to say. And while Charlie and his exploits were usually passed off as merely part of Taylor's overworked and incurably noxious imagination, even those who doubted Taylor's narratives the most reluctantly admitted there was a modicum of proof for Charlie's existence in the legendary Whore House Charlie—Computer Death Duel, which, if mentioned at all, was usually spoken of only cautiously and in whispers.

The five of us walked to Club Victory. Four of us entered the Club while Patterson remained behind to check the bulletin board. Just as Patterson was about to open the door, Blinky approached from the direction of the swimming pool. I could see what was happening from a window next to our table. Patterson couldn't make it into the club without saluting.

Blinky returned his salute and then Patterson entered the Club.

Blinky was standing near the window, which had been cracked the day before by a Singha beer can, and I could hear him talking to himself. He took out a small notebook and began writing. "That man is one of the best saluters in the unit. Definitely officer material." He put the book away, rubbed his hand along his regulation haircut, and stared meditatively. "If only all enlisted men saluted like that this war might have been over a long time ago."

The enlisted men's club had a bar to the left of the door. Thai bartenders and waiters worked in the club while American GIs—some in fatigues and some in civilian clothes—sat around tables playing cards, drinking and talking. A jukebox was usually playing and all three slot machines were constantly in use. The noise level was always loud.

Wat, a Thai bartender, walked in carrying a tray of beer. "Quiet everybody!" he shouted. "Meeting of the Tennis Elbow Club!"

As soon as Wat gave out his call, everyone stopped what he was doing and moved tables together and positioned a chair in the center of the room for Patterson. Taylor walked to the bar and picked up a small black book which Wat had placed on the counter for him. I reached into the drawer next to the cash register and pulled out the large, wrinkled, black-and-white illustration of Abraham Lincoln. None of us were certain where it had come from or even whether or not it was drawn after an actual photograph, but, for as long as anyone could remember, the photograph was hung above all sessions of the Tennis Elbow Club. The illustration showed Lincoln with his gaunt bearded face above a crooked bow tie and collar. Over the years, his visage had yellowed with age suggesting either that he had come down with a severe case of hepatitis or else was himself the product of a Thai mother and a GI father. His expression seemed to be that of a man who neither approved nor disapproved of the proceedings, but who was intensely interested in the outcome, as a bargirl might watch a fight between two GI customers only one of whom ever bought her drinks.

I stood on a stool near the quarter slot machine and taped the portrait in its place of honor, affording our welcome and distinguished *amicus curiae* an unobstructed view of American military justice. Several GIs crowded around Taylor as he sat with solemn countenance behind the table facing Patterson. Taylor tugged at his mustache and looked meaningfully around the room and at the juke box. A GI quickly pulled the plug out and the room went completely silent. Patterson began squirming. Taylor then, with due solemnity, opened the black book.

"Aw, Christ," Patterson said, "I was gonna' report it."

"Like hell you were," Freeman said.

Taylor began speaking in a solemn magisterial voice. "Hear ye, hear ye, hear ye. The 16th meeting of the Tennis Elbow Club is now in session. Specialist 4th-Class Roy Patterson, finance clerk, man of olive fatigues, college dropout, debauched devotee of Happy Hour, and known participator in PX privileges, the charge against you is a serious one." He looked toward Wat. "When did it happen, Brother Wat?"

"About 45 seconds ago, Brother Taylor."

"What is the charge, by the way?" asked a GI new to our unit.

Taylor gave the GI a disdainful look. "Wat, would you tell this ignoramus the charge?"

Wat mimicked a serious salute. Taylor pointed to Patterson who continued to sulk. "This man willingly, deliberately, unashamedly and without justifiable cause," here he paused for effect, *"saluted an officer!"*

A wave of shock and indignation swept the group. Everyone gathered even closer together around the tables. Taylor raised his right hand and spoke directly to the accused. "Do you solemnly swear that every day in every way the war is getting better and better?"

Patterson raised his right hand. "I do."

"State your name, rank and degree of inebriation."

"Roy Patterson, Spec-4, completely sober."

"Do you recognize the accused?"

"Fuck you talking about? I *am* the accused."

"Irrelevant and immaterial. You show the wrong attitude again and this court might well find you in contempt, soldier!"

"I *am* the fucking accused!"

"This court will determine who the fuck is the accused and who the fuck isn't the accused! Not you!"

"Well, am I the fucking accused or not?"

"That will be determined according to the time-tested methods of military justice. Anyway, moving right along, whether you're the accused or not, how do you plead?"

"I need more time to prepare my defense. I need a postponement."

"Postponement! How do we know you'll show up for trial!"

"Hey, man, I'm in the fucking Army! Where the fuck am I gonna go? Just release me on my own recognizance."

A GI at the back turned to the guy next to him. "What did he say he owns?"

"A recognizance."

"No shit. I had one of them once. I souped up the engine and that baby could take off from a red light faster than—"

"A recognizance ain't a car, asshole, it's a kind of border collie; mean motherfuckers too. Ours bit my little brother's finger clean off!"

Another GI yelled out. "What's a recognizance?"

Another answered. "If it was up your ass you'd know what it was."

"Oh yeah? Who the fuck's gonna' put it up my ass?"

"I will, asshole."

"You and whose army?"

Taylor spoke in a controlled scream. "Anytime you gentlemen would like to pay some respect to this court, you just let me know, because if you don't shut the fuck up, I'll have Hogbody clear the court." Taylor took a deep breath and turned back to Patterson. "Sorry, Roy, but it seems this court is fresh out of recognizances. So let's continue along the line of march. How do you plead?"

Patterson swallowed his anger and managed to speak contritely. "Guilty."

"In that case—"

"With extenuating circumstances," Patterson added in a tremulous but loud voice. His plea was met with an immediate outburst of raucous jeers and obscene gestures.

Taylor held up his hand. "Remember, brothers, this is *military* justice. We must hear the extenuating circumstances and all the evidence before we dick him away. You may proceed, Specialist Patterson."

Patterson was at his plaintive best. His southern accent reeked with ingenuous sincerity. "I didn't see him coming until it was too late. I wasn't carrying anything. There was no way out."

Taylor looked around the room. "What do you say, brothers?"

"Why him no pretend to faint!" shouted Wat.

Immediately everyone agreed and began crying for blood. Taylor made an entry in the book. "Guilty as charged. Free drinks on Roy." Cheers filled the room.

"Shit," Patterson said. He climbed unsteadily onto a chair. "Wait one olive-green minute. Out of the 16 sessions of the Tennis Elbow Club this is only my second offence. And Rick is a hanging judge. He's never found anybody innocent of anything. I demand another judge review the case."

Freeman ran over to Taylor's seat and pushed him out of it. He began speaking in an exaggerated black accent. "All right, bo'. Here de' judge. How you plead?"

"Not guilty," Patterson said.

Freeman looked at him for several seconds before speaking. "Brother Patterson," he said at last, "you are aware are you not that this is a military court and any plea in a military court must be relevant."

Patterson seemed confused. "What's relevant?"

"Anything that aids in dicking away the accused," said Freeman. "In this case, you. Anything that doesn't is irrelevant. So, Brother Patterson, if you're not going to help hang your ass, you're no friend of this court. So pay for the goddamned beer and shut your goddamned mouth."

"But I didn't even have a goddamned lawyer!"

Taylor was thoughtful. He leaned over and spoke to Freeman. "Maybe he's right, Freeze." He called to Wat behind the bar. "Brother Wat, you have just been appointed as Roy's lawyer. Raise your right hand. Do you solemnly swear that every day in every way the war is getting better and better?"

"I do."

"How should he plead?"

Wat's face broke into a broad smile. "Him guilty!" Patterson's protest was drowned in the applause.

Patterson was adamant. "If he's my lawyer, he can't testify

as a witness; so you got no witness. So there!"

Freeman thought for a moment. He looked at Patterson. "Does the accused have his own lawyer?"

Patterson became confused. "Of course I got a lawyer. You just appointed him."

Freeman continued. "And does the accused have his own witness?"

"Have a witness? What the hell you talking about?"

"Very well. This court will appoint a witness for the accused. Hogbody, you have been appointed as witness for the accused. Please raise your right hand."

Patterson was too nonplused to speak. Hogbody stood and raised his right hand. Freeman continued. "Do you solemnly swear that every day in every way the war is getting better and better?"

"I do."

"Please be seated."

"I am seated."

"Are you showing contempt for this court? Because if you are—"

"I'm saying, moron, that I *am* already fucking seated!"

"Fine, be a hostile witness for all I give a shit. In any case, you are now a court-appointed witness in a court determined to seek out justice, that is, military justice. The court assumes, therefore, that you do, in fact, agree with the prosecution."

"I do."

"Specialist Patterson, both your lawyer and your witness say that you are guilty. Therefore this court has no choice but to find you guilty as charged. You will not converse with any person whatsoever outside this courtroom regarding the proceedings inside this courtroom."

"Fuck you and the horse you rode in on! Hogbody's right; you're a moron."

"Hearsay is not admissible evidence."

A GI in khakis opened the door. He was working for the orderly room as charge-of-quarters for the day. For a few moments he watched as everyone called for free beer on Patterson while Patterson screamed obscenities at the court's 'witless witness.' He finally shouted above the noise. "Hey, Rick! Blinky wants to see you."

"Oh, Christ," asked Taylor, "now what?" Then the C.Q. spotted me. "You too, Pineapple. He said he wanted to see both of you. On the double!"

Taylor and I followed the C.Q. out of the Club. Halfway across the court, I spotted the Thai neighbor's kid hiding in the leaves of a jackfruit tree on their side of the fence. His grenade (always some kind of fruit depending on the season—this time a banana) finished its wobbly arc and tumbled near me. I quickly shoved Taylor to the ground, threw myself to the ground, and drew my imaginary .45.

I shouted. "VC!"

Taylor immediately joined in, drawing his own imaginary .45. He spoke to the C.Q. "Get down, you fool! VC!"

The C.Q. was new to the unit and apparently hadn't gotten the word that a few of the kids in the neighborhood enjoyed hiding in palm and jackfruit trees and picking Taylor and me off with their fruit-flavored weapons. He panicked and hit the dirt. His glasses flew out and landed several feet from him. Taylor and I made appropriate sounds of weapons being fired as we aimed at the kid who also made appropriate sounds of a weapon being fired. As the kid drew back to throw another grenade (banana), we got off several imaginary rounds and he screamed and fell from the tree out of sight, hidden by the fence. Taylor and I knew the kids had set up a mattress there specifically for the purpose of happily being shot dead by American finance clerks.

Taylor stood up. "Got the sucker."

I stood up, grabbed the banana and started peeling it. "How many's that?"

"Thirty-four."

"Body counts sure do add up." I chomped down on the banana and offered some to the C.Q. "Thai bananas are good, man!"

The C.Q. stood up, retrieved his glasses, and brushed off his now dirt-streaked khaki uniform. "Jesus Christ, you people are nuts!"

Taylor shook his head and walked toward Blinky's office. "War is hell."

We crossed the court and walked up the stairs to Blinky's office with the self-pitying attitude of a prostitute who's just learned her biggest spender's being transferred to another duty station. I was silent but Taylor swore all the way. We sat in the orderly room outside Blinky's door.

"Now what did I do?" Taylor asked, more to himself than to us. The C.Q. shrugged his shoulders. "Beats me." Taylor spotted a *chinchook* lizard on the wall and began sticking his tongue out at it whenever the lizard stuck its tongue out. He continued this for a few minutes. I happened to glance behind us and noticed that Blinky had his door open and was watching Taylor.

Taylor spoke to the clerk. "Hey, I think I've learned to communicate with Bangkok's lizard population."

Blinky exploded. "Specialist Taylor!"

Taylor jumped up and turned around. "Yes, sir!"

"If you're finished!"

"Yes, sir!"

We entered Blinky's office and stood in front of his desk as he sat down behind it. Out of the corner of my eye I saw Sgt. Bumbles smirking at his desk.

31

Blinky was short but not excessively fat. He just looked pudgy. His accent and build always reminded me of George Wallace. Blinky was only slightly less abdominous than Butterball, and when he smiled, which was only to an officer of higher rank, his teeth reminded me of an uncooked corn-on-the-cob; small, even, close together and in alternating patterns of white and yellow. There was also one tooth which had a greenish cast to it, which may have confirmed Taylor's claim that Blinky had become so enamored with the olive-green color of fatigues that he had olive green fillings placed in his teeth.

Except during inspections and sessions in which he could give vent to his hatred for enlisted men, the only time we saw Blinky out of doors in Bangkok's heat and humidity was when he put on his enormous red, white and blue swimming trunks and climbed into the pool. Blinky always wore his oak leaves well-polished and perfectly positioned and, occasionally, after an evening of little sleep and a great deal of booze, he would show up wearing enormous aviator spectacles, the type designed for use when witnessing atomic explosions or when forced to gaze upon an enlisted man.

Bumbles was a bachelor and a First Sergeant, and his sign of rank, which appeared on each of his sleeves, was a diamond located midway between six yellow stripes; which for us always represented a GI at bay surrounded and hounded by Army Regulations. He was thin to the point of emaciation with a long nose, a prominent forehead, and a nasty pair of hard black eyes that were constantly on the lookout for 'discrepancies' which he would write up in his discrepancy book. Bumbles was the only Vietnam veteran who was actually stationed with our unit. Not that he had ever fought in Vietnam or anywhere outside of a bar; rather, every month he would hop a military flight passing over Vietnam or making a ground stop in Saigon on the way to Taiwan. Then he'd come right back again. In that way, military personnel could get out of paying taxes for the month. Bumbles was a veteran of thirteen trips passing over or briefly through the war zone. His increased take-home pay appropriately reflected his valor.

In addition to the military, Bumbles had delved deeply into other areas of life as well, including political science, philosophy and theology. As far as political systems were concerned, socialism was "a pain in the ass" and communism was "a royal pain in the ass." Regarding the possibility of other forms of life in the universe, Bumbles was very open-minded on the subject, although he was heard to say that "man for man in a fair fight, the American fighting man can whip the ass of any bug-eyed being or space-man stupeedo on any planet, gravity or no gravity." (Steven Spielberg take note.) And, of course, his faith in the Almighty was absolute although he did feel our unit had more than its share of "dickhead chaplains" whose "candy-ass sermons" were so vague that sometimes one could hardly tell whether they were "serving in God's cause" or "rooting for the gooks." And even his enmity toward "the gooks" was tempered with a modicum of respect. Whereas Dr. Kissinger was later to describe Vietnamese as "just a bunch of shits; tawdry, filthy shits," Bumbles once praised "the gooks" because they fought well even though they "couldn't even speak bargirl English."

His often-expressed views on abortion were simultaneously diametrically opposed to one another. On the one hand, he would often end a discussion by shrugging his thin shoulders and murmur, "that's the way the cookie crumbles." On the other hand, he often bemoaned the fact that "if some of those kids had lived they would have made fine soldiers." Apparently, everyone deserved a chance to live to kill.

Wherever Blinky went Bumbles was sure to go. He was so

often peering over Blinky's shoulder to give us menacing looks that we began to think of Blinky as a dicephalous ogre having one pudgy body and two heads.

Like all American military officers, both would pronounce Vietnam to rhyme the 'Nam' with 'slam'. And, of course, Thailand became 'thighland'. Blinky's voice was even deeper than Hogbody's and he had a southern accent besides. He was a master of barely controlling his nearly uncontrollable anger. The angrier Blinky became, the more he spoke from the side of his mouth until finally, as he approached apoplexy, it seemed as if a disembodied voice was speaking from somewhere off to the side and to the rear while Blinky himself only pretended to be pronouncing the words.

Whenever one of us was called before him to account for our actions, he worked his emotions like a puppet show—first red-hot anger entered stage left, then a trace of sympathy. Next came the man-to-man, "you-can-talk-freely-to-me" discussion, and, finally, the concluding delivery wrapped in no-nonsense, military bearing. It was the Blinky symphony, in four unvaried movements.

Whenever he talked to enlisted men not only did his accent get deeper—his grammar got worse. I guess he figured that way we'd feel he was on our level, so that we enlisted men could identify with him even if we could never hope to understand the crises he faced and the solutions he found on our behalf. His blinking was probably the result of a nervous condition, although he gave the impression that only by blinking frequently could he hope to keep the necessary but regrettable sight of enlisted men from forming too lasting an image on his brain.

Taylor saluted. "Specialist 4th-Class Richard Taylor reporting as ordered, sir." I also saluted and just started to speak.

He held up his hand to stop me. "One at a time," he said,

"one at a time." Which was exactly the phrase used by upper-class prostitutes in Bangkok's Chinatown area when rejecting innovative GI proposals for group-tour 'special service.' He began drumming his fingers and searching for words. He was looking through a file on his desk. Finally he began to speak in an I-loath-you-but-am-too-fine-an-officer-to-ever-show-it voice. "Specialist Taylor, I see you have a university degree in *Chinese* Studies. That right?"

"Yes, sir."

Blinky continued as if uncovering a particularly insidious communist plot. "Took a lot of *film* courses, too, didn't you?"

"Yes, sir."

Blinky finally closed the file with a nod that clearly indicated that whatever we had done hadn't fooled him. Not by a long shot. He folded his hands on his desk. "Specialist Taylor, it has been brought to my attention by another member of this command, . . ." he looked toward Bumbles who continued to smirk, ". . . that you have been spreading the idea of changing our national anthem from the 'Star Spangled Banner' to 'America the Beautiful'. Is that correct, Specialist Taylor?"

Taylor seemed bewildered. His luxuriant chest hair sprouted above his civilian shirt in disordered confusion. "Well, yes, sir, but I just thought that we could demonstrate our loyalty better by—"

A red-faced Bumbles erupted from behind his desk. "Demonstrate! Did you hear that, sir? He admits he wants to demonstrate! Of all the communist stupeedos I've ever—"

Blinky spoke firmly. "Sergeant, *I* will handle this matter."

Bumbles continued to glare at Taylor but reluctantly resumed his seat.

Blinky continued his interrogation. "Specialist Taylor: I am fully aware that you have never had officer training but don't you see how your suggestion plays into the hands of the communists?"

"Communists? Sir, I—"

"Have you given any thought, Specialist Taylor, to what the consequences would be if we changed our national anthem to America the Beautiful?"

Taylor turned to me for assistance but I had already put my mimetic ability to good use by becoming a pen-and-pencil set, or water cooler or desk and chair, which was what I became in any potentially volatile situation involving military officers.

Even for trained soldiers there are only four human responses possible to serious crisis situations: attack, retreat, paralysis and manipulation. As Blinky made it clear that enlisted men are unable to see the Big Picture, it naturally followed that we didn't know when to attack and when to retreat; hence, attack and retreat were not for us. The ability to manipulate one's surrounding was also clearly not for those expected to unhesitatingly follow orders from above; hence, manipulation was only for officers and civilians. That left only one possible reaction for an endangered enlisted man; also the one most commonly employed by Thailand's ubiquitous wall lizards—paralysis; and we had become adept at it. Hence, our situation was not a tetralemma, or even a dilemma, as our *only* hope during such crises was to remain absolutely still and to noiselessly transform ourselves into innocuous inanimate objects which might escape the notice and, hopefully, the wrath, of our superiors.

Taylor turned again to face Blinky. "Sir—"

"No, Of course you haven't." His tone varied between unspeakable anger and unutterable sorrow, promising both spittle *and* tears. He looked down at his desk, scratched the back of his red neck, and gave an I-try-my-best-but-can't-seem-to-get-through-to-them sigh. Then he looked up at Taylor and spoke in a bombs-bursting-in-air voice. "As you're not an officer, you're not in a position of command authority and so you're unable to see the big picture. But, God, man, *think* before you make such statements! If we change our beloved anthem to one which is easier to sing, then just about *anybody* could sing it. Right, Specialist Taylor?!"

"Major, if—"

"*Right,* Specialist Taylor?"

"Yes, sir."

"Isn't it possible," continued Blinky, "that under those conditions even—even—even *enlisted men* would be able to sing our national anthem! Didn't think of *that,* did you? *GIs* singing our national anthem! You didn't, did you!"

Taylor's mouth opened and closed several times before any words came out. Unnoticed to anyone else in the room, I had transformed myself from a pen-and-pencil set into the most unobtrusive lamp in the entire court. I was convinced that my camouflage rendered me completely invisible to all enemies—foreign or domestic.

"No, sir, I—"

Blinky nodded and held up his hand to cut off any apology or defense Taylor might have offered. It was a now-you-see-what-I've-been-trying-to-tell-you nod. "Of course you didn't, man." He tapped the file. "You're educated but *untrained.* But let that be a lesson to you to leave the decision-making to your superiors. There's a war on, you know."

"Yes, sir."

For a moment, Blinky's eyes began to cloud over, and his expression was that of a man who knew he was equal to a great task set before him, like a prostitute who has just learned that her bar is once again on limits to the military. "Fortunately, every day in every way that war is getting better and better." He placed his hand on a book on his desk. It was *The Power of Positive Thinking.* Next to the book was a red, white and blue sign which read: 'He can who thinks he can,' and his name plate: 'Major John Thompson.' He continued to speak with his nervous habit of blinking frequently. "Now, raise your right hand and repeat after me," he said. "Every day in every way. . . ."

After a split-second hesitation Taylor raised his hand and responded, "Every day in every way. . . ."

"The war is getting better and better."

Taylor spoke as solemnly as Blinky. "The war is getting better and better."

Blinky then stared at Taylor for a few moments, like a mama-san might stare at one of her bargirls who forgot to ask for money after a screw, infuriated but still capable of giving absolution. Finally he shouted: "Dismissed!"

Taylor saluted, turned and exited. Bumbles's eyes followed Taylor out the door with a long you-commies-think-you're-smart-trying-to-fuck-with-our-national-anthem-but-God-and-the-Army-will-show-you-in-the-end glare.

Blinky patted the book a few times. Then he turned to me. His blinking increased. "Specialist, it has been brought to my attention that you failed to salute an officer last Thursday at the operations compound, is that correct?"

"Sir, I—"

"Specialist, you may be a finance clerk and Bangkok may not be the center of the war, but there is a war on and we've got a job to do, is that clear?"

"Sir—"

Blinky began shouting. "You men are soldiers first and finance clerks second. I suppose you think this war isn't vital to the security of your country, is that it? Is that why you didn't salute?"

"No, sir," I said. "As a matter of—"

"You may not respect me but you've got to respect my uniform and by the same token you may not respect the men fighting in the war but you got to respect the war. Is that clear?"

"Yes, sir, I do respect the men fighting in the war very much, sir."

"Good." Blinky continued to speak with more than a trace of spittle. "It's not the glove that counts, it's the man behind it. When the going gets tough the tough get going. Now repeat after me." Blinky again placed his left hand on the book and raised his right hand. "Every day in every way. . . ."

I immediately raised my hand. "Every day in every way. . . ."

'The war is getting better and better."

"The war is getting better and better."

Blinky managed a smile. "That's the spirit, soldier. A little positive thinking. I know you're doing a fine job, checking the finance records of our boys in Vietnam, but remember, there are no boys in my outfit only *men*—and *men* salute! Is that clear?"

"Yes, sir!"

Blinky saluted and I returned his salute, and on a scaffolding, outside the window behind him where he could not see, smiling, dark-skinned, male and female Thai workers in wide-brimmed hats and sarongs also saluted.

"Dismissed!"

"Yes, Sir!"

I turned to go, walked to the door, opened it and walked into the C.Q.'s office. The door remained slightly ajar and I turned to close it properly. Just before I did, I saw through the crack that Blinky was now standing in front of the mirror on his office wall. In his hand he was holding the book: *The Power of Positive Thinking.* He was staring intently into his own eyes. I could barely hear the words: "Every day in every way the war is getting better and better. Every day in every way the war is getting better and better. Every day—"

No freelance prostitute stealing the wallet of an inebriated, snoring GI in a short-time hotel room ever closed a door more quietly.

2

BANGKOK WARRIORS
18 September 1967

Jack's Off' bar was about the same as all the other bars in Bangkok catering mainly to *farang,* or foreigners, except that there were paintings of buxom nude Asian girls hanging on the wall. And Jack, the owner whom no one ever saw because he was always "off," apparently paid the local police enough so that he could ignore the latest police ordinance which insisted that people's faces must be recognizable at a distance of six feet. New lights had been added but they were still kept lower than Blinky's I.Q. We would crowd into one of the booths inside the dimly-lit room, and imbibe several quarts of Singha beer as bargirls and customers crowded around the bar or sat around in other booths. On the wall behind the bar was a large rectangular sign which read: "Free Beer Tomorrow!"

Each and every time we visited the bar, Taylor would approach the obese middle-aged mama-san and point to the sign. "Hi, Mama-san, how about some of that free beer?"

The mama-san would always turn around to look at the sign, lines of puzzlement appearing on her forehead, as if she and Taylor had never indulged in this ritual dozens of times before. She would turn back to Taylor and say—not without a certain amount of irritation at his inability to understand simple English—"Tomorrow!"

Needless to say, the day never came when we got the free beer, but, according to Hogbody, there was a valuable life lesson to be learned here.

I especially remember the night we had Wat with us. He walked up to the booth, arms laden with beer. "Why we celebrate?" he asked.

Taylor punched Roy in the shoulder. 'This lucky son-of-a-bitch is going on leave tomorrow."

Patterson hesitated. Despite his indifferent shrugs his handsome, narrow face creased with concern. "Oh, I might not go," he said.

"Why the hell not?" asked Taylor. "You've been saving for six months."

Patterson began to squirm. "Well, I haven't really got enough."

"How much you got?" Hogbody asked.

Patterson sighed. "It's a matter of 'how much did she get'."

Freeman began laughing. "Jesus! Don't tell us Superstud got rolled!"

"It's all Doc Spitz's fault," Patterson said. "I decided to try his kill-the-Clap theories so after I finished I went into the shower to 'wash thoroughly'. That's when she made off with my wallet."

Hogbody was incredulous. "You went to a short-time hotel with your savings in your pocket?"

"And his head up his ass, no doubt," Taylor added.

"I was smashed," Patterson said in defense.

"Which bar did you take her from?" Freeman asked. "We can find her."

Patterson slunk lower in the booth. "She wasn't from a bar."

Hogbody was more incredulous. "You took a *freelancer* to a

short-time hotel with your leave money in your wallet?"

Patterson repeated his litany with no hope of salvation. "I was smashed."

"Jesus Christ, Roy," Taylor said. "How could you keep that much money on you? I mean everybody has an asshole, but not everyone is one. You may qualify for the flying, gaping, screaming, diarrhetic, dripping asshole award."

"Nice of you guys to try to cheer me up," Patterson said.

Suddenly a bargirl walked quickly by the booth. Butterball grabbed her and pulled her onto his lap. Her name was Dang and she was one of our favorites—learned, wise, cagey, foul-mouthed, hot-tempered and unable to hide a heart of gold. Dang's only problem was that she was something of a schizophrenic. Like many Bangkok Thais, one of her parents had actually been a Chinese who had immigrated into Thailand, and one had been a native-born Thai. Dang would wake up one day and, even before climbing out of bed and starting negotiations with her bed partner, she would be consumed with a sudden and intense hatred for Thailand's Chinese community as they had taken complete control over the country's economy and, as everyone knew, were grasping, cunning and treacherous. Every other day she would wake up seething with a fanatical and barely controllable loathing for the Thais, whom she said wouldn't even have an economy at all if it weren't for the country's Chinese population, and, as everyone knew, the Thais were unsophisticated, ignorant and downright obtuse.

Butterball began the usual question-and-answer opening. "Where's Jack—"

Before he could finish Dang completed the sentence, "Off." She began feeling Butterball's stomach. "God, Butterball get fatter all the time. Hey, when you tell me what you *do*?"

Taylor spoke up, "We're freelance latrine inspectors temporarily attached to the T-69th mess kit repair squadron. We unbend spoons, sharpen knives and count forks."

Butterball began fondling her ass. "Listen, why don't you and I—"

Dang pulled his hands away. "Never happen, GI. You number ten butterfly. Butterfly he go flower to flower but no love any. Same same you. Go girl in bar to girl in next bar but when come time to make your mind, you no can do. Butterfly same same Butterball."

As both bargirls and GIs are relegated firmly to the lowest point on any society's totem pole, any sustained relationship between members of the two groups encountered more than the normal share of male-female entanglements, including consecutive and even simultaneous displays of genuine affection and intense loathing, unshakable fidelity and casual betrayal, cunning deceit and childlike candor.

Butterball mustered his most pained expression. "Dang, you know I'm always on standby for you."

"Yeah, that your problem," she said. "It can only stand by." She yelled to another bargirl. "Hey, Noy. Bring one beer." Then she turned to Hogbody. "Noy just come this bar. She got big tits. You like her, I know. She married Air Force but he go States now. Send her money sometimes. She got baby by him. Name Robert."

"I suppose he sends her money to help buy medicine for her poor mother up north and to help put her younger brother through school," Taylor said.

Dang tilted her head and looked at Taylor suspiciously. "How you know she have sick mother up north and brother in school?"

"Every bargirl has a sick mother up north," Taylor said. "How else can she get money from her boyfriend to buy lots of new dresses? Right?"

Dang punched toward him but missed. "Shit! GIs know too much."

"But not Air Force?"

Dang smiled maliciously. "No. Zoomies believe everything pretty face say."

Noy brought the drink and sat on Taylor's lap. A fight between R&R GIs broke out near the door. Everyone turned briefly to look. Although there was little contact between R&R GIs and GIs stationed in Bangkok, the inevitable brawl did occur. For our part, we were seldom happy to see GIs from Vietnam in Bangkok because with their (sometimes accurate) 'today-we-live-tomorrow-we-die' attitude, they spent so freely the bargirls became used to Big Spenders, making us look like "number ten Cheap Charlie Bangkok GIs."

But the main war was less overt and far more deadly, in that it was not the threat of physical violence that made us shudder when GIs on leave from the 'Nam entered our favorite nightspots; rather, it was the knowledge that the venereal diseases they passed on to the girls we screwed would undoubtedly reach us. And as Doc Spitz had said on more than one occasion, with a mixture of pride, defiance, and bewilderment, "I don't give a damn how many new miracle drugs they come up with, some of the strains of VD coming out of this war are fantastic, and no son-of-a-bitch, candy-ass, test-tube analyst will find a cure in our lifetime. You can bet your ass on that."

It was, of course, a different part of our anatomy that lay more directly in the line of fire, whose fate, as it were, hung in the balance. But like the VC, VD was now presented as a kind of familiar, old-world underdog struggling heroically against an insentient scientific adversary, and its persistence in the face of all odds seemed, to Doc Spitz, at least, if not cause for rejoicing, at least deserving of respect.

"Shit! Another fight," Dang said disgustedly. "Why they no save fight for the war?"

"Cause Charlie won't fight in bars," Taylor said, "only in jungles."

"I think that why Charlie win," she said.

The fighting behind us increased in intensity as American MPs and Thai police arrived to break up the brawl. Taylor was upset because a German tourist had taken one of his favorite bargirls to Pattaya Beach for the weekend just when he wanted that particular girl the most. A German tourist on Patpong was a rarity then; little did we know that in the years to come, when the last American GI was long gone from Thailand, Germans and Swiss would not only crowd the bars as tourists, but would also jointly own most of those same bars with their mandatory Thai partners. But it was Patterson's long face that caught Dang's eye. "Why Roy sad tonight?"

"Some Superscrew took Superstud for all of his leave money," Butterball said.

"How much he lose?"

"About four hundred and fifty dollars."

Another bargirl called for Dang and Noy to take care of new customers. Dang got up. "We go now."

Butterball was outraged. "Hey, our two girls are deserting us for somebody else because we're broke."

"Yeah," Patterson added. "Number ten girls and number ten bar."

Dang was indignant. "This number one bar!" She said proudly. "I number one girl. We come back." Her shapely hips and sexy legs carried her off into the darkness of the bar.

"Goddamn women," Wat said. "All butterfly." Wat's engaging coprolalia was not his only benefit from American GI-Thai bartender acculturation. In no time at all, he began exhibiting other identifiable traits of the American enlisted man: a studied interest in and obsession with the size of mammary glands; the ability to both recognize and dispense with untruths with a terse and somewhat common one-word description of taurian excrement; and an attitude toward military officers which matched and, perhaps, even exceeded our own in antipathy. Hence, "big tits," "bullshit," and "lifer puke" were now the mainstays of his conversation.

"How come every Thai around American GIs swears more than I do?" Taylor asked.

"Goddamn!" Wat said. "I never swear on the farm. Only after I come to goddamn GI camp to mix your goddamn drinks. My father want me to be monk or teacher or farmer. Now I bartender. Shit. I had to go, anyway. Goddamn."

"Why?" Taylor asked.

"My father want me to marry goddamn ugly girl. But maybe after working bar for goddamn American GIs, I be ready to marry anybody."

"Come on, Wat, knock it off," Taylor pleaded. "If I laugh too hard I miss my period."

Dang, Noy and the bar's mama-san suddenly returned to the table and handed Patterson a fistful of Thai money. "Here money for your trip," Dang said. "All no good number ten girls got most and number ten bar put up the rest. You pay back when you get, OK?"

As Dang sat on Patterson's lap, Taylor took the money and thumbed through it. "Well, come on, Roy, what do you say?" Taylor asked. "This fistful of play money is worth about four hundred and ten real dollars."

"I love you, Dang," Patterson said. He leaned forward to kiss her.

"Hey!" she pushed his face away. "You can bullshit some bargirls all time, and you can bullshit all bargirls sometime, but you no can bullshit all bargirls all time."

Patterson spoke more to himself than to us. "Haven't I heard that somewhere before?"

Taylor got up. "Whiz time."

"Good idea," I said. "I'll join you."

Dang yelled to us just as we went in the door. "Mention my name and you get good seat."

We stood in front of the urinal pissing. My eyes were on a level with the largest of the wall's graffito, three meticulously printed words in blue ink informing all who presented their johnsons that, 'dinks don't bleed.'

Two young Americans entered the men's room behind us. They were neither very old nor very drunk but there was something about their eyes and even their movement which made them appear as old men made up to look young. Finally, as they moved closer, the cumulative effect of their pallid, grey skin, the fixed gazes, and the invisible but almost tangible aura of death and decay embalming them spelled out what disease it was that separated and isolated them from others: *too much war.*

And they were threatening; not in a physical sense, but because they looked to have traveled beyond the pale of human values and seen how delicately those values were constructed and how easily they could be unraveled. Although they couldn't articulate their psyche's voyage through the obscenities of war, they had been irrevocably altered by it. It was a hideous perversion of Maugham's reflection: "I do not bring back from a journey quite the same self that I took." What we saw of them was only what was left.

One took a place beside Taylor and one beside me. They also began pissing. The first one had a beer can in his hand. He was thin, wiry, and a nervous twitch tugged at one side of his mouth. He looked at Taylor, then spoke across us to his friend. "That's one of them, all right. Bangkok Warriors." Then he spoke directly to us. "How long you been here?"

"A long time," Taylor answered. "R&R?"

"On R&R from the big, bad war," said the first GI. "And I'm supposed to try to make up for a lost year in five fucking days." He stared at Taylor. "Yeah, I know. My hair turned white and I'm supposed to be shell-shocked. All fucked up!" He hadn't pissed but he flushed his urinal by pulling a chain. He put his tool in his pants and zipped up. "I was sitting in a Saigon bar feeling up a bargirl and I heard a clump on the other end of the bar near the door. So I turned to see what made the clump and it was a grenade that done that."

The second GI walked toward him. "Fred," he said. "I'm all set if you are. Let's call it a night."

But the first GI ignored his companion's advice, and continued. "It rolled down between my beer bottle and glass. I said: 'I'll be damned. A grenade.' The bargirl froze up with fear but I figured Charlie had my number so I just picked up my glass, took a swig, stood up and walked out. But the damn place didn't blow until I was outside. The bargirl—" before he could finish his sentence his throat and face tightened and he rushed to the sink to vomit.

His companion held his shoulders in a way that suggested he'd done it a lot of times before and turned to Taylor to finish the sentence. 'The bargirl got hers ducking behind the bar. She didn't have a face left."

The first GI turned around. "And she got it because she had been near me; because of all of us over there!" Then he spoke more quietly. "I guess I snapped after that. They told me I ran around screaming and swearing." He put his arm around his companion's shoulders. "Bill, here, had to tackle me. Didn't you, Bill?"

"Yeah, Fred."

"But you remember what you said?" Fred continued. "About how I didn't scream 'that bastard gook' or 'those bastard Charlies.' What'd I scream, Bill? Tell him. Tell the Bangkok Warrior what I said."

"You said, 'that bastard, Johnson,' Fred. Now let's—"

Fred interrupted. "And who'd I say I was gonna' kill when I got back to the real world? Tell 'im, Bill. Come on."

"'John Wayne', Fred. You said you was gonna kill John Wayne."

Fred looked at Taylor, and then at me. "Can you imagine that?" He attempted to take a drink from the beer can but his hand began to shake violently.

Bill spoke softly. "Fred."

Fred tried to steady himself. "You know, it's a joke. We can't find Charlie." Bill began leading him out. Fred continued speaking as Bill helped him toward the door. "Fighting for peace. Do you believe it? That's like fucking for virginity." He crushed the beer can in his hand and threw it across the men's room.

When Taylor and I returned to our booth, Fred was just following Bill out the door. Fred stood for a moment in the doorway like an illusory spectral warrior, turned to us and gave a slow salute. Taylor and I returned the salute and the door closed. We sat down again at our booth which, thanks to more rounds of beer, and an influx of bargirls, was now the liveliest in the bar. No one had noticed Bill or Fred. I suddenly felt the need to celebrate being alive. I raised my glass of beer and said: "A toast! A toast to the Bangkok Warriors!"

In the sudden silence that followed, Taylor picked up his glass and held it high. "The Bangkok Warriors!"

Among officers it is not necessary to know the strategic value of a village in order to bomb it, and, among enlisted men, it is not necessary to understand the meaning of a toast in order to drink to it. Hogbody followed our lead immediately. "Bangkok Warriors!" And in the wake of Hogbody's booming voice we all drank up.

3

THE CHAPLAIN'S LAST SERMON
25 September 1967

Those of us stationed in Bangkok during the 1960s did not have the advantage of a plethora of books, plays and films to interpret to us the Why and Wherefore of 'our' Vietnam experience. But we did have one great advantage over those who have never experienced military life: we had the complimentary (and mandatory) service of an interpreter who alone, in the face of doubt and confusion, understood fully, and, in the presence of ignorance and error, revealed patiently why America had decided to challenge the process of Vietnamese nationalism.

And perhaps it is precisely because those of us stationed in Bangkok during The War were merely on the edge of the action, that I can see clearly that multi-media coverage of America's longest nightmare—then and now—has failed to do justice to the one man whose task it was to interpret the slaughter to men no longer open to interpretations. I mean, of course, the chaplain. The man who succeeded in splicing together the ultimate feature-length Gothic of Christian faith and saturation bombing into one meaningful and desirable double feature. The assistant director who helped advance God's celestial plan with its celluloid layers of light-sensitive emulsion by means of interpreting and defending the paradisiacal pull-down claw as it locked onto the sprocket-holes of 58-thousand American, and one million Vietnamese, hearts. The running-gag narrator who promoted the story line, approved the shooting script, applauded the rushes, defended the answer prints and successfully engineered a B-grade exploitation film into a box-office spectacular. The undespairing adjudicator and supernal connoisseur whose swish-pan promises provided smooth transitions between more than one million wipes. The man who told us—who *dared* to tell us—why.

But the chaplain—at least, 'our' chaplain—always seemed prepared for disaster. And, in its immediate absence, he was well prepared to give detailed notice of its malignant effects. He would begin training sessions by discussing the dangers of bacterial inflammatory diseases of the genital tract which resulted from indulging in sex with Bangkok bargirls. Although he never actually suggested any concrete alternative to male-female relations, sometime during the session, he would invariably shuffle his notes, look us over for several seconds, and finally, speak confidentially, soldier to soldier, sinner to sinner; "Remember, men, you don't get this kind of stuff from just looking at girlie magazines. Magazines can't hurt you. Think about it."

Even as we thought about it, curtains were closed, lights were dimmed, doors were locked, and the chaplain expertly prepared and projected what we dubbed 'blue movies,' slides of the faces, breasts, arms, mouths, lips, tongues and intimate anatomical parts of both men and women who had contracted particularly horrible and presumably incurable sexual diseases. The chaplain never mentioned where or when the slides had been taken but we suspected they actually portrayed the effects of some great epidemic which had struck an especially sinful and hedonistic European community in the Middle Ages. Nevertheless, for those tempted to abandon magazines in favor of more perilous forms of stimulation, the wrath of a righteous, no-bullshit God was clearly in evidence.

At one session, three of the newer members of the unit fainted during the first ten minutes. As Hogbody, Butterball, Taylor and myself sat well toward the back of the day room, we seldom had a clear view of the screen. But unlike during the sermon itself, the chaplain took considerable interest in what effect the blue movies were having on his congregation. As he knew Hogbody was a 'breast man' during the screening of one disease-ravaged breast enshrined in a colorful but slightly unfocused close-up, the chaplain turned to him and said, "What do you think of *that* breast, eh, Hog? I wouldn't be very anxious to get *her* bra off."

After several moments of observing the screen without any visible emotion, during which we assumed he was asleep, Hogbody turned to the chaplain and said, with unaffected dignity, "It has been my experience, sir, that a breast in the hand is worth two in the bra."

The chaplain never spoke to Hogbody again.

As for the quality of the chaplain's sermons, it was never easy to judge. What does one look for in a sermon—correct grammar, ironclad logic, eloquent appeals, mass conversions? But, as it was 'in' in the 'Real World' at the time to be 'relevant,' the chaplain often tailored his sermons—and God's plans—to his military audience. Unfortunately, he often traveled to Vietnam and some of his sermons had obviously been designed for those about to be blown away in battle zones. He never did understand that for GIs stationed in Bangkok, The War might as well have been on the far side of the moon.

Thanks to a very banged-up tape-recorder which Taylor swore had once belonged to Whore House Charlie (so corroded that even the Black Market refused to take it), I can give the reader an accurate account of what was to be the chaplain's last sermon.

It was usual for the chaplain to ignore his inattentive and inconsiderate audience. He habitually spread the Word of God in the face of hostility, derision and other obstacles painstakingly prepared by the Antichrist such as Butterball's burps, Hogbody's snores, Taylor's running comments on the sexual proclivities of chaplains, and heated arguments over both clandestine and overt card and dice games, none of which ever once caused him to shoot a glance in our direction.

Indeed, each time he returned from Vietnam, his sermon was shorter, less audible, and less coherent—and his concern for our salvation less evident. His eyes seemed less able to focus, his face appeared more drawn and pallid, and his uniform seemed both too big and too small for him at the same time. He would prop up his notes, place his Bible on the lectern, blow his nose repeatedly, clear his throat nervously, shift from one foot to the other as if trying to keep warm, and address himself to the few pairs of eyes which remained open.

It was only during this last recorded sermon that there was no blowing, clearing or shifting. It wasn't until years later that I realized why this particular discourse had seemed so singular and unnatural. It was that it was missing the one ingredient a congregation always expects to find at even the most soporific sermon—an attempt at communication.

A speech delivered for humorous effect which fails in its goal results in embarrassment. A serious speech which produces hilarity may be even more embarrassing. But this was not the resignation of one who has tried to share an important message with an insolent audience and failed; rather the ingenuous manner and sincere tone of one whose speech conveys utter madness with an excruciating ignorance and unspeakable equanimity surpassing, in horror, despair and shame, the most deliberate obscenity, the most catastrophic defeat and the most poignant embarrassment. It was precisely this unexpected abeyance of resolve and unintended display of humor that, only moments into this speech, achieved for the chaplain's last sermon both total silence and rapt attention.

"Men, I want to talk to you today about prayer. I know many of you—as professional soldiers—may feel ill at ease when humbling yourself before God. But I have a pleasant surprise for you. Because praying to God is not unlike stepping on a land mine. Yes, that's right: there is nothing more explosive than faith in God. Now, I know you cannot always tell a good gook from a bad gook. But God can. God knows which gook plants rice and which gook plants mines. I do not have to remind you that planting rice is Good and planting mines is Evil. And God wants you to recognize Evil when you see it; that is why He created land mines in such a way that when you step on them they blow you away.

"Of course, I do not mean to imply that land mines planted in His name are Evil. (But, don't forget, those too can blow you away.) But, remember, all personnel blown away in His Name have Life Everlasting.

"You cannot see God—and you cannot see a land mine; but both are there and both are capable of responding. This is because both have *power. Enormous* power. But God has far more power than ordinary land mines. Land mines can blow you away when you step on them. But the power of God is *unlimited:* He can blow you away anytime, anyplace, under any conditions, war or peace, out on patrol or while cleaning your rifle, standing in the chow line or marching in a parade, engaged in a firefight or walking to the latrine, combatant or non-combatant, officer or enlisted man, mama-san or baby-san, soldier or queer. Even, somewhat unfairly, perhaps, in a demilitarized zone.

"Now, men, I want you to think of God as a powerful weapon. Because God is smarter than the smartest bomb, more powerful than the most destructive artillery, and don't forget, He can see in the dark.

"Think of God as a Great Being looking at us all through an infra-red starlight sniperscope. Wherever we are, the eyes of God follow. We are forever lined up in His sights. And one day this Supreme Being will peer through those sights, squint through that scope, slowly squeeze the trigger and neutralize each and every one of us—regardless of race, color, creed, sex, age, I.Q., name, rank and serial number.

"God needs no illumination rounds or saturation bombing to rubbish His chosen targets. His rifle never jams; His ammunition is Everlasting. The day will come when each and every one of us will be trapped in one of God's multi-divisional search-and-destroy sweeps, or by angels deployed by God to mop up. And let me assure you that God's angels are perfectly able to bomb and strafe any pockets of resistance that hold out, however briefly, against them.

"Let there be no doubt about it, the day will come when God will frag all of us. And when that day comes, when God in His wisdom springs His ambush, when God booby-traps your trail, when God chooses to evacuate you from the battle zone forever, when He discharges you from our army to reinforce His own celestial combatants, be absolutely certain that you have been adequately briefed for your new mission.

"Because on that final Day of Judgement, when what we call our universe is finally and utterly defoliated for all time, God will gather the elite troops of his most crack division around him, while those soldiers who surrendered to temptation, or who performed unnatural acts, will be condemned to a free-fire zone forever.

"And of those who still feel they might escape God's Incoming Rounds, remember, even Jesus was not issued a flak-jacket. Quite the contrary. Out of His Great love for the world, God fragged His own son. And that is something to think about.

"Now, men, even after the war is over, people will still have faith in God—and they will still have children, some of whom will become soldiers themselves, and some of whom will be blown away by stepping on leftover land mines—regardless of race, color or creed, boy or girl, tall or short, military dependents or draft resisters, students participating in R.O.T.C. or deserters, applicants to O.C.S. or queers. God calls everyone. And he who steps on a land mine hears the Call of God. But how many who have ever stepped on a land mine have actually paused to consider . . . consider how one path can lead back to base, and how one path can lead to Life Everlasting.

"As I've said, men, land mines cannot be seen, neither can God; but both exist, and both are waiting—Out There. Now, you may never step on a land mine, but that does not mean God does not love you. Let us pray.

"O Lord our God, Thou who art greater than any weapon yet conceived by man, Thou who exist in greater depth than any land mine yet planted by man, Thou who has blown away more soldiers on more battlefields, than even we are able to do, give us this day the power to tell good gooks from bad gooks, and to know which gooks serve in Your Name and which gooks should be neutralized . . . in Your Name. Give us the firepower to destroy Thine enemies. Give us the strength to understand Your Wisdom, to glory in Your Plan, and—when that time comes—to readily and gratefully allow our bodies to be rubbished in Your Name.

"When you call us back to base, oh Lord, when we stand before you in Divine Interrogation, lead us not to report that our mission was aborted or that our air-strike against Thine enemies was canceled because of unfavorable weather conditions. Let us salute proudly and smartly and with confidence our Supreme Commander-in-Chief; and let us never stoop to inflating a body count in order to make a favorable impression.

"And give us this day the ability to recognize that beseeching

59

Thy aid is—if we sincerely and humbly request it—as simple and as uncomplicated as stepping on a land mine. We ask this in Your Name and in the Name of Your Only Begotten Son. Whom You saw fit to rubbish on our behalf. Amen.

Dismissed!"

At the following training session, a more conventional chaplain delivered a more conventional sermon. After he'd finished, Hogbody asked him what had happened to our usual chaplain. The man smiled knowingly, and said that our "usual" chaplain had apparently become quite unusual in many ways, and had deliberately walked across a minefield in Vietnam; when, before he could be rescued, he had stepped on a land mine. But he added that it might have been just as well that God had called him home: The man was a lunatic, because there was no sense in what he did."

Hogbody fell silent for several seconds, but when he spoke it was with the quiet confidence and artless candor of a man who knows he is stating a Truth: "I think, sir, that a chaplain who believes that praying to God is as easy as stepping on a land mine, is worth two chaplains who don't."

The chaplain never spoke to Hogbody again.

4

THE PX CRISIS
10 October 1967

It was during the fall of 1967 that all hell broke loose. Officers and senior NCOs from all over Thailand and, finally, from all over Asia, began flying into Bangkok to meet with Blinky and Bumbles. Top secret telexes submerged deep in cryptographic codes flashed urgently to and from American military bases around the world. It was one of the greatest crises in American military history, far surpassing in importance, excitement and desperation the TET Offensive which was not to hit until early in the following year.

Dozens of high-ranking officers were huddled in meetings which often lasted through the night. The crisis was real: a congressional committee had suggested that PXs be made to *pay for themselves.* Although the meetings were conducted with the greatest regard for secrecy, an alert C.Q. had overheard Bumbles referring to the congressmen on the committee as "communist congress faggots" who had "infiltrated our home front" and had "betrayed" America and everything it stood for. Facing a frontal assault on American PXs around the world, those flying in for the meetings arrived in the same hurried manner, and all wore the same expressions of unswerving resolve, righteous indignation and gnawing fear—not unlike a bargirl who has just learned that her bar has been placed off limits to military personnel because of accusations involving venereal disease.

There were representatives from the intelligence sectors of all American military agencies, from MACV (Military Assistance Command Vietnam); MACTHAI (Military Assistance Command Thailand); CORDS (Civil Operations and Revolutionary Development Support); DEA (Drug Enforcement Administration); CIA (Central Intelligence Agency); NSA (National Security Agency); U.S.AID (United States Agency for International Development); COMNAFRV (Command Naval Forces Vietnam); CINCPAC (Commander-in-Chief of all Military Forces in the Pacific Region); and, if rumor-control was correct, there was even a very concerned delegation from COSVN (Communist Headquarters for military and political action in South Vietnam).

If the congressional committee's viewpoint succeeded, it would mean that, in order for PXs to pay for themselves, not only would prices rise, but the goods on the shelves which were the most exotic, indescribable and worth their weight in gold on the black market would disappear. Expensive and sophisticated cameras and stereos ("How much is it in the States?") ("How much am I saving by buying it here?") would be replaced by boot blousers, army fatigues and other items of value only to the military. One more "benefit" would be lost. No longer could constantly inebriated American sergeants in debt to the world's bars pay off their debts in PX goods worth a small fortune on the black market. It was probably the greatest challenge to America's military establishment since Harry Truman decided that after all, he, and not General MacArthur, was running the country.

Fortunately for Blinky, Bumbles and military leaders around the world, although MacArthur had failed, the military had not; and it was a fact that the United States Army had more than enough power to stop congress or God himself

from modernizing the Army or any other branch of the service
if said modernization threatened entrenched privileges, particularly the most sacred privileges of all, *PX privileges.* Had the
Vietcong attacked PXs rather than bases, The War might well
have taken a very different turn and thousands of beautiful peas-
ant girls near Hanoi would have, like their Saigon counterparts,
found new and rewarding careers, rewarded in part by Dior perfumes, Seiko watches and Salem cigarettes.

None of us thought it in any way odd that those gathered in
crisis never once attempted to win the hearts and minds of enlisted men in the struggle to protect PX privileges even in the
face of America's number one enemy: Congress. Officers like
Blinky and NCOs like Bumbles were aware that we often used
the PX and that we even bought cigarettes for bargirls to resell
on the black market for themselves and their fatherless half-
American kids. They knew we too were addicted to America's
cornucopia and would never willingly sever the umbilical cord
with the shelves full of baubles and various and sundry *divertisse-
ments.* But they also understood that we were far from being in
their camp; for we did not *worship* PX privileges. This lack of reverence toward the lifers' Church ("Thou shalt not purchase any
single-lens reflex or Johnny Walker Black Label for other than
thine own use nor shalt thou covet any big-busted, smooth-
thighed, almond-eyed bargirl who requests that the PX card be
so used as to transgress PX commandments") was what pre-
vented them from initiating us into their conciliabule, and re-
questing us to write letters against Bumbles's "creeping, congressional communism" and the rampant attempt of "congressmen
dupes and stupeedos to subvert and overthrow our established
institutions."

It was Freeman's belief that just as tourists loved postcards
of beautiful scenery and pear-breasted women, officers and
their 'leeches' (wives) and 'rug-rats' (children) would love to

buy postcards with pictures of PXs: "No shit, man, postcard scenes with shelves full of all the discounted shit they can buy to send back home to make their civilian acquaintances green with envy! 'Having wonderful time—wish you could buy here too.'"

Unfortunately for those of us working the swing shift out at the compound, Blinky and Bumbles had to fabricate a reason for acting as hosts to a conclave of military personnel from all over Thailand, lest they raise the suspicions of yet another committee infiltrated by communist faggots. The rationale was fabricated, written down, approved with changes, re-typed, analyzed, approved with suggestions, rerationalized, reapproved, stenciled and made its appearance on our bulletin board in time for afternoon formation.

ATTENTION! ALL PERSONNEL!
THERE WILL BE A BRIEFING BY MEMBERS OF THIS COMMAND AT 2000 HOURS. ALL OPERATIONS PROCEDURES WILL BE REVIEWED BY COLONEL GUTHRIE AND COLONEL MYERS. NO-*REPEAT-NO* PERSONNEL WILL BE EXCUSED.
(SIGNED)
MAJOR JOHN THOMPSON, COMMANDER

By 8 p.m. a dozen officers' vehicles had pulled up at the operations compound. Their presence greatly excited Lt. Pearshape who tried valiantly to appear competent and worthy of a promotion; and also Agent Orange, the pregnant Thai bitch, who liked to beg for scraps outside the operations mess hall.

Agent Orange was aware from past experience that whenever Blinky and Bumbles brought other military officers out to inspect the compound, in order to impress the visitors with the fine food situation in his command, Blinky would order only the best beef. Blinky did this especially during the visit of the Inspector General. The I.G. would leave impressed with the quality of food and the cleanliness of the dining area, and the fact that not one man had made an appointment to see him during his stay to complain about anything. No one ever did, of course, because in order to get to the office set aside for the I.G., we would have had to pass through Blinky's office first. In a few areas, even *enlisted* men were capable of seeing the *Big Picture*. No complaints.

Each day we were bused to the area where we worked on the outskirts of Bangkok. It was a beautiful rural setting with the round floating trays of water lilies arranged like stepping stones down the center of a canal running, or rather, stagnating behind the area. And all around were betel nut and cocoa palms, breadfruit trees and banana plants. During the rainy season, the water smashed into the palm fronds and banana leaves, tearing the leaves and making an unholy sound not unlike a Thai bargirl trying to sing along with Jimmy Hendrix.

Taylor said that before the Army came, the whole operations compound used to be a countryside whorehouse and the briefing room had been the mama-san's room. Some of the local Thai men resented us not because we were Americans but because they now had to walk to the next village to go to a brothel. As always, we were never certain how much truth and how much fiction was embedded in Taylor's Tales of Old Siam.

Hogbody, Freeman, Taylor and I slouched on a bench outside the briefing room waiting our turns to speak. The schedule of those who would address the VIP guests was distributed by Bumbles. In descending order of worth, the announcement stated that first to speak would be majors and above; then GS11 and above; next, second lieutenants and above; then any remaining civilian personnel; then non-commissioned officers; and then, last and certainly least, "all others."

Bumble's cadaverous head finally appeared in the doorway and, almost beside himself with a sense of urgency, he ordered us into the room. It was time for the "all others." We filed into Mama-san's Room and smiled unrequited smiles. Hogbody was first to give his briefing. He was pretty sharp. He turned on his macho attitude which the lifers mistook for military bearing, his voice was deep, his tone was confident and the houseboy had managed to scrape off most of the green grime encrusted on his belt buckle and brass.

Freeman and I had gone to Bangkok's Chinatown area the night before and had been introduced to Chinese centipede wine. It was an actual bucket of red wine with centipedes floating on the top. About three swallows are enough for a drunkard's nirvana, but I couldn't feel any immediate effect and had consumed about two large glasses of it. I turned to Freeman and told him that the wine seemed to have no effect on me—when I realized I was lying on my bunk back at the court with a large bandage on my head; the result of attempting to fly from the top of a set of stairs in a Chinatown brothel while flinging centipedes at frightened prostitutes. My abortive volitorial experience had already made me something of a celebrity at the court as, it was said, nothing that exciting had occurred in our unit since Lt. Pearshape, Corporal Napalm, Thai and American guards and Agent Orange attempted to intervene in the Whore House Charlie—Computer showdown.

The memories returned slowly and painfully. The bandage had been changed to a Band-Aid, and handfuls of aspirin, Bufferin, Anacin and Chinese powdered dragon's horn competed to relieve me of my headache. But as Hogbody was nearing the conclusion of his brilliant snow job, the headache returned in force. My eyes got heavy and the uneven lighting reflecting off the green walls began to make me nauseous. I rested my head in my hands.

GIs from the computer section kept barging into the room by mistake. As they couldn't be spared from work, they didn't know or care about the briefing so they'd open the door, look in and shut it fast. A practical joker must have taken the 'briefing' sign down so everyone would blunder in.

I was almost asleep when through a misty vision of giant centipedes terrorizing officers' naked wives inside PXs, I heard Colonel Guthrie's voice asking the "soldier by the door" to "hit the switch." I jumped up and immediately hit the light switch. Mama-san's room suddenly appeared as it must have night after night long before—completely dark. For a moment, I bathed in the pride of having reacted without hesitation to an officer's command even though I had been more asleep than awake. But then a small light went on in my head and showed me that I had done a very stupid thing. I somehow controlled a sudden urge to run out the door and puke. In three sweat-filled seconds I was able to review my entire life and I was convinced that I would never see the beaches of Hawaii again. It must have been only about that many seconds before I had flicked the switch on again. I looked dumbly at the many pairs of eyes staring at me.

Taylor had become a table; Freeman a chair; Hogbody was now a lamp; some of the lifers were books while others had transformed into pen-and-pencil sets. Just before Bumbles changed into a telephone stand, I saw his face register so much anger I was afraid he might actually explode. So it was only Colonel Guthrie and me.

He raised his hand and pointed to the door. I went over to push the switch which locked the door and then sat down. Several eternities later, Hogbody started where he had left off. Then it was my turn. I decided on a blitzkrieg attack to try to get back a few of the many points I had lost. I explained how most of the vouchers came in on Wednesday afternoons and how they were processed in two or three days and how since I was on break Thursday and Friday, if I was lucky I'd have an easy week. That's when I knew, as every great comedian learns, that there are certain audiences which see humor as only one step removed from communism.

I immediately recovered and filled in the silence by pointing out the areas I checked in my section. I told my audience that it was amazing that in spite of all the new people entering and the veterans leaving the sectors of Vietnam which I covered, very few errors were made by the personnel people in Vietnam. I threw a little more bull—a little faster and bolder than normal thanks to the wine—and then asked if there were any questions. There weren't so I sat down.

But just as Freeman walked to the front of the room to deliver his message, Colonel Myers rose and walked to the map. He picked up the pointer, tapped it on the map and spoke with a barely intelligible southern accent. "Now, the tew of yew have indicated that most of the new arrivals with whom yew're concerned, yewse routes A and B. Yet this here rail line seems much less tortuous than either one. Can either of yew tell me why this isn't yewsed? Or is this only for returning personnel?" He looked straight at Hogbody and then at me.

In my crapulous condition I thought I saw a chance to get all of my points back and then some by showing the lifers that I was really up on the area. The split second thought went through my head that Hogbody should have known the answer but I was in no condition to realize that his silence, which I attributed to ignorance, was, in fact, the product of great wisdom.

"Sir," I said, as loudly as any fool who ever spoke, "that isn't a rail line, it's a line of latitude."

I was right in what I'd said, but dead wrong in saying it. I knew something was wrong when, from the corner of my eye, I saw that Taylor had become a table again. This time it was Freeman who had transformed into a lamp and Hogbody was the chair. Just before Bumbles assumed his disguise, I saw his face contort with hate, anger and frustration, and blood vessels reached out attempting to strangle me. Once again it was only a colonel and me and a room full of furniture, books, lighting fixtures and pen-and-pencil sets .

The colonel eased a pair of glasses out of his pocket, put them on, and examined the map at close range. Finally he turned to me and said: "So it is, Specialist; my mistake." Then he walked to his seat and sat down.

With the centipede wine now throbbing at my temples, I felt a warm friendship grow between the colonel and myself. I smiled modestly and forgave him his mistake. I almost wanted to shake his hand and say: "Forget it, sir, it's no biggie."

I was to learn that Thai elephants, Chinese centipedes and American officers *never forget*.

5

DOC SPITZ
19 October 1967

Doc Spitz was not thought to be the best doctor in the Army, nor did he even like sick people coming to see him; it made him nervous. Rather, Doc Spitz had done something no other officer had done before him and none have done after him: He risked both his rank and his ass to help enlisted men.

It seems there are three signs of the clap. One is the pain while urinating; the second is the drip itself; and the third is something that only occasionally appears on a slide under a microscope. Doc Spitz decided that if a man had the first two symptoms without the third, then it shouldn't be classified as VD. So, leaving his microscope covered in dust, he classified all VD cases as non-specific urethritis, NSU, and saved dozens of enlisted men from being harassed by their statistics-conscious officers. So while our VD rate fell flat on its ass to ten percent, our NSU rate erected to about sixty percent. This went on for months until some officers in other units in the Asian area got jealous and then suspicious. Soon military-type industrial spies began appearing in Bangkok to find out how it was that 'Bangkok Warriors' had all suddenly become model soldiers, or voyeurs, or impotent or whatever.

Finally the trail led to Doc Spitz and the lifers at other units demanded his blood, VD-tainted or not. And, once again, in much-lengthened training sessions, with even more graphic 'blue movies' than before, we were warned about the evils of Bangkok's nightlife. But Doc Spitz remained unrepentant, unbowed and ungovernable. And he was never happier than when his "boys" came to see him. As his wife was Thai, she didn't fit in with the lifers' wives and their catty and often vicious 'teas' anymore than Doc Spitz fitted in with the lifers and their meticulously planned 'dickaways.'

His office was a cubicle separated from his waiting room by a divider, and all sounds in the office could be heard in the waiting room. A large calendar with a drawing of a bare-breasted Pacific islands girl hung on the wall. Beside it was a chart illustrating the steady increase of cases of venereal disease in the Asian area. Written diagonally across the chart in Doc Spitz's handwriting was the sentence:

> Because nocturnal emissions shot up during
> the month of September, no—repeat—no
> member of this command will be allowed to
> have titillating dreams until further notice.
> (signed)
> Doc Spitz

Doc Spitz was endowed with enormously bushy white eyebrows and a sparse mustache. Taylor always claimed the different layers and configuration of white hair on his face made him appear as a moving pallet or sculpture for various styles of Chinese calligraphy, extending chronologically from the ancient seal form protruding from his nostrils, to the elegant and running cursive-script eyebrows, down to the modern short-form mustache bristles.

Another unusual thing about Doc Spitz was that he believed in a 'group therapy' method. If anybody was sick (and he made it clear that he didn't like anybody who was sick to visit him), he always liked to have the patient surrounded by several GIs with whom he could discuss the patient's case. When everyone reached agreement on the nature of the sickness and how best to treat it, all was well. If anyone failed to agree on either point, however, Doc Spitz would accuse the patient of malingering, and throw him out of the office without so much as a pill.

One afternoon in late October Taylor, Freeman and I sat in his office and presented ourselves for duty. He lit his cigar and stared at us. "Goddamn it all, you're supposed to be my main assistants."

"We are, Doc," Taylor said.

"You shitheads couldn't diagnose your own clap if it was coming out of your ears." His gaze remained fixed on me. "And you! What are you always so happy about? You figure if Charlie ever takes over this country they'll take one look at you and figure you're one of them?"

Before I had a chance to respond his Thai nurse entered the room. "Excuse me, Doctor, Major Thompson's wife has arrived with her son, Tommy. She says he has a stomachache."

Taylor stopped ogling the nurse's curvaceous brown legs and turned to Doc Spitz, terror replacing lust in his eyes. "My God," he said quietly. "That's Blinky's wife out there."

'There is also an enlisted man," continued the nurse. "A Private First Class Philip Barber."

"Send in PFC Barber," Doc Spitz said. As the nurse exited he turned to us. "All right, today you're going to be my chief assistants and, by God, you'd better be good or I'll call the shithead who runs that useless unit of yours and tell him-"

Just then there was a soft knock at the door.

"Come in!" Doc Spitz rose. "Sit down, PFC Barber, sit down."

PFC Barber moved diffidently into the room. He was young,

red-haired, bespectacled, freckled, and extremely nervous. Doc Spitz pointed to his own chair. PFC Barber hesitated but Doc Spitz led him over to the chair then sat down on a corner of his desk. He then introduced everyone as his assistants.

"Now then, Phil," he said, in a friendly, let-it-all-spill-out manner, "what seems to be the problem?"

"Well, Doctor, I . . . that is, what I mean to say is I went out the other night. Downtown, you know."

An incredulous look spread across Doc Spitz' face, as if no one had ever done that before. His eyebrows rose and snowy-white Chinese characters in running script form rearranged themselves. *"Downtown Bangkok?"*

"Yes, sir, downtown Bangkok. And I went into a bar."

"You did?"

"Yes, sir. And well, sir, I got me a girl."

"A girl?"

"Yes, sir, a real pretty one with long black hair and real nice tits."

"Real nice tits?"

"Well, yes sir. I mean, breasts."

"Her name wasn't Lulu, was it?"

"No, sir, it was Katy. And she was real nice. So I sort of suggested we go to a hotel. You know what I mean, sir?"

"And she accepted?"

"Oh, not right away she didn't sir, no sir. She said she wasn't that kind of girl."

"But she was?"

"Well, yes. I mean she did go to the hotel."

"With you?"

PFC Barber's tone reflected both pride of accomplishment and fear of censure. "Yes, sir."

"Did you sign your name in the hotel book?"

"Yes, sir."

74

"Your *real* name?"

"Oh, no sir. She said it wouldn't be wise."

"So whose name did you sign?"

There was a long silence. PFC Barber blushed.

"Come on, son," continued Doc Spitz, "you're among friends here."

Barber finally spoke without looking up. "Mickey Mouse, sir."

We started to chortle until a steady wilting gaze from Doc Spitz silenced us. He chomped on his cigar. "Mickey Mouse."

The "yes, sir" was almost inaudible.

"That was your idea?"

"Oh, no, sir. It was Katy's idea. I guess . . . I guess it wasn't the first time she suggested it."

"No?"

"No, sir. I mean, the book I signed in was full of Mickey Mouses and Donald Ducks. And even one Lone Ranger."

"How much did you pay her, Mickey?"

"Twenty dollars, sir."

Doc Spitz now became even more incredulous. *"Twenty U.S. dollars!"*

"Yes, sir."

"Don't call me 'sir', I work for a livin'. Twenty dollars for all night?"

"No, sir, a casual stay."

Doc was dumbfounded. "You paid twenty U.S. dollars for a *short time?* You ought to be ashamed of yourself; court-martialed, in fact."

"Well, yes, sir, but I'm new here."

"Where're you from?"

"Virginia, sir."

"Only two things come from Virginia, son. Portholes and assholes, and I don't see any water through you." Doc had a rebuke ready for whatever state a GI mentioned. He paused to take a smoke. "Well, did you just come to pimp for the girl or you got a problem?"

"Well, sir, I think I might have picked up something off her, you know what I mean, sir?"

"Drop trou', Mickey."

Barber looked confused. "Sir?"

"Your trousers, Philip, drop 'em!"

"Oh! Yes, sir."

Doc walked over to Barber. "Now, let's see."

"Sir?"

"Your tool, boy, your johnson! Let's see it!"

"Oh! Yes sir."

Doc began to examine him. "Felt any pain while urinating?"

"Yes, sir. Started yesterday."

"When did the drip start?"

"Yesterday, sir."

"Why in hell didn't you come in yesterday?"

"I wasn't sure what it was yesterday, sir."

"And today you found out?"

"Well, sir, some of my colleagues in my unit told me it was the clap. I mean, VD, sir."

"You don't have any," Doc Spitz said evenly.

Hope springs eternal in an enlisted man's breast. "No VD, sir?"

"Of course you've got VD, you idiot! I'm talking about 'Colleagues!' Who told you you can have *colleagues,* Mickey? *I* can have colleagues. Your mother can have friends, but for as long as you're a GI, you can have only *buddies.* That's the American Way, got that, Mickey?"

"Yes, sir."

Doc Spitz looked at me. "Pineapple, get over here."

I walked over to where Doc was standing. "What's your diagnosis?"

I looked at PFC Barber's green-stained underwear. I thought for a moment and then said, "Headache."

"Right you are, Pineapple, probably caused by fatigue." He pulled out his prescription pad and a syringe and filled the syringe as he talked. "Now, PFC Barber, I'm going to give you a shot of penicillin. And I want to see you in here in two day's time. Haven't had headaches like this before, have you?"

"Oh, no, sir."

'That's good, Phil, that's real good. You're off booze and sex until further notice, get it?"

"Yes, sir."

"Now, face the door. This won't hurt a bit."

Barber faced the door and Doc Spitz proceeded to give him a shot in the ass. The door opened and a dumpy, middle-aged woman rushed in with her son. Her eyes were red and she appeared about to cry again.

Mrs. Mary Thompson had a fleshy face with sad green eyes and a drooping mouth which she attempted to brighten with liberal application of dabs, dots, dapples, speckles, smears, smudges, and daubs of make-up. Her smile was of the sticky, red, carefully planned, often-used-but-seldom-felt variety, and her personality clearly reflected the type of person who would give a kid an apple instead of a candy bar on Halloween.

Despite her kaleidoscopic patterns of make-up and free-swinging opalescent earrings, she always appeared harassed, harried, and overworked, as if she'd just stepped out from a hot and steamy kitchen. The haggard appearance was largely due to her constant apprehensive expression and her full but bedraggled head of hair which she brushed up to great heights before allowing it to level out toward the rear. Her long, narrow eyes were surrounded by thin, horizontal lines of make-up running parallel to one another; blue, green, purple and violet. It was something like looking at a map of a city with well-planned boulevards, with her blinking eyes in the middle of each section representing the 'you are here' light. The deep, uncolored, well-entrenched lines of age which ran beneath each eye and diverted from the multicolored boulevards across the cheeks, appeared as 'roads under construction.' The thin, tightly drawn lips were always colored with fire-engine red lipstick, and in the heat and humidity of Bangkok, we were often afraid that her masses of facial color might indeed burst into a conflagration at any moment, but no one wanted to tell the Commanding Officer's wife that her face was a fire hazard. As the modern world increasingly transgressed, flouted, and even ridiculed her narrowly defined and obsolete rules of propriety, she was in an emotional state constantly bordering on sniffles, snuffles and tears, all of which earned for her the unit's sobriquet of Lachrymary Mary. Her wrinkled neck boasted a small but active dewlap which, whenever she spoke, sniffled, snuffled, wept or bawled, moved erratically back and forth in the heat like a fan attempting to cool her enormous, securely bound and properly concealed breasts.

Lachrymary Mary spoke to her son peremptorily. "Tommy, come along!" Then she turned to look toward Doc Spitz. "Excuse me Doctor Spitz, but I was—" It was then that she noticed PFC Barber facing her with his pants down. Her sudden scream sent several wall lizards scurrying for safety. "Aggghhh!"

Doc Spitz ignored the social situation and concentrated on giving the shot. "Be right with you, Mrs. Thompson."

"Doctor, I-" Her voice trailed off and it was only a matter of seconds before the flood broke.

Doc Spitz quickly walked to her and put his arm on her shoulders. "Now, now, Mrs. Thompson," he said, "it can't be as bad as all that. Sit down, sit down." He pulled the last empty chair in the room over by his desk and sat her in it. Then he opened a drawer and brought out some tissues. As he handed them to her, he sat on the corner of his desk again. "Now, Mrs. Thompson, try to pull yourself together." Suddenly he noticed PFC Barber. "PFC Barber! Will you pull up your goddamned trousers! Unless you're some kind of exhibitionist in which case you came to the wrong kind of doctor."

"Oh, yes, sir. I'm sorry, sir, I didn't know you were through with me."

Lachrymary Mary continued. "Oh, Doctor, it was terrible."

"Now, just what was so terrible, Mrs. Thompson? Can you tell me?"

"First, Tommy . . . became sick. And then while we were in your waiting room . . . your waiting room. . . ." she began crying again.

"Now, now, Mrs. Thompson," Doc continued. "It can't be all *that* bad."

"Oh, Doctor Spitz, it was just terrible. There were . . . there were . . . there were *GIs! GIs* around my baby!" Lachrymary Mary buried her face in her hands and bawled again, while Doc Spitz put out one cigar and lit another. He handed a prescription to PFC Barber who moved quickly and quietly out the door. Tommy stood against the wall looking sullen. Taylor and I exchanged glances.

Doc Spitz spoke slowly. "Well, Mrs. Thompson, sometimes even officers' wives and their children find it necessary to mingle with the common soldier."

She began to dry her eyes with the tissues while she looked at Doc Spitz. "Oh, but Doctor, you know better than anyone how many . . . filthy diseases Asians and enlisted men have." She suddenly glanced at me, both Asian *and* enlisted, as it were, but, fortunately, like Taylor, I had already become a made-in-America floor lamp with a gold American eagle painted on its red, white and blue base. She continued: "It's their fault my little Tommy—"

Doc Spitz took a long puff on his cigar as he looked over at Tommy and back to his sniffling mother. "Your little Tommy what, Mrs. Thompson? I guess we'd better be checking that stomach of his."

"Well, Doctor, it's not really his stomach that's troubling him."

"But, Mrs. Thompson, I thought you told the nurse-"

"The truth is, Doctor, Tommy . . . went out at night against his father's wishes and, well, Doctor, he must have had relations with a *Thai* girl. You know these girls here, Doctor. Oh, I get so angry, I really do."

Tommy spoke up. "Mom, I already told you she was an American girl from the International School. She's a punchboard for all the—"

Lachrymary Mary grew red in the face and her increasingly agitated dewlap nearly spun out of control. "You just keep quiet, young man. Your father will deal with you later."

Doc Spitz rose and walked toward Tommy. "Drop trou', boy, now. Pull down your trousers."

"Yes, sir," Tommy said.

"Don't call me 'sir', I work for a livin'. Face the wall."

He started to examine Tommy. "Taylor, come over here. . . . Oh, Mrs. Thompson, I haven't introduced my colleagues. Fortunately, they're specialists in venereal diseases here from the States for a visit. What do you think, Doctor Taylor?" Doc pulled Tommy's shorts out and let them snap back.

"Acute Gonorrhea." Taylor said solemnly.

"I think I concur in your findings, Doctor. Any suggestions as to treatment?"

Taylor thought for a few seconds before speaking. "Well, Doctor Spitz, the treatment of your patient is, of course, up to you. However, with an advanced case like this one, in the States we would have no choice but to sever the offending member."

Tommy panicked. "Mom! He wants to cut it off!"

"It's all right, Mrs. Thompson, my colleague is just having his little joke." Doc Spitz picked up a syringe. "I rather doubt that a penectomy is necessary."

"Doctor," Lachrymary Mary said quietly attempting a smile. "I was hoping it might be possible to—"

Doc Spitz continued to prepare the injection. "Be right with you, Mrs. Thompson, Tommy!"

"Yes, sir?"

"Bend over."

She spoke up again. "Doctor, perhaps I should wait outside."

"No, no, Mrs. Thompson; you wait right there. This will only take a minute."

Tommy yelled. "Ouch! It hurts!"

Doc Spitz spoke to him quietly. "Give me your tough shit card and I'll punch it for you. Now then, Mrs. Thompson, you were saying?"

"Well, Doctor, I was hoping that you could, for Tommy's health record, I mean, list his, uh, problem as, perhaps, stomach trouble or—"

Doc Spitz looked up from his RX pad. "Or headache maybe?"

Lachrymary Mary's heavily made-up face brightened. "Why, yes, that will be all right."

"Sorry, Mrs. Thompson, I'm afraid VD is a very serious matter. And, besides, if I were to do that, I'd be falsifying records. You wouldn't want me to do that, I'm sure."

Doc Spitz handed her the RX and escorted her to the door. She made one last try. "Doctor, about Tommy's health report—"

"I'm sorry, Mrs. Thompson, but don't you worry; your Tommy's secret is safe with me."

She then spoke in her normal haughty manner. "Well, then, come along, Tommy, we'll speak to your father about it when we get home."

Doc Spitz' eyebrows angrily rearranged themselves; elegantly formed Chinese calligraphic patterns jostled wildly for position. "Yes, you do that, Mrs. Thompson, you do just that." He slammed the door, walked over to his desk, pulled out a bottle of red wine and a telephone book. He turned to me. "Pineapple, hold this against the wall." He slammed the bottom of the bottle against the book several times, stopped, looked at it, and saw that the cork was almost out.

He spoke as he poured the wine into cups and handed them out. "Goddamn officers and their wives make me sick! Are you aware that your swimming pool will be closed for a week?"

We shook our heads.

"Well, it will be. Some full bird colonel's daughter caught a case of the clap and since she's a full bird colonel's daughter she couldn't possibly have caught it from somebody's pecker. So her daddy says she must have caught it from the pool in your useless outfit."

"Can anybody catch clap in a pool?" I asked.

"Only colonels' daughters and Mickey Mouse," Doc answered.

6

PREYAPAN SRIYANANG
22 October 1967

Three days later, in a convoy consisting of a jeep with Blinky and Bumbles and three open trucks of grumbling Army personnel from the court, we were on our way to a rifle range somewhere in Thonburi, across the river from Bangkok. I was in the second truck. We were dressed in fatigues, boots, helmet liners and we held tightly to our M-14s. To the Thais selling vegetables and fruit along the road, and to those who stared at us from porches of houses, we might have been mistaken for actual soldiers.

As Blinky was the kind of officer who would climb a tree to tell a lie, he continued to lead us as if he had not been lost for nearly an hour. When we passed an elephant, we knew for certain we were lost. They had been banned from the Bangkok area for years as, according to Taylor, Volkswagens had been steadily losing out at intersections.

"Jesus Christ!" Freeman spoke as the truck sped on down the road. "We're lost. The rifle range is in the other direction."

"We can't be," Hogbody said. "We've got Blinky and Bumbles guiding us."

We stopped in front of a sprawling, wooden Thai house with a slightly more modern building adjacent to it. The buildings were almost completely surrounded by rows of jackfruit, breadfruit, various palm trees and assorted vegetation with only the narrow dirt road in front to suggest that the occupants maintained contact with the outside world. A Thai flag drooped on a flagpole, its red, white and blue stripes faded from the sun.

We're stopping," Taylor said.

"No shit," Freeman said. "You should apply for officer training."

"Oh, bend over and crack us a smile will you, Freeze?"

"Bite my-"

Blinky's figure suddenly appeared at the back of the truck, looming like a malevolent target on a firing range. His face was covered with sweat and he was gritting his teeth in despair. Rivulets of perspiration coursed between reddening layers of fat surrounding his eyes and chin. "Taylor!"

"Yes, sir!"

"You speak Thai?"

"A bit, sir."

"Take one man and see if anyone in that house or school or whatever it is knows where the goddamn firing range is."

Taylor hit my shoulder, left his M-14 on the floor of the truck, and jumped down. "Yes, sir!"

As we walked to the house I spoke to Taylor out of the corner of my mouth. "How do you say 'rifle range' in Thai?"

"How should I know? At least if we get invited in we'll get out of the sun for a few minutes."

We heard shouts and laughter and walked around to a back yard protected from the sun by strategically placed fan-shaped traveler's palms. About a dozen children were playing. Some of them were sitting quietly, holding timeworn dolls, and some were holding onto each other as they ran around the yard, laughing and falling. They stopped suddenly as we walked closer.

"Look at the way those kids are looking at us," I said. "They must think we're about to attack."

Taylor stopped in front of a little boy and spoke in Thai. "Hello, young fellow, how are you?" He stood up and looked at several of the other children. They stared back at us. "Wait a minute," he said. He walked over to a little girl about four years old and put his face close to hers. "These kids aren't just scared; they're blind."

A slender and attractive Thai woman of about 35 in skirt and blouse walked out into the yard from the house. She walked gracefully and confidently to meet us and her slight, quizzical smile broadened as she approached. She addressed us in perfect English. "May I help you?"

"Well, we're lost," Taylor began. "I mean, we're after a firing range that seems to have disappeared."

"I'm not sure. Come, we can ask my husband." She picked up a small child and started into the house. The child's eyes never left us. "My name is Mrs. Jayasutra. Please come in. Never mind about the boots. I know they're too much trouble to unlace. My husband is retired from the Thai Army."

We took off our helmet liners, wiped our boots thoroughly and entered the house. She led us into a small living room where her husband was sitting. He was small, dark and wrinkled but very polite. A bronze Buddha gazed at us from a shelf decorated with flowers and large pictures of the Thai king and queen were prominently displayed on the wall.

She spoke with her husband in Thai, and then turned to Taylor. "My husband wants to know if you wish to shoot rifles in the same place where the Thai army sometimes practices."

"Yes, that's right."

"Then you are only about three miles out of your way. Go back to the road which crosses the *klong,* I mean, 'canal,' and then, once over the canal, turn to the right. It is straight ahead."

"Thank you very much." Taylor started to turn.

"But my husband insists that you cannot go until you have had some Thai fruit."

"That's very kind of you but there are others waiting."

"Never mind. A little wait won't hurt them, and you can take them some fruit."

The four of us sat around a small table eating the fruit and making small talk. They began asking us how long we had been in Thailand and if we liked it. The kitchen door opened and a young Thai woman with high cheek bones and extremely delicate features entered. She was dressed in a blue-and-white sarong-like *phasin* and sandals. Her black hair was down to her waist and her skin was a light brown. As Taylor was speaking, the girl gracefully walked to our table and set down a tray and cups and poured the tea in an extremely accurate way, measuring distance between cup and plate with her hands; accurate through practice not through sight. Mrs. Jayasutra guided her hands when necessary.

Taylor stopped talking in mid-sentence, "Well, Connecticut is about—Jesus!"

"Oh, no, she is Buddhist," Mrs. Jayasutra said pleasantly.

Taylor stared open-mouthed. I turned to him and spoke quietly but quickly. "Rick . . . Rick!"

His fingers were unintentionally squeezing the lime meant for the reddish-pink pulp of his papaya into his tea.

"Oh, Preyapan speaks English quite well now," Mrs. Jayasutra said. "She is our oldest student. More like a daughter. Preyapan, this is Pineapple and Rick, two American soldiers."

Preyapan placed the palms of her hands together before her face in a Thai *wai* and gave us a slight bow. There are feminine smiles that can light up the sky's most overcast corners on even the darkest night, and other feminine smiles that can light up the neglected, almost forgotten, wholesome corners of even the most lecherous heart. Preyapan's smile—complete with full lips, perfect teeth, and the loveliest labial form imaginable—could do both. It was, quite simply, glowing, sincere, natural, innocent, uncorrupted, virginal, divine, honest, unadulterated, artless and ambrosial. In other words, it was everything Taylor was not. For Taylor, it was like confronting a being from another planet. He had developed no defense against it because he had not known such a creature could exist. Her smile was for Taylor a sudden and nearly apocalyptic revelation of a *terra incognita,* in which not all attractive members of the opposite sex need conjure up sensations of lust. His mouth now hung open in abject astonishment, and for the first time since he reached puberty, the vision of a beautiful girl did not cause his lips to twist into an expression which could only be described as lustful, concupiscent, lascivious, salacious, lewd, impure, obscene, prurient, debauched, dissolute and licentious. The tuning-fork vibrations which began passing between them were both visible, audible and, if Taylor's later description of the event is to be believed, edible.

It was during the late fifties and early sixties that Thai tourist promoters woke up to the fact that not every woman in the world has a ready and alluring smile like that of a beautiful Thai woman; hence, airline brochures, hotel booklets, tourist office posters, and multi-visual advertising agency presentations began belatedly promoting the 'natural Thai smile' as a tourist attraction at a time when the incredibly brutal but always impersonal forces of the 20th century were already relegating it to a rapidly growing list of endangered species of Asian mores. Although more delicately beautiful than anything which had ever appeared in an advertising campaign, one peculiarity of Preyapan insured that she would never be a typical example of the admittedly glorious Thai smile. To put it simply, from somewhere in her past (we were to learn later that it was from her grandfather) there had been a Muslim racial contribution. In the case of Preyapan, any trace of Muslim features had recessed and nearly disappeared. But, like the word 'almost,' 'nearly' counts only in horseshoes, grenades, and atomic weapons. Because above the incredible charm of the unaffected smile, and enhancing the allure, grace, and charm of one whose faith is alive and whose customs are still practiced, were the two largest, blackest, and most outrageously beautiful eyes I had ever seen. It seemed impossible to believe that those eyes, which could change the outlook of anyone who gazed upon them, could not see.

Despite their incongruous setting, amidst the artless smile and gentle manner of perfect innocence, Preyapan's penetrating gaze spoke of intense but concealed passion, a dormant sensuality, and hinted of the fires of a defiance almost to the point of an outright challenge.

It was as if one had walked into a remote Thai village temple and instead of experiencing the soothing and soporific effect of Buddhist chanting and bells ringing in the breeze, one came face to face with the barely controlled frenzy of an excited *muezzin* calling his Islamic congregation to a holy war. The invincible, magnetic and totally irresistible combination of Islamic fervor and Buddhist gentleness, presented in the guise of feminine pulchritude, had stunned Taylor with the force of a physical blow. We returned Preyapan's *wai* more in abject surrender than as a courteous gesture.

"Jesus," Taylor said again. And then perhaps as proof that his knowledge of Christianity was extensive, he added, "Christ."

"I am very glad to meet foreigners," Preyapan said, or rather, sang. "I badly need to practice my English."

"Your English sure sounds good to me," I said.

"Fantastic," Taylor said. "Succulent."

"Thank you. Please excuse me." She turned and walked toward the kitchen, lifting her arm up a little sooner than necessary to push open the kitchen door.

"Her name is Preyapan Sriyanang," Mrs. Jayasutra said. "She is twenty-two now. When she was five she was blinded by disease. But there has been no disfigurement and she is able to see shadows and forms. She came to us about eight years ago from northern Thailand. She had no family."

Suddenly we heard a horn blow several times. An image of a furious and sweating Blinky loomed before me in my mind's eye. I put my cup down and rose. "I guess we'd better be off now, Mrs. Jayasutra. I'm full as a tic. Many thanks for the fruit."

Taylor took a bite of papaya, chugged his tea as if Preyapan were swimming in it, and got up. "We sure do thank you," he said.

Preyapan returned to the kitchen doorway to say goodbye. Taylor spoke to Mrs. Jayasutra while glancing at Preyapan. "If we come back this way, off duty, I mean, would it be all right to stop in and say hello?"

"Of course. And if you have time, well, the truth is, we need someone to teach English to the children just for an hour or so on weekends. But I suppose as soldiers you would be too—"

"What time?" Taylor asked.

"Saturday at two in the afternoon."

"Right. Many thanks and goodbye. *Sawasdee,* Preyapan. See you again."

Preyapan *waiied* us again. "*Sawasdee, kha,* " she said.

"Goodbye, Mrs. Jayasutra," I said.

She handed me a bag full of rambutan, custard-apples and bananas. "Call me Watana, please. We're friends now."

We grabbed our helmet liners and ran toward the jeep as someone's hand continued to lean on the horn.

"Jesus!" Taylor said.

"Not bad, huh?"

"Not bad! The most beautiful girl in the world and all you can say is not bad?" Taylor pinched his eyelids as he walked.

"Christ! She's so beautiful she melted my contact lenses into my eyeballs." He grabbed my shoulder. "Not a word about that angel to anybody."

I smiled. "Sure, pal."

"I mean it, Pineapple."

"Sure. If you can't trust your buddies who can you trust?"

He thought for a moment. "Army recruiters, Army officers, Army computers. . . ."

7

CURTAIN CALLS
26 October 1967

Inspections were, for those forced to participate in them, absurd, excruciating, a waste of time, and a pain in the ass. For those who gave them, however, they provided a weekly dose of power, where none was desirable, a sense of purpose, where none was evident, and a renewal of martial spirit where none was needed. But to the Thais in the neighborhood, our weekly inspections were looked forward to as a combination circus-carnival, a westernized (but equally stylized) *Khon* dance-drama, and, as we all stood rigidly at attention in the Bangkok heat and humidity—proof that foreigners were totally, undisputedly mad.

Children and adults from all over the northern section of Bangkok—fruit and vegetable vendors, bargirls, samlor drivers, laborers, students and housewives—would jostle for position on chairs and boxes just outside the fence eating, depending on the season, papaya, longan, durian, bananas, jackfruit, guava, mangosteens, rambutan, mangoes, beetles fried in oil, and, in the dark shade of palm trees, watch the *dramatis personae* with dark, damp circles under their Khaki armpits torture themselves.

At the conclusion of each inspection when we were

"dismissed!" a great roar of approval and sustained applause would go up from the audience as is natural for any successful performance which has had a run of several years. No Broadway smash hit ever received more enthusiastic acclaim or more loyal support. Other occasions which were cause for noisy approbation among the appreciative audience were the vociferous and lengthy tirades of Bumbles as he chewed out a GI for an infraction of the rules, and (always sure to bring the house down) a GI fainting from the heat.

The spectacle of an imported, non-profit, show business extravaganza, in which among the performers' repertoires were such wondrous and risorial acts as swooning, bellowing and marching, was one that tore the elderly from their sick-beds, the young from their playgrounds, and the middle-aged from their shop counters.

The Show of the Week that I most remember was at the end of October—supposedly part of the cool season. Just as Blinky and Bumbles began their walk in front of the first of four rows, Freeman ran up and jumped in line.

"Where you been?" Bumbles shouted.

"No excuse, Sergeant!"

"That's no excuse!"

"Yes, Sergeant!"

Bumbles walked to a Jewish GI, new to the unit. "Is that mustache on your ID card, soldier?"

"Yes, Sergeant!"

As Bumbles passed down the rows of sweat-filled uniforms stuck fast to overheated bodies, it was clear that, as always, Jewish soldiers stood the greatest chance of having their names entered in the Discrepancy Book. Not that Bumbles was anti-Semitic. Indeed, it was difficult to pass normal value judgements on the beliefs and actions of someone like Bumbles. Nor did he dislike Jews because of their longer noses, or doctored penises, or sense of togetherness, or fatter bank accounts, or whatever it is that in-sures that a certain percentage of good Christians will always dis-like Jews. He did not even bear Jews a grudge for killing Christ, for, as Bumbles once pointed out to a bespectacled and bemused Jewish assistant C.Q., "He would have been dead by now, anyway, so don't sweat it. Just carry on with your work as if nothing hap-pened."

It was when Bumbles learned from a Master Sergeant on R&R from Vietnam that a Jew by the name of Arnold Rothstein had once fixed the World Series that he began inspecting soldiers with Jewish names—or those he believed to be Jewish names—a bit closer. How could any red-blooded, baseball-loving Ameri-can forgive them for *that*? Unfortunately, precisionist that he was in military matters, Bumbles had almost no ability to distinguish a Jewish name from a non-Jewish name, and was usually in error at least fifty percent of the time. Still, a .500 batting average is nothing to be laughed at in any league.

Bumbles was quick to point out that some very fine Jewish officers—and even enlisted men—had been rubbished in Viet-nam (presumably by the enemy). And when once asked what he thought of the Nazi's killing six million Jews at one go, he re-plied with genuine anger and deep-felt outrage that "communist bastards are all alike and that just proves the domino theory."

On another occasion, in a boisterous Sukhumvit Road bar, to an audience of perplexed bargirls and other NCOs, Bumbles expounded at length to say that Christ had "fought the wrong war with the wrong people in the wrong place at the wrong time." Apparently, now, in Vietnam, was the proper time and place for Christ to make his stand not "fucking around with some candy-ass Roman stupeedos baring their knees for all to see," and Bumbles confided that he "wouldn't be at all surprised if the Al-mighty didn't correct his first mistake in the very near future and send another one or maybe even the same one to do it right this time." Although Bumbles did express the hope that at his next coming Jesus might exhibit a bit more military bearing, or at least show up with a regulation military haircut. In Bumbles's words, "each and every one of you swinging richards can be goddamn sure that no dickhead gook is gonna' nail Him to no fucking cross while I'm around." Which was the clearest statement I'd ever heard as to why Americans were in Vietnam.

Blinky closely inspected Freeman's brass. "What's your third General Order, Specialist Freeman?"

I heard Taylor whisper to Patterson. "Oh, Christ! He's asking Orders, Code of Conduct and Chain of Command!"

"I'm not sure of the third one, Sir," Freeman said.

"Are you sure of any of them, Specialist?"

Freeman was suitably repentant. "No, Sir."

Blinky grimaced, stared and cleared his throat the way big league pitchers do when they've got a full count on a batter who keeps hitting foul balls no matter what the pitch. "You men may be finance clerks," Blinky said for the hundredth time, "but you're soldiers first and clerks second!" *Scattered applause from the audience.* He moved on down the second row as Bumbles glared at Freeman and wrote something down in the sweat-stained Discrepancy Book. Blinky stopped in front of Patterson. "Soldier, your shoes look like they've been shined with a Hershey bar and a wire brush. It is your responsibility that you look like a soldier, not your houseboy's! There's no rule that says—"

Suddenly Taylor started shouting. "Don't anybody move!"

All heads turned to face him with Bumbles peering over Blinky's shoulder. Taylor was stooping over, staring intently at the ground. A GI near him started to move. Taylor bellowed in an even louder voice: "Don't move, goddamnit!"

We had all heard rumors of activity on the part of Vietcong sympathizers in our area of Bangkok; in fact we had quite happily embellished and spread them ourselves; but had someone managed to plant land mines inside the court itself? No one moved an inch.

"Wait a minute, here it is!" Taylor reached down and retrieved something invisible from the ground. "Goddamn piece of junk!" Taylor spat on the space between his fingers, rubbed his contact lens on his sleeve, replaced the lens in his eye, and snapped back to a position of attention. Other GIs also returned to positions of attention.

Blinky looked at Bumbles who began thumbing through his book of army regulations to see what had been written on how to punish GIs who lost contact lenses during inspections. Blinky continued on down the row trying to recover military momentum while Bumbles fingered his discrepancy notebook and gave Taylor a you-think-you're-smart-losing-a-lens-in-formation look. *Moderate applause from the audience.*

As Blinky walked between the first and second row, every now and then he leaned forward to tap the shoulder of a man in the front row and mumble the word, "haircut." Bumbles would then make a note in his Discrepancy Book. As Blinky and Bumbles passed down the row behind Freeman and continued on, Taylor leaned forward and tapped Freeman's shoulder. He spoke in a low, military voice, perfectly imitating Blinky: "Haircut."

Freeman spoke loudly but without turning around. "Haircut! I just got one this morning, Sir!"

By the time Blinky and Bumbles turned, Taylor had already resumed his position of attention. They moved around Freeman's row and stood in front of him. Blinky waited a few moments before speaking, his nasute, perspiring face only inches in front of Freeman's rigid form. "Freeman, I don't know what your problem is but I intend to find out. You've got grass-cutting detail out by the front gate for two weeks. And I don't give a damn if the grass needs cutting or not. Is that clear?"

"Yes, sir!"

At the conclusion of that particular inspection, just as we were being dismissed, Patterson staggered forward with one hand on his forehead and the other thrust forward, as a man might totter blindly when he has soap in his eyes, or upon learning that the bargirl he was mad about, the one he had bought countless drinks for, was actually living with a guy in the Air Force, and then, with unrehearsed histrionics, promptly passed out from the heat; or rather, from the effect the heat had on thirteen cans of Singha beer consumed on an empty stomach and no sleep. This unprecedented combination of simultaneous dismissal and collapse, which would be told and retold by generations of families inside squatter huts, canal-side houses-on-stilts, and dingy dockside bars, brought about such a tremendous outpour of zealous, near-hysterical acclaim, that, after carrying the fallen warrior into the shade and air-conditioned coolness of Club Victory, several of us propped the weak but partly conscious star of the show between us, and took him back out into the heat to acknowledge his acclaim.

This process was continued for no fewer than three curtain calls and was carried out amid showers of exotic fruit slices, seed and skins, and even strands of flowers which left dozens of children's and adults' sticky fingers to land near our feet.

In the tradition of the theater, we waved, bowed, and modestly shared our glory with one another. And as wave after wave of applause rose to feverish pitch and even beyond, it was clear that, although the final chapter of American military involvement in Asia had yet to be written, there would never be another performance quite like the one we had just given.

An hour later Taylor and I were drinking soda while leaning on the rail of the fourth floor. We watched Freeman below pushing a non-motorized lawnmower by the front gate, sweating profusely as he worked. Taylor yelled to him. "Hey, Spearchucker!"

Freeman looked up, wiping his face. "What?!"

Taylor couldn't resist the smirk. "I wish there was something I could do."

"You could bite my ass." Freeman said, throwing him a bird.

"I said I was sorry. We'll save some soda for you."

Taylor was sitting on his bunk staring at his collection of stuffed animals when Freeman finally finished the lawnmower detail and walked into the room. He lay silently on Butterball's bunk for several moments, his eyes focused on Taylor's newest wall slogan: 'Every day in every way I'm getting closer to my discharge.' Taylor rose and began tugging at the door of his wall locker. Freeman finally spoke. "It was a real shitty thing to do."

"Freeze, how many times do I have to tell you? It was the sun. The Bangkok heat makes a man a bit crazy. You know how it is. Anyway, as Bumbles would say, it's good training."

Taylor pulled furiously on his locker door. Freeman seemed to direct his anger more at the Army than at Taylor. "Goddamn! Stay in the Army and scarf up on all the benefits. That's like saying 'collect enough cigarette coupons and get a free cancer operation.'" He unbuttoned his shirt. "Anyway, I've only got 515 days and a wakeup till civilian status, if you'll check it.

As Taylor opened his locker, a great avalanche of junk fell out including cartons of cigarettes, a bottle of liquor, stuffed animals and books. A rusty, incomplete mess kit with knife and fork scattered on the floor.

"What we need in here is a white glove inspection for Taylor like they have at West Point," Freeman said. Then he noticed the cigarettes. "Hey, what are you doing buying cigarettes? You don't smoke."

Taylor began throwing things back into the locker. "Helping the war. With every puff and every drag, the war is getting better and better."

"Could you explain that a bit?"

Taylor's face lit up with a big grin. "Sure, Freeze, I buy up all the whiskey and cigarettes my PX card will let me buy." He began shining his belt buckle on his undershirt. "Then I sell it for Thai baht which I trade for dollars. I'm reclaiming dollars for America."

'You're a real patriotic son-of-a-bitch."

Taylor spoke solemnly. "Not everybody is called upon to make the sacrifice."

"Why didn't you sell the stuff to the taxi driver on your way back from the PX?" I asked.

"Because on Sundays I go down to the Weekend Market and buy old Buddhas or stuffed animals in exchange for cigarettes and whisky. I buy lots of made-to-look-old Buddha statues and antiques to sell at ten times the price I paid to little old ladies at antique fairs in Connecticut who are crazy about antiques because they're afraid of their uncertain future, and because they live in a machine-disposable container age which makes them crave for something carved by hand or jaded by age or—"

"Somebody ought to put you in for a medal," Freeman said.

Taylor sighed. "I regret that I have but one PX card to use for my country."

Freeman picked up an ant-infested stuffed mongoose. "What the hell you saving all these ugly stuffed animals for?"

Taylor indignantly grabbed the mongoose out of his hand and lovingly placed it on a shelf. "Cause those ugly stuffed animals as you call them, Freeze, remind me of how it feels to be in the Army." Taylor finished changing into his fatigues, grabbed his hat and walked toward the door of the room. As he adjusted his contacts, he tripped over the houseboy who was polishing the floor on his hands and knees. He got up and brushed himself off. "Jesus. These little brown people really know how to fuck a guy up."

"LBJ couldn't have said it better," Freeman said.

I took a long, thoughtful drag on my cigarette. "Freeze, what do you make of the black market, anyway? I mean, the way the lifers try to make you look like a traitor if you get caught?"

"I think the army, as usual, overdoes the whole thing."

"I could use some money right now."

Freeman looked into his wallet. "My wallet offers us two dollars till payday."

I counted money from my pocket. "I've got about twice that. Just enough for a couple bottles of booze and a couple cartons of cigarettes."

Freeman jumped off the bed. "What are we waiting for?"

"You to get dressed."

After we bought the booze and cigarettes we stood outside the PX near the fence looking over the taxi drivers hanging about like flies on a carcass. We chose one who looked like he might know the score. Once inside, Freeman leaned forward to talk to the driver. "Hey, slow down. You want to buy some booze?"

The driver was a very old man with friendly eyes completely encircled by dozens of undulating wrinkles, like two temporary helicopter pads carved out of luxuriant jungle growth. As he drove he looked back at the open bags. "I buy," he said, "but no money here. My friend buy. OK?"

"Sure," Freeman said. "Let's go see your friend."

The driver pulled up near other taxis in front of the Temple of the Emerald Buddha. He got out and talked to three other drivers. All four came back and looked over the bags and talked among themselves. At last, the driver got back in and a dark thin man got into the passenger side. As we pulled out he turned to us and smiled. He reached out to shake hands. "My name Slim," he said. "I think this your first time sell on black market."

I briefly shook his hand. "What makes you think that, Slim?" I asked.

"Cigarettes and liquor you buy not Thai favorite. Next time you buy Salem and Johnny Walker. OK?"

"Sure, sure," Freeman said. "Where we going now?"

"We try bars. See how much they pay. Better to shop around. Get you good price."

The taxi pulled up in front of several bars but each time Slim shook his head at the offer or the customer would decline and the search continued. Finally, the taxi pulled up in front of a bar located in a crowded shopping area. Slim entered the bar and came out with the burly Thai manager. Other taxi drivers and children began crowding around the taxi as we bargained. The manager looked through the bags. "I can offer you two dollars and fifty cents American money for the whiskey and two dollars for each carton."

I smiled politely. "That's not what a friend of ours said he's getting."

"But you bought the wrong kind," he said. "Didn't you do any market research?"

"No," I said. "Where'd you learn your English?"

"L.A."

"But the stuff is worth more," Freeman said. "Look, your customers pay about an American dollar for one drink. You get at least 35 drinks out of a bottle."

"Yes. But I have to pay for the girls and lights and rent and bribes to the police."

As we talked, more people began crowding around the car and some started debating the price in Thai and broken English.

Children began moving among the crowd, trying to sell gum, candy and flowers. The debate continued and began to attract attention from passersby including police.

Finally, Freeman handed the manager the bags. "Jackshit! All right! Quiet down. This isn't a public debate. Give me the money; it's a deal."

The manager began counting out some American money from a wad of bills. Freeman started to hand him the bottles and cigarettes over the seat but the manager held up his hand and ran into the bar. "What's he doing?" Freeman asked.

"I don't know," I said. "But if he's calling the police be ready to run and if he's not going to pay, be ready to fight."

He came back, got into the front seat and leaned toward Freeman with a fingernail file pointing at his chest. Freeman doubled up a fist. "What's the problem?"

"You have to scrape the numbers off the label so that if the police raid the bar, they can't trace to see who buys." He held up a bottle. "See? Right here. They wrote these numbers in the PX book when they sold the bottles to you. Can't be too careful."

Freeman relaxed his fist and gave me a sheepish look. He then began filing off the numbers. "What about the cigarettes?"

"No numbers, no problem. Here's your money."

We finished our transaction and finally made our way through the crowd. Cheering children reached in to shake hands with us and waved goodbye; some even threw flowers. We got back to the court and began checking figures off on a piece of paper. "We paid one dollar and forty cents for a carton of cigarettes," Freeman said. "And a dollar sixty-five cents for the booze. That's six dollars and ten cents for our expenses. We got two dollars a carton for the cigarettes and two fifty a quart for the booze. That's nine dollars. We paid seventy cents to get to the PX, one dollar and seventy-five cents for the ride all over town and your good will gesture of fifty cents to Slim for helping us finding a buyer. Plus gum and flowers, fifty cents. That means we spent three hours to lose fifty-five cents."

Even as I approached Club Victory to begin some serious drinking, Freeman's expletives could still be heard from his third-floor room clear across the northern side of Bangkok.

8

OVER SPILLED MILK
5 November 1967

Although there was abundant evidence to the contrary, Butterball maintained that he was not only a vegetarian but that he rigidly adhered to a program of fasting as well. When mercilessly cross-examined between huge mouthfuls of mess hall beef and lengthy eructations, Butterball assured his audience that he was a vegetarian because he never ate more than one helping of meat per meal, and he considered that he was on a strict fast as he never ate any snacks between between-meal snacks. Indeed, by his definition, he was in fact on a dangerously radical crash diet.

Although for Butterball the mess hall represented *nirvana* for his polyphagian orgies, for Taylor, the mess hall often became an unlikely but inevitable battleground between Blinky and himself. The inordinate amount of collisions which took place there were usually of two kinds: Those Taylor brought upon himself by not thinking before speaking, and those he brought upon himself by thinking before speaking. A simple example of the first kind occurred when Blinky was strutting across the mess hall with a huge amount of food heaped on his plate and a self-satisfied expression which curved his thick lips into what passed for a smile. He stopped by our table to give us the benefit of his observation.

"Do you men know how much a meal like this would cost on the *Outside*!?" (American military officers' fulsome praise for the American (military) way of life invariably had an ironic corollary in unconscious but highly perceptive criticism of the American (civilian) way of life which they were sworn to defend.)

Taylor tugged at his mustache. "Well, sir, food may not be free on the Outside, but at least *people* are."

An example of the more complicated run-ins, in which fate played a role, occurred one day when Patterson, Taylor, Freeman and I were just placing our trays on a table and sitting down to eat. We had two choices. We could either sit under the ceiling fans and be cool but accept the bugs blowing into our food, or we could sit away from the fans and avoid the bugs but be uncomfortably hot. Battles were fought daily between those who would be hot and have bugless food and those who would be cool and have food with bugs. As we argued the point, light brown Thai waitresses in dark blue-and-white uniforms were walking about serving food, cleaning and giggling among themselves. Taylor's faction was finally outvoted by Patterson's faction and we sat in sweat enjoying bugless food. To be more precise, Taylor's faction lost because Freeman agreed to cross over to Patterson's side for part of Patterson's fruit-and-insect Jell-O which made it three to one. As a lover of the democratic process, an inveterate foe of corruption, and a sore loser, Taylor began harassing Patterson. He picked up his tray. "Roy, baby, I think you crushed some mosquitoes when you slammed your tray down."

"What, are you on a Buddhist kick or something?" Patterson asked.

"No, but I was teaching some of the precocious ones to bite officers and NCOs only. Anyway, fucking move your tray, will you?"

"Hey!" I said, "you can't swear like that in front of God and these young ladies."

"I didn't swear," Taylor said.

"What do you call it?"

"If I said: 'move your fucking tray,' then that's swearing. I only said, 'Fucking move your tray.' That's just adverbial emphasis, nothing to do with profanity."

"That's pretty sloppy linguistic analysis," I said.

"It defies linguistic analysis," Taylor answered, while making birdcalls to a perplexed but smiling young waitress who, from both warning and experience, kept her distance from Taylor.

As Patterson ate, he continually took pieces of food out of his mouth, glared at them, and placed them in formation on the side of his tray. I turned to Taylor. "How's your campaign coming to teach the waitresses English?"

"Fantastic! most of them can say 'The war sucks' or 'the Army sucks.' "

"Do they know what it means?" Patterson asked.

Taylor pointed to the divider with a sign 'Officers and NCOs only'.

"They know it has something to do with the folks who eat over there. That's enough for me."

Taylor got up to get a glass of milk. As he started back toward our table with the milk, Blinky and Bumbles walked from the officers' side of the mess hall toward the door. At the same time, one of Taylor's favorite waitresses also walked by Taylor. She looked thoughtfully at Taylor and then at Blinky. Her pretty, nut brown face lit up and she began to speak as she pointed at Blinky who was now almost next to Taylor. "The war—"

If ever there was a time for a display of cryptic coloration, it was at that moment. Taylor, however, reacted true to form. He immediately threw his arms around her and kissed her hard, spilling some milk over her uniform onto the floor. He then turned to Blinky and Bumbles, with an exultant and lofty smile on his face. ". . . is getting better and better. Thai girls are with us all the way, sir, I'll say that for them."

Blinky's jaw dropped and his eyes widened. He quickly recovered, said nothing and walked on. Even Bumbles seemed uncertain as to exactly what had happened, let alone how to respond, but certainly the war was getting better and better and nobody who was teaching Thai waitresses *that* could be all bad— not even an enlisted man.

9

LOY KRATHONG
15 November 1967

To be popular in Thailand one need be neither rich nor hand-some, merely hirsute. As Thai men have only a modicum of body hair, a hairy Westerner, particularly in the countryside, is a walk-ing tourist attraction, a one-man carnival act and for small chil-dren, definitely something to run home to mother about.

No Rorschach inkblot test could hope to match the effi-ciency of a hairy foreign traveler in 'upcountry' Thailand, where his very crinite presence could cause hilarity, fear, admiration, envy, astonishment, resentment, delight, disbelief and, often enough, insoluble traffic jams.

For the kids at the School for the Blind, no amount of new toys or amusing games could evoke from them the undisguised awe and indescribable glee the feel of a GI's hairy arms and legs could bring. At the sound of our voices, they would run in groups of four or five, holding onto each others' shoulders or wrists, and at the last possible moment, would throw out their arms, and with the complete trust and final act of faith known only to children, leap through darkness into ours.

In the beginning, the silent, even reverent, manner in which they ran their tiny hands slowly and meticulously over our ex-posed limbs left us with awkward embarrassment; but we were soon responding to the joy we brought to them, and our awkwardness was swiftly replaced by a disguised pride and undisguised pleasure which they brought to us.

On the day of the Loy Krathong Festival, Freeman, Patterson, Taylor and I visited the school. The rice-planting was over and the reaping would not begin for a few weeks, so everyone in the countryside was taking his month of rest. The festival was in honor of the mother goddess of water and in a few hours every canal, stream, river, pond and lake in Thailand would have thousands of banana leaf (or, in recent years, plastic) cups with flowers, candles, and joss sticks floating on them.

While the four of us submitted to the usual ritual with the children, Taylor walked to Preyapan, touched her cheek, and held her hands. She moved one of her hands quickly over his face and down his neck. The gleeful shouts of the kids always insured that no one could hear any of the delicious intimacies of their conversation.

After only a few of our visits, the children soon realized that (as a Hawaiian) I had far less hair than the other incredible beings who came to play with them, and after a cursory tactile search revealed that they had grabbed onto the least incredible of the foreign walking wonders, I would be summarily abandoned and left to myself, like a disgraced God who can no longer respond to his supplicants' prayers. The only exception was one beautiful little girl with a slight smile and knowing look on her dark brown face and an insatiable desire to feel my nearly glabrous skin, as if she alone understood that an angel with clipped wings might well have a more interesting story to tell than those who had never fallen from grace.

As I wheeled out the mower from the shed, Watana stopped me and admonished me for attempting to work on a festival day. I replaced the mower in the shed and, ten minutes later, we were sitting in the shade of traveler's palms watching the children play a variety of Thai instruments. While this was happening, other children, under Watana's guidance, brought two long bamboo poles and a drum out of the shed. Some of them knelt down and picked up the poles at each end. While the children clapped and beat the drum, the poles were hit together close to the ground in time with the beat. Preyapan appeared in a yellow and gray sarong, with a strand of red flowers in her hair. She began dancing in and out at one end and a young boy danced in and out at the other. When the four foreign walking wonders were encouraged to join in, the inevitable happened, and the poles continually clamped upon several ankles and toes of owners too slow and clumsy to perform the dance successfully.

Preyapan approached a small spirit house on a pole and made her offering of incense sticks and flowers to the *phra phum,* insuring the continued protection of the guardian spirit of the house. We then followed her to a table where she gave each of us a banana-leaf cup and told us to follow her to the canal. The leaf cups had incense, coins, replicas of temples, and, in the center, candles. The four of us shouted goodbye to our attentive audience, and followed Preyapan through thinly scattered jungle growth and along banks of ricefields until we reached a wide canal. As the sun set, we sat together on the bank of the canal, watching and listening.

A small bright spot of reflected sunlight to the west soon revealed a temple's orange-and-green tiled roof rising from the surrounding branches of a solitary but massive flame-of-the-forest tree. As Taylor described the scene to her, Preyapan began bending one of her thumbs back to touch her wrist, in the manner of Thai dancers.

"Rick," I said, "I hate to say anything, but when she does that it gives me the chills."

"OK, Sarge," Taylor said. "I'll ask her to stop."

"Thai dancers do this from when they are very young," she said.

For awhile, we sat silently watching the Thais paddle the vegetable boats up and downstream. All would whisper something about the *farangs* to their companions.

As the darkness relentlessly devoured the canal's bright colors, Taylor continued his description. "And some of the kids in the boats are imitating the cries of birds. And there's a small boat with a sluggish long-tailed motor moving downstream. It's barely keeping ahead of floating weeds and purple flowers." After it passed only the sounds of paddles entering and leaving the water were heard along with the cries of birds.

"This is the first boat on this canal with a motor," Preyapan said. "Some of the people here do not like it. They say it is too noisy."

"Maybe like in our country when cars replaced horses," I said.

Preyapan slipped out of her sandals and waded barefoot across a shallow branch of the canal. I remember how impossibly beautiful she looked dressed in her clinging yellow and gray sarong. Her long black hair cascaded across her light brown bare shoulders and down to her waist. As she adjusted the sarong, her dark eyes seemed to stare into the growing darkness, and her face lit up with a smile of delight.

She waded back to shore. "It's almost time," she said.

"For the *krathongs*?" Freeman asked.

"No," she said. "Time for snake to come."

All four of us stood up immediately. "It's only a little snake," she said. "It comes by here very often after it wakes up from sleeping during the day. Many snakes sleep in the daytime. I have heard this one many times. Very friendly."

"I think I'll stand awhile," Freeman said.

"You're not afraid of a snake, I hope."

"A Bangkok Warrior?" Taylor asked. "Afraid?! Impossible!" He carefully searched the ground and then sat down again in the growing darkness. Cooking fires lit up the night on the other side of the canal. A woman began brushing her teeth in the water.

"Do Thais really brush their teeth in *Klong* water?" Patterson asked.

"Of course," Preyapan said. "In the countryside, we brush our teeth in it, wash and take a bath in it, and swim and work in it. I think maybe that's why we are so happy."

"Is that the secret of the Land of Smiles?" I asked.

Preyapan only smiled.

Taylor spoke again. "Preyapan, many people are floating the *krathongs* now. There are candles along the shore and up and down the canal. It's getting dark."

"Then it is time," she said. She picked up her *krathong* and we followed her down to the water. "When Lord Buddha floated his rice bowl it floated upstream against the current," she said.

"We don't have to make our *krathongs* do that, do we?" Taylor asked.

Preyapan began laughing. "No, of course not. But tonight all our faults and all our troubles will float away with our *krathongs*. And the legend says that when two young people put their *krathongs* into the water, if they float close together, it means the two lovers will stay together in a happy future. If the *krathongs* separate, then they will not."

"Well," Taylor said, "let's see what we can do."

I turned to Freeman and Patterson. "We'd better send ours first," I said. "If one of ours stays closer to Preyapan's *krathong* than his does, he'll claim we're after his girl."

"Now you fellows know I'm not like that," Taylor said. "But go ahead anyway." The three of us lit our candles and put our *krathongs* into the water. They stayed a few feet apart and headed on a safe journey as far as we could see.

Then Preyapan took the flowers from her hair and put them on Taylor's *krathong*. Within seconds, Taylor's had gone over toward the other bank and either lost its candle or else the candle had gone out. The *krathong* began breaking up. Preyapan's stayed close to the near bank and swirled along at a slow rate.

"Are they together?" Preyapan asked.

I began to speak. "Well, they—"

Freeman held up his hand. "They sure are, Preyapan."

"Right," Taylor said quickly. "They're so close together it's hard to tell if there's one or two."

Preyapan raised her hands together in a *wai* in respect to the *krathong* and in gratitude to the water spirits. She spoke softly. "Their journey will probably end downstream where children swim out and collect the *krathongs*. I'm glad ours will first share a long, safe voyage."

I watched the *krathongs* floating downstream and into the blackness of the night, and in the silence that followed, I got the impression that Preyapan had detected our fabrications about the confluence of the leafcups, and had concluded that this was likely to be the first and only *krathong* festival she and Taylor would ever share together.

10

BLINKY'S HYPNOPEDIA
8 December 1967

What information we were able to come by regarding Blinky's life, or rather, shadow existence, outside the military, was provided by one of Hogbody's Thai girlfriend's sisters who happened to be the fourth (simultaneously) wife of Blinky's eldest servant. Information obtained through such a makeshift relay system was understandably sketchy, scant and, to be fair (who wants to be fair?), suspect. But endless stories of a domestic life becoming every day in every way less blissful were naturally eagerly received, highly treasured, frequently retold, and greatly embroidered. Breakfast-table arguments centered on Blinky's supposed neglect of his spouse in favor of his military career. Afternoon phone calls, before they were abruptly terminated by one party or the other, dealt with Lachrymary Mary's supposed neglect of their four children who were—from little Nancy's nocturia, pretty Patty's paruria, Ellen's persistent enuresis, to Tommy's seemingly incurable gonorrhea—inevitably described as "impossible, unruly, undisciplined, and just like their (multiple choice) father, mother, father's mother, mother's father."

Evenings were devoted to the burdensome duty and vicarious pleasure of all American military officers stationed in

Bangkok: watching the Battle between Good and Evil televised from the War Zone which according to Hogbody was how Blinky was able to know for sure that there was a war on in Vietnam. Hogbody's supposition might have been incorrect but it was true that, with the exception of finance records, at no time while any of us served as C.Q. or assistant C.Q. did our unit receive any information, instructions, queries, acknowledgments, or, in fact, any form of communication whatever from any other military unit.

More than a little was said about what effect the daily battle reports from the War Zone had on Blinky's sex life although, to be sure, what was said was based less on informative reports than on speculative malice. Nevertheless, it came to light that Blinky was a faithful devotee of learning while asleep, or at least the use of constant repetition on the subconscious as a manner of forming positive attitudes. His hypnopedia took the not unexpected form of a tape cassette with only one sentence repeated endlessly: "Every day in every way the war is getting better and better."

I don't recall exactly whose suggestion it was to alter the tape but, with the aid of the elderly quadrigamist, a briefly empty house, and four of us specially chosen by drawing straws, Blinky's tape underwent modifications. The first half was left unsullied as it was felt that he might still be awake and perhaps even *active* during that period. But during the second portion of the tape, when Blinky's exposed subconscious mind was being bombarded by American optimism courtesy of Japanese equipment, a quiet, calm and nearly imperceptible voice cut into the second half of each endlessly repeated sentence bearing the news that "Every day in every way the war is 'going to hell in a handbasket.'"

As children with new games are seldom satisfied without still newer games, yet another suggestion reared its ugly head and a brief but well-rehearsed taping session provided the final chapter in Blinky's nocturnal onomatomania. It was, as we all readily acknowledged, a vicious, malicious, and, one might even add, sick way of harassing an American military officer. Indeed, there was no way of knowing if what we were planning would have permanent effects on Blinky's nervous system, mental stability and marital harmony.

Nevertheless, three days after Wat, Preyapan, Dang, and six of us on break completed the taping session, the new tape was smuggled into Blinky's house and substituted for his now hopelessly contaminated tape which, he still believed, provided an undiluted power source of positive thinking. And so it came to pass as Blinky's hand hit the light switch, and his head hit his pillow, the most heinous act of treason in the annals of military warfare was shamelessly consummated. Above the ticking of the clock, the snores of his wife, and the hum of the air-conditioner, one Thai bargirl, one Thai bartender, one Thai orphan and six *enlisted men* raised their orotund voices in unison to reverently, fervently, and (one likes to think) movingly, sing our National Anthem.

11

THE BATTLE OF OPERATIONS
21 December 1967

Five days a week we would climb on one of the leased tour agency buses lined up in front of Club Victory and ride to the northern outskirts of the city to our work at the operations compound finance offices, which, because of the Vietnam connections, were designated 'restricted areas.' A few of us would be sober enough and interested enough to look out the window as the sights and sounds of the City of Angels sped by; the rest would play cards and talk of assassinating Blinky and Bumbles, read and daydream of assassinating Blinky and Bumbles, or sleep and dream about assassinating Blinky and Bumbles.

As the bus left the congested quarters of the city, it traveled through some of the more scenic areas. For many the trip was usually a hangover blur of traffic jams with motorized samlors and entire families hanging onto speeding motorcycles; Thai monks with rice bowls walking precariously near the road; small temples surrounded with towering banyan trees; children on water buffalo; and attractive half-coy, half-come-hither country girls working at roadside food stands selling rice wrapped in banana leaves and, when their boyfriends weren't around, waving to us. Although I seldom took notes on the bus itself, those I took on the day of the now legendary 'Battle of Operations' are completely reliable and unusually accurate.

Freeman woke up as the bus turned sharply off the highway onto the road to the compound. He leaned forward to see if Taylor was awake. "Hey, Rick. Rick!"

"Huh, whazzat?"

"Listen, man, when we get back to the court tonight I want to use your porch for a minute, OK?"

Taylor yawned. "To look or to jump?"

"Bite my ass," Freeman said. "I want to see if the army of ants on my wall is coming down from your room or not. I think they plan their campaigns from your porch."

"Move your nose over," Taylor said. "My porch is not a battle-free zone for your mother-fucking ants."

"Hey, speaking of mother," Patterson said, "my mom's birthday is coming up. I've got to send her some perfume or something. What time's the PX close tonight?"

"You can't," Freeman said.

"Can't what?" Patterson asked.

"What Freeze is trying to tell you," Taylor said, "is that you're not married so you're not allowed to buy anything feminine because the lifers are afraid you might give it to a *Thai* girl. It says right on your PX card that your tour of duty is 'unaccompanied'. So don't try to buy anything for any females."

"Well, what the hell am I supposed to buy my mother for her birthday?"

"Oh, cigarettes or cigars," Taylor said. "They make a nice gift. Boxing gloves are good for the mother who has everything. I gave my mother a nice set of canteen covers and a mess kit with her name engraved, one brand new olive green helmet liner and the latest copy of the *Army Digest*. She loved it."

Although Taylor still sent his mother gifts on special occasions, he had long ago given up writing to her as, whatever he said he had done or was going to do, she would invariably reply, "get out of it all you can, son; take advantage of your unique experience." So, finally, when in a particularly foul mood, he wrote his mother and mentioned that he would be going to an especially notorious brothel after which he was defecting. Her reply was delivered with the same unmistakable enthusiasm and maddening equanimity: "That's wonderful, son; be sure to get out of it all you can." He swore his mother had either stopped reading his letters or had become a computer in his absence.

Butterball was awoken by roadside branches hitting the sides of the bus and the faces of sleeping GIs who inadvertently leaned too close to the windows. Several such rudely awakened GIs began swearing. Butterball sighed. "What is it with this Thai driver that he always takes the highway instead of the shortcut?"

"He says too many people have died in accidents on the old road and their ghosts are there." Taylor knew a lot about ghosts. He was always dreaming either about ghosts or about God. For the rest of the journey, those of us not asleep were treated to the latest of Taylor's dreams. In this one Whore House Charlie and God were sitting at a booth inside Jack's Off Bar where the lights were still not quite bright enough to reveal God's face clearly. As sexy bargirls walked away, disgusted by the adamant refusal of both God and Charlie to buy them drinks, Charlie attempted to talk God out of re-enlisting in the Army to collect temporary duty pay. God was being very cagey about why he needed the money, but if he was willing to re-up for TDY pay, Whore House Charlie knew it was serious. Charlie also had the feeling that it might be somebody pretending to be God, and everyone knows that for an enlisted man to pretend to be an officer is a court martial offence. In any case, God tried to borrow Charlie's ration card so he could buy some cigarettes at the PX and Charlie told him the regulations say that GIs can't sell or even give the stuff away; especially not to foreign nationals.

Taylor's recounting of his dream was briefly interrupted by Freeman who expressed astonishment that God might not be an American and that he'd been praying to a foreign God. Butterball commented that God sounded straighter than the erection a lifer gets when he visits a new PX. Butterball's comparison of The Almighty with an erection brought forth streams of invective from Fat Eddy which, undoubtedly due to their disparity in size and to Fat Eddy's good sense, stopped just short of a scuffle.

Fat Eddy was a short, freckle-faced GI with the kind of perfectly-formed pot belly that was as much a distinguishing part of him as his face. There was no doubt that his civilian calling would eventually be that of a department store Santa Claus. He had very beady eyes and a very red face; sort of a miniature Butterball with freckles. He always looked a bit like an all-American boy up to mischief. If he wasn't in one of his 'religion-is-where-it's-at-why-haven't-you-tried-it' moods, he was a hell of a guy. Eddie's problem was that he blushed at even the mention of a girl's intimate parts, and this insured that whenever he was present, such mentions were made especially for his benefit.

Fat Eddy was deeply in love with Noy the Laundry Girl and he would daily, sometimes hourly, tear a button off a sleeve or rip a small tear in his shirttail and then stand in line in front of the laundry to ask Noy to sew a button on his sleeve or to mend a small tear in his shirttail. As all other members of the unit sent their houseboys to the laundry, Fat Eddy was subjected to discreet snickers from the houseboys, and raucous and often sustained ridicule from GIs who passed by.

Noy the Laundry girl was a verecund, diffident, portly, 28-year-old virgin from Thailand's impoverished Northeast region, the sixth of eight daughters and three brothers. Whenever another GI asked her how Eddy was, she would invariably giggle behind the back of her raised hand and sew a button on the wrong sleeve.

Fat Eddy had lost a great deal of face with Noy when he first arrived at the court and had brought in a beautiful Thai girl for a drink in Club Victory. He stopped to chat with Noy while the girl went off to the ladies room and asked Noy her opinion of his date. After an embarrassed silence, Noy lowered her eyes, blushed deeply and spoke softly: "You know that's not a girl, don't you?"

Thai transvestites, known as *katoeys,* as with many other glabrous, fair-skinned Asian males, are notoriously difficult to distinguish from the real thing. An Adam's apple here, a deep voice there, a rather large foot under there—all present, to the discerning observer, telltale clues as to sex. Although Eddy was definitely not the keenest of observers, according to those who claimed to have seen 'her' leaving the ladies room, Eddie's 'girl' had almost no Adam's apple, relatively small feet, a feminine wiggle, and, when 'she' returned Eddy's heated accusation with a "Well, if that's the way you feel about it," and strutted off, a moderately feminine voice as well.

Such was Eddy's love for Noy the Laundry Girl and her "deep, almost religious insight into people and things," that he remained her tireless, devoted, undaunted admirer. Noy the Laundry Girl remained a virgin.

He had just returned from a leave in the States, his first trip back to 'The Real World' in four years and he had confirmed what other longtime residents in Asia discovered upon their return to the States: Americans look very much alike. He had also discovered that when people on the Outside make mistakes or totally fuck up a project, rather than get promoted or reassigned as in the military, they can *fire* you. This message was cautiously and obliquely relayed to Bumbles who immediately made it clear that he regarded such a practice as "unfair, unAmerican and unfuckingconstitutional," and was a "perfect example of what prolific (he seemed to have meant 'profligate') communist stupeedos will do unless the military takes over."

Taylor then began relating how God told Whore House Charlie he had the clap and had to see Doc Spitz. Here, the story of the dream was abruptly ended by Fat Eddy who had to be restrained from attacking Taylor with the last of his bananas.

About five miles north of Bangkok, not far from the Chao Phraya River, The bus turned off the highway onto a wide dirt road which eventually turned into a narrow dirt road which eventually led us to the front gate of our compound. A Thai guard shack and an American guard shack were sited side by side at the gate.

The compound enclosed a communications center and a finance office and a computer room. The finance office was located in an old modified Thai house and the communications center and computer room were in a modern but unsightly concrete building attached to it. Whether to protect us from VC-sympathizers, aggrieved bargirls or lost water buffalo, the compound was surrounded by a high wire fence on three sides and in back by a high wooden fence. Behind the fence was a dirty but scenic canal and beyond that nothing but ricefields. Large antennae, our communications link with our Saigon counterparts, were also visible at the rear of the compound. Inquisitive Thai farmers and villagers nearby had been encouraged to believe that it was an American TV station. If it had been, it probably would have done more that we did to ensure that every day in every way the war was getting better and better.

We stepped off the bus, and looked as much like professional soldiers as we could in our wrinkled olive-green fatigue work uniforms. We lined up at the gate to pick up our badge from Lek, the Thai guard on duty in the Thai guard shack, and a second badge from Corporal Nathaniel Alan Palmer, known, of course, as Corporal Napalm, the American M.P. on duty in the American guard shack. Corporal Napalm was always too engrossed in pornographic literature to respond to greetings but as we passed Lek, Freeman spoke. "Hi, ya, Lek. How's the boy?"

Lek handed him his badge and grinned. "You two late," he said. "I think also drunk."

Freeman was contrite and indeed a bit tipsy. "I try my best to be a good soldier, Lek."

"If the Lord wanted you to be a soldier," Taylor said, "he would have made you with olive-green, baggy skin."

The finance office was crowded with desks of all sizes, and long tables lined the walls. A water cooler, a table with a coffee pot and cups, and several filing cabinets lined the back wall near Bumbles's well-isolated desk. On the walls were charts, graphs, maps with pins in them, photographs of those in the Army chain-of-command and several signs including 'Buy U.S. Savings Bonds', 'Write down your suggestions', and, near the door: 'Fire Exit'. There was a poster on the wall with a father zebra with lots of stripes and a sad-faced young zebra with no stripes. The sympathetic father zebra was saying: 'Stick with the team, son, your stripes will come'.

As we entered we placed our fatigue caps on a rack and took off our fatigue jackets to work only in our undershirts.

"I suppose we should start cleaning for the inspection," Butterball said.

"What inspection?" Patterson asked.

"Look at the damn walls. Full of snowjob signs. Whenever Blinky gets interested in our suggestions that means some superlifer is coming to inspect. When the superlifer's gone, the signs come down."

Patterson stood before a cabinet door with his long arms full of charts and books. "Hey, there's no room in this cabinet," he shouted.

"Pile them on top of the cabinet and balance them on the door," Butterball said. He got up to help. "Leave it slightly ajar . . . like this."

Patterson shook his head as he saw the way Butterball was preparing the trap. "Whoever opens the door is gonna get himself a big headache."

Butterball spotted Freeman and began shouting and blinking in imitation of Blinky. "Hey, you guys are late. You should 'a been on the first bus."

"You mean the war's over?" Freeman asked happily.

"We had to help Doc Spitz with some tough cases," Taylor said. "Where is everybody?"

Butterball pulled a chart out of the drawer and read from it. "Two men on quarters due to unknown strains of sexual diseases, one man down with Bangkok belly and one man last seen on a water buffalo heading north."

Hogbody walked to Bumbles's desk and picked up Bumbles's brass nameplate on which was engraved the names of the different countries Bumbles had been stationed in and the dates. Hogbody began to smear the nameplate with his hands. I suppose to a civilian the ritual may have seemed a bit bizarre. In fact, it was the only sort of real communication we had with Bumbles. Every day when Hogbody came in, he would smear the nameplate with his fingerprints; every day when Bumbles came in, he would take out a cloth and a can of Brasso and polish it. Exactly what was being communicated through this ceremony, none of us ever discussed. But I suspect that, among other things, it revealed to each side that although they were enemies, there would be limits on the weapons deployed; on his side, Hogbody would not damage or dispose of the nameplate, and, on his side, Bumbles would not seek to press charges against the man responsible. A tacit acceptance between two sworn enemies—American officers and American enlisted men—that even in the face of irreconcilable differences life must go on.

For a few minutes, we proceeded as usual; checking and rechecking the finance records of men stationed in northern Thailand and central South Vietnam while recounting and, no doubt, embroidering, our latest adventures in Downtown Bangkok the night before. As always, Patterson had far more to relate than others and it was a fact that, although he knew Bangkok after Dark better than any man alive, as soon as the morning sun ended the rule of the neon signs, Patterson could not travel more than one block from the barracks without getting hopelessly lost. Hogbody and Butterball began playing chess on the squares of the paper cutter with the caps of soda bottles, pausing only occasionally to make derogatory comments on Patterson's adventures.

Suddenly the room began shaking as if a locomotive were passing through it. Loud whumping and whirring sounds came in quick, successive waves, and pins from maps began dropping to the floor. "What the hell is that?" I asked.

"Somebody probably pissed off the computer," Taylor said. "Sometimes they forget to feed it and the computer gets nasty."

Army computers of the 1960s, designed by amoral scientists for immoral military officers were not the 'user friendly' variety which would appear in the homes, offices and schools of the world in the1980s and which would take over the homes, offices and schools of the world in the 1990s. Years before the microchip reduced the computer's enormous size, before *Time* magazine would hail the computer as 'Machine of the Year,' and long before the word 'apple' meant anything but the fruit Thais loved but couldn't grow in their climate, specially designed 'user unfriendly to enlisted men' computers were assembled to aid Americans in their war effort. These computers were olive green, huge, wily, menacing, malevolent, ill-tempered, disagreeable, and surrounded by a series of trip wires to protect their software, hardware and apertures.

Taylor's eyes began to glaze over in poignant memories. "Ever since Whore House Charlie ambushed the computer, the fucking machine is suspicious of everybody."

Although the computer was well-guarded from further attacks by Corporal Napalm and his specially trained commandos, so little was known about it that hardly anyone would know when the computer needed repair. It was certainly true that the computer's actions had become increasingly erratic from about the time of the alleged Whore House Charlie— Computer Death Duel. For one thing, as its operations were classified, no one other than Lieutenant Pearshape and a few computer personnel even knew exactly what type of computer it was. Some said, "digital," others whispered "analog," and Taylor, constantly complaining of its lethargy, said "backlog."

Whereas most computers perform high-speed mathematical or logical calculations and assemble, store, correlate, and otherwise process and print information, the operations computer seemed to actually pass judgement on information it received and, with ironic twists of black humor, to deliver only what information it deemed fit to print. It was a censor, and a temperamental one at that. It once claimed that the American military owed 30 million dollars in back pay to men fighting in Vietnam in a province which had no American men in it. No matter how the information was programmed into the machine, the computer steadfastly maintained that the money had to be paid even if it went to the Vietcong, upon which Bumbles had declared the computer a traitor and a "perfect example of computerized, communist stupeedos at work." The computer retaliated that Bumbles was the one with a screw loose, whereupon specialists were brought in from the States to repair the machine, and as they could find nothing wrong with the computer they began to examine Bumbles. The report was classified.

Taylor was interrupted by a loud series of knocks on the other side of the wall. It was the call for battle stations. Hogbody hurriedly pushed the bottle-cap chessmen into a drawer. All other non-military paraphernalia was similarly concealed. Freeman jumped up and ran around the room and began flapping his arms like a bird's wings. "Enemy in the compound! Enemy in the compound! Officer Alert!"

Everyone began looking studiously professional and working in a very concentrated manner on Army finance records and charts. Rechecking a soldier's finance records for accuracy of payment had in the early 60's been fairly routine; now the process often ended with yet another 'File Terminated.' Those two words on the badly typed information sheets sent from Saigon bloodlessly summed up the death of an American in Vietnam. It always brought images to my mind of a sudden and vicious firefight in a ricefield, or the fireball of an exploding Huey gunship, or the screams of someone my age as a Bouncing Betty exploded on a jungle trail and destroyed his private parts. As the war progressed, more and more 'FT's' appeared. And more and more we developed the

Bad Attitude of Bangkok Warriors.

After a few seconds, Bumbles stalked into the room. He sat down at his desk, glanced quickly through his 'in' file, then poured a bit of Brasso onto a cloth and began polishing his nameplate. Suddenly, his eyes narrowed, and he jumped up and walked over to Taylor's desk. He reached under some papers and pulled out three books. He held in one hand *Democracy in America 1840* by Alexis De Tocqueville, Herndon's *Life of Lincoln,* and *Flora Fleshes It Out* by X. Bumbles replaced *Flora Fleshes It Out* but waved *Democracy in America* and *Life of Lincoln* in Taylor's face. "Taylor, how many times have I warned you not to bring non-military reading material to work?" He then attempted to tear the books and finally managed to tear the bindings and some of the pages. He threw them in the wastebasket, walked over to his desk and sat down.

Taylor seemed genuinely perplexed. "Excuse me, Sergeant, but why did you throw out the book on Abraham Lincoln?"

Bumbles glared at him. "Why? If you could see the Big Picture you'd know why. Lincoln was tryin' to keep a country together; we're tryin' to keep one apart. Lincoln ain't relevant!"

"Well, excuse me again, Sergeant, but I think you forgot about *Flora Fleshes It Out.*"

"It ain't revolutionary, is it?"

"Well, no, Sergeant, it's more evolutionary than revolutionary."

"Then I don't give a damn. And I want to tell you people," Bumbles continued, "that there won't be any promotions in this section until I see certain people get rid of their bad attitudes. Certain people here seem to forget there's a war on; or maybe they think it's a wrong war! Well, let me tell you it's no one's right to question whether the war is right or wrong; the right question is whether or not the war is won. A right war is a won war and so too is a won war right. And two wrong wars don't make a right war. Is that clear?"

Our response was instantaneous and simultaneous. "Yes, Sergeant!"

Bumbles stood beside the cabinet, his elongated head drooping over his thin shoulders. "I expect and will get respect!" he said. He hit the cabinet for emphasis, closing the door, setting off the shower of charts and books on his head. Butterball's trap was a stunning success. After a shocked silence, Bumbles grabbed his hat and stalked out.

"I bet he's off to tell Blinky," Freeman said.

Taylor began looking into the middle distance. "That will be one of the finest memories of my military experience: watching a military officer tear up a copy of *Democracy In America* because it's a non-military book. The only—"

Taylor was suddenly hit hard on the side of the head with a rubber band. Others sailed past him. Several GIs had quietly entered the room from the door adjoining the communications center.

Freeman began screaming: "Computer Section attack! All hands at battle stations!"

We dove behind desks, chairs, filing cabinets and the water cooler. We took off boot blousers (a piece of twisted elastic with two small hooks, one on each end) and, by placing one of the hooks in our fingernails, fired them as weapons. Boot blousers and rubber bands were bouncing off the charts on the walls and knocking pins of various colors out of maps onto the floor. Entire American divisions in Vietnam were decimated.

Surprise attacks by marauding bands of Computer Section personnel were nothing new. They had long been the Vietcong Guerillas of the Operations Compound. These shadowy figures and their hit-and-run raids had caused havoc with our finance operations dating back to the days of Whore House Charlie and possibly before. Not unlike John Wayne in 'The Green Berets', what we most resented was that we were never allowed to launch retaliating attacks on *their* side of the border as, first, the computer was in their area and nobody wanted to piss off the computer by accidently slapping it with a runaway rubber band or wapping it with a misguided bootblouser; second, their highly unpredictable, and always eccentric officer, dubbed Pearshape, was usually in their room; and third, the compound's one civilian and her children (Agent Orange and her pups) slept in the computer room ensuring that their entire area was an unattackable sanctuary perpetually out-of-bounds to all forms of violence.

"Hey!" Freeman yelled. "They just shot Roy with a paper clip from a rubber band. We outlawed that."

"They've escalated the war," Hogbody said ominously.

"It just goes to show you," Taylor said. "You give a soldier a tactical nuclear weapon and if he's losing, he'll use it."

Taylor braved a blizzard of paper clips and boot blousers to grab the fire extinguisher. "Freeze! Get your ass over here! You and I are about to perfect the ultimate weapon."

Taylor rolled up a page of *Democracy In America,* stapled it, and capped it off with a pointed paper cup nosecone from the water cooler and another cup inside. He then placed his creation in the funnel of the fire extinguisher. "Here it is, boys," he said proudly. "Our missile and missile launcher. Let's see how the computer boys like a taste of this."

He pointed the fire extinguisher funnel toward the Computer Section GIs. "You boys surrender?"

A volley of rubber bands, boot blousers and paper clips hit Bumbles's desk and the wall. "All right, mothers," Taylor said. He turned to Freeman. "Freeze, you figure you can handle a missile firing?"

Freeman saluted. "Yes, Specialist!"

"All right, countdown. Ten, six, five, three-and-two thirds, fire!"

Freeman closed the top lever of the extinguisher to meet the bottom lever. For about three seconds nothing happened. Then, slowly and stately, the paper missile rose and shot out across the room. The entire center of the room was filled with white gas from the extinguisher. Taylor was amazed. "So Blinky is right. There is white at the end of the funnel after all."

It was obvious to all combatants that, despite having the computer on their side, the computer personnel had lost the arms race, and the breakthrough of the ultimate weapon gave both the battle and the war to the finance section. Cries of surrender filled the air. Some computer personnel began to escape through the door. Hogbody ordered them to stop. They returned—but not because Hogbody ordered them to. Blinky and Bumbles entered the room. "Adiese!" Bumbles said.

"As you were!" Blinky yelled.

No one moved as Blinky, blinking furiously from anger, from habit, from the gas, and from the presence of enlisted men, walked over and picked up the missile. I stretched my memetic, procryptic ability to the limit and furtively disguised myself as one of the cups in the water cooler rack. Blinky looked at Freeman who was still holding the fire extinguisher. "Did you fire that, soldier?"

Freeman was at his sequacious best. "Yes, sir."

"You be in my office tomorrow morning at eight o'clock, Understood?"

"Yes, sir."

Blinky then looked at all the GIs in the room. As always, Bumbles's thin head peered over his shoulder giving the impression of one body and two heads. Bumbles was so angry he was almost in tears. Blinky spoke slowly and deliberately. "The rest of you *men* seem to have forgotten our motto: *Zero Defects*. You understand what that means? It means 'no mistakes'. And your playing at war is a mistake; a defect. Is that clear?"

"Yes, sir!"

"You men play at war," Blinky continued, "because you don't respect *real* wars. Real men respect real wars, not play wars. Real wars have real casualties, not play casualties. If you were real men in a real war some of you would be dead now: Real wars have *real* body counts with *real* body bags!"

Those of us who had not immediately become office furniture as soon as Blinky had entered glanced sheepishly and shamefully at one another for not having acted like *real* men by having been blown away in a *real* war. Just in case my camouflage was not working, I remained motionless and gazed straight ahead with a fixed, unblinking stare, attempting to look as dead as possible. Blinky's widened, reddened eyes continued to survey the battlefield in disgust and anger at not finding even one *real* soldier (corpse) in his outfit. "Is that clear?"

"Yes, sir!"

"You obviously don't have enough to do," Blinky continued. "So I'll find something for you to do. You can train for a real war at the go-go school. Then maybe you'll have more respect for *real* wars. Now clear up this *play* war."

"Yes, sir!" Blinky turned to leave and his ventripotant belly immediately bumped into Bumbles's cadaverous form lurking in his path. Bumbles ricochetted backwards and, after prolonged and spirited jostling, finally managed to get out of Blinky's way and together they left; but not before Bumbles gave us a you'll-be-hearing-from-me-about-this sneer.

"How come Blinky only picked on Freeze?" Patterson asked. "We were all doing it."

"Lifer psychology," Taylor answered, as we began picking up and replacing some of the pins and charts instantaneously reestablishing American military power in Vietnam. "They figure if they yell at a group it will only unite the group and give it strength. But if they single a guy out, then everybody will say to himself: 'Oh, Jesus, it could be me next; I'd better shape up.' They learn that stuff in lifer school."

Patterson was impressed. "You should have been an officer."

"I'm not officer material," Taylor answered. "I'm not aggressive enough."

"Aggressive?"

"Yeah, you know. All those euphemisms the Army uses for when a guy is a real bastard and dicks everybody away to get promoted: aggressive, born leader, natural leadership ability."

"Jesus," Freeman said. "The go-go school. Would he really send us there?"

"Never mind that now," Taylor answered. "Where the hell was Lek with the warning signal?"

We charged out to the Thai guard shack and surrounded Lek. No one bothered with Corporal Napalm as his obsessive perusal of pornographic literature had long ago precluded his participation in military duties of any kind. "Where the hell were you?" Freeman asked.

Lek's eyes widened in surprise. "I leave for just one minute. Go to pees."

Freeman grabbed his collar and pulled his face close to his. "Oh, you had to go tinkle in the little boy's room, did you? I guess you think we'll just let bygones be bygones, is that it? I mean, if you want to take a piss and you don't get a replacement at the guard shack, well, so what? We're all buddies, right?"

"But also have Thai guards at entrance to road," Lek said. "No Communist can get in compound. I—"

"Communists!" Freeman yelled. "Who the fuck is talking about Communists? I'm talking about the *en-e-my*!" After a pause Freeman let go of Lek's collar and smiled as he began to straighten it out. "Lek," he continued patronizingly, "you know what the punishment is for failure to warn your buddies, don't you? The same punishment we all get from time to time for dicking our buddies away."

Lek grinned a huge Thai grin and started backing off but six hands grabbed him and in a minute he was carried through the compound and through the back gate to the canal at the rear of the house.

As we began to swing him, Hogbody counted. "All right. One .. two . . . *three.*"

Lek sailed out over the canal and splashed in. Although it was only fair that Lek should receive the same punishment as the rest of us, Lek had been born along a canal and spent most of his childhood swimming in one, and as we watched him happily ca-vort about in the water before clambering up the bank, I couldn't escape the feeling that we had done him a favor.

12

THAI ORPHANS
28 December 1967

From somewhere, Taylor had learned that 'typhlophile' meant 'friend of the blind.' Hence, he now sprinkled nearly every conversation with 'typhlophile' and, as befitted his new role of 'typhlophile-at-large,' Taylor decided that we had to raise money for the School for the Blind. And he decided the best place to try this was during one of our training periods when the room would be full of GIs worked to a fever of excitement by the chaplain's 'blue movie'. He stood on stage and began giving his speech on the status of the School-for-the-Blind fund. The overheated slide projector was still set up and he began showing slides of the school. As he spoke, Patterson, Freeman and I collected funds from the GIs in our fatigue caps.

". . . and we've been building the wading pool for some of the younger kids as you can see here. Thanks to your vote, we are now getting three day's worth of takings from the club slot machines each month. Now, however, we need to buy a lawnmower. The one the school has now is a fucking mess. And we need to get some extra cribs and other items. But for this we need a bit of extra money." As the hats were passed, GIs gave money reluctantly.

"One of our biggest problems is rice. We've got the money to buy the rice but we need to be able to deliver rice and other items ourselves if we're really going to save money. We used to deliver three kilos of rice in a jeep that Hogbody had but Hog's Thai girlfriend's American husband came back from a job with Philco way over in the war zone and wanted his jeep back!"

"What about his *wife?*" a GI asked.

"Nope," Taylor answered. "Only the jeep. And now, before I wrap this up, I'd like to ask that we have one more pass of the hat while the orphanage committee shows some other interesting Thai orphans." Taylor began showing slides of nude Thai bargirls in sexy poses. As the GIs began cheering and applauding the 'orphans,' the hats quickly filled with money.

Taylor stood quietly on stage, his posture revealing his sense of accomplishment and his lips in the same broad smile of approval a mama-san displays when she sees that every one of her girls has a lady's drink in front of her.

13

SGT. JIGABOO
15 January 1968

Unfortunately, Blinky had meant exactly what he'd said about the go-go school. The 'school' was on the Thonburi side of the river and consisted of a wooden barracks building and various methods of torture including a track and athletic field. It was surrounded by the usual lush vegetation and by an NCO quarters. About twenty-five of us were lined up in front of the building and several sergeants—none it seemed at the time under nine feet tall—started walking about. One huge black sergeant walked up and down in front of us and looked us over as we stood at attention. Every now and then he shook his head and muttered, "Bangkok Warriors."

The other sergeants stood ominously near. The black sergeant finally began to deliver his speech. "So you're the ladies who played war games. Well, ladies, your officers have been kind enough to give you to us for a little re-conditioning training. You are going to be our guests for the period of two weeks. Now, it is already obvious to my command and to myself that there is not one real soldier among you. I don't know what it is that you've been doing to earn your pay, but I'll tell you one thing: it ain't soldiering. Well, let me tell you, that's going to change right here and right now. Because for the short time you gentlemen will be with us at our little a-go-go-school, you will relearn the art—I say *art*—of being a soldier. Which you might need should you be sent to the war-zone. This damn fool jungle war is not the way wars were meant to be fought, but we're stuck with it and we will *adapt*. Everybody got that?"

"Yes, Sergeant!"

"That's good," he said, cupping his ears with his huge hands, "except I can't hear you."

"Yes, Sergeant!"

He again cupped his hand at his ear and shook his head in bewilderment. "Now, maybe we've got a bunch of WACs here but I just can't hear anything."

"Yes, Sergeant!"

"That's a bit better, ladies. Although if Charlie Cong ever saw you ladies, he'd just laugh himself to death and we could end the war tomorrow. You ladies notice I said your schedule starting *tomorrow*. Maybe you're all thinking to yourselves (and here he used an exaggerated negro accent), 'Wat 'bout today? How come dat dere jigaboo didn't tell us 'bout what we goin' to be doin' *today?*'" He stopped and put his face about one inch from Freeman's. "That what you thinkin', boy?"

"Yes, Sergeant!" Freeman said.

He moved his face closer. "Who told you to think, boy? Did Sgt. Jigaboo give you permission to *think?*"

"No, Sergeant!"

Sgt. Jigaboo spoke softly but menacingly at all times. "Soldier. There is a *banyan* tree over by the barracks. Can you see that?"

"Yes, Sergeant!"

"Soldier, that banyan tree is lonely. You march over there, stand in front of it at parade rest, and speak romantically to it. That banyan tree is the sexiest woman you have ever laid eyes on and you will proceed to whisper sweet nothings to it. Now, you've got ten seconds to get over there and nine of them are gone. Ready? Move out!"

Freeman moved out and as Sergeant Jigaboo continued talking, Freeman held his largely one-sided romantic conversation with the Banyan tree.

"All right, gentlemen," he continued. "Let's see if we can get you into shape in two weeks. So that just in case you actually had to go to war, you'd have an outside chance of making it back alive. That, gentlemen, is the reason for this school. You won't like us. Especially you won't like me. 'Cause I'm Sgt. Jigaboo! And I'm black and I'm mean. Now, let's move!"

The next two weeks I remember as being perhaps the most torturous weeks of my life. They were filled with running, exercising, push-ups, calisthenics, marching and rifle-firing. During the few moments I had to myself at night before I collapsed from exhaustion, I made several half-hearted attempts to continue with the diary. But even after a long shower, the sweat which dripped, or rather, splashed, onto the page made it impossible to write, and, in any case, described far more accurately and meaningfully than I could what an a-go-go school is all about. But even during the worst of times we behaved exactly as 'Bangkok Warriors.' It began when Sgt. Jigaboo was inspecting rifles. He stood in front of Freeman and looked at his M-14. "You call this clean, soldier?" he asked. "How often you clean this?"

I clean my gun once a day, Sergeant."

"Your *what?* Did I hear you say 'gun'?" Freeman's term was not the 'correct military nomenclature.' In any case, he was soon standing again in front of the banyan tree, this time holding out his rifle with his left hand and pointing with his right hand. He again spoke to the tree. "This is my weapon," he said, pointing at his rifle. "This is my gun," he said, pointing toward his penis. "This is for killing," he said, pointing at his rifle. "This is for fun," he said, pointing toward his penis. And then he continued. "This is my weapon, this is my gun, this is for killing, this is for fun."

A few hours later we were lining up on the firing line in a prone position with our rifles pointed down-range. The sergeants were walking back and forth behind the line. Instructions were being given over a microphone system from a tower. The voice from the tower was metallic and hard. "Is there anybody down range? . . . Is there anybody down range? . . . Is there anybody down range? . . . Ready on the firing line—"

Suddenly a shot rang out. The voice in the tower panicked. "Hold your fire! Cease fire! Cease fire! Who fired that shot?"

Several sergeants ran over to where a GI had put his hand in the air. It was Butterball. Sgt. Jigaboo ran up and stood directly in front of him. "Like to jump the gun, do you, ma'am? Well, you jes' come right this way, ma'am." They walked several yards behind the tower to where there were several large holes. Sgt. Jigaboo pointed. "You see those holes, soldier?"

"Yes, Sergeant."

"I want you to use your entrenching tool and—very gently—move them three feet to the left."

"Yes, Sergeant." Butterball took out his entrenching tool and began to dig.

The following morning we had bayonet practice and a sergeant with what looked like a bayonet scar on his forehead stood on a platform calling out orders. Suddenly he held up his hands. "Hold it, men," he said. "Hold it. We have a genius among us. Hold up your rifle, son, and show us what you've done."

A crimson-faced Patterson held up his rifle. He had placed the bayonet on backwards. Within minutes, Patterson joined Butterball in his task of 'moving' holes three feet to the left.

An hour later, as we sat on bleachers, a short, squat, squint-eyed sergeant was standing below us doing his best to teach us guerrilla tactics. "The problem with constant tension is, of course, constant fatigue. If you give yourself up to it, you're very likely not going to wake up at all." I was beginning to fall asleep. Several others were also drowsy. The sergeant's monotone continued. "So that's why the smart soldier is always alert." Then he spoke quickly but a bit softer. "And now all men who are mentally alert, disregard my next command. All WACs," then he screamed, *"on your feet!"* Taylor and I jumped up.

All eyes and sadistic grins turned toward us. We joined Butterball and Patterson in 'relocating' holes three feet to the left.

About half an hour later at the training ground we were all standing at attention. Sgt. Jigaboo stood in front of Hogbody who was sweating profusely. After a few moments of ominous silence, he spoke. "Soldier, didn't I tell you yesterday that I wanted the Bangkok heat lowered to a reasonable temperature? And didn't I forbid you to sweat?"

"Yes, Sergeant!" Hogbody said.

"Did you carry out my order, soldier?"

"No, Sergeant!"

"You disobeyed a direct order from a non-commissioned officer? From 'ol Sgt. Jigaboo?"

"Yes, Sergeant."

Butterball, Patterson, Taylor, Hogbody and I continued 'moving' holes three feet to the left. Butterball's now enormous hole disappeared into the earth to such an extent that, had they known, speologists the world over would have gathered to observe the experiment.

The following morning Freeman sneaked into the barracks where Patterson and I were cleaning. He walked over to a bunk. "Damn Taylor suckered me into a detail," he said. "I'm going to fix his bunk for him." He grabbed Taylor's pillow and covers and threw them on the floor. "There. Now when Taylor gets back from a hard day of training he'll find his covers on the floor and think his bunk didn't pass Sgt. Jigaboo's inspection."

"Jesus Christ, Freeze," I said. "The inspection was postponed this morning. They'll be in any minute now to inspect the bunks."

As Freeman's face drained of color, a door slammed and Sgt. Jigaboo and one other sergeant walked in. "Adiese!" Patterson yelled. Freeman continued to stand in shock looking down at Taylor's covers sprawled out on the floor.

The sergeants walked up to him. "You do that, boy?" Sgt. Jigaboo asked.

"Yes, Sergeant."

Sgt. Jigaboo began to nod. "You know," he said, "when I first joined this army, my daddy looked at me and he said: 'Son, you're a black man. When you do a thing it got to be right or else all black men look bad.' I suppose all that's changed; and it's good that it has. But the last thing my daddy said was that, like the warriors of long ago, I was to come back with my shield or else carried on it; but he told me never to come back without it. But you, my good man"— he put a hand on Freeman's shoulder— "you gonna' go back with *your* shield shoved up your ass. So after you remake every bunk in the barracks, we'll let you help your buddies."

And sure enough, it came to pass that Freeman began helping Butterball, Patterson, Taylor, Hogbody and me as we 'moved' holes three feet to the left. Butterball's hole was now bottomless.

The following day we again lined up in front of the barracks and the sergeants again moved around us ominously. Sgt. Jigaboo finally spoke. "Now you men been with myself and my command for a training period of two weeks and, no doubt, some of you are wondering about something. That right, Freeman?"

"I got no wonders, Sergeant."

"Well, that may be, but I been hearin' your little minds working ever since you got here," Sgt. Jigaboo continued. "Your minds are thinkin', 'Well, if dat dere jigaboo is such a great soldier, how come they pulled him out of the war to come here and teach finance clerks?' Well, Sgt. Jigaboo is gonna' enlighten you; 'cause it's the most important part of your training."

Sgt. Jigaboo walked slowly up and down the first line and then began speaking as he walked. "Gentlemen, it was . . . it was a time when there were so many Vietcong around that we were showing our ration cards in Vietcong messhalls and eatin' with them to save us the trouble of goin' back to camp."

Some of us laughed. Sgt. Jigaboo continued. "One morning I was out alone in full combat gear rounding the bend of a trail in the jungle. Two Vietcong were rounding the same trail heading right for me. Most 'Cong quieter than a fart in a windstorm, but these two were teenage girls with pigtails and funny conical bamboo hats and rifles . . . who should a' been giggling in a schoolroom somewhere . . . but they was giggling at the wrong place at the wrong time. The rifles were a bit big for them; they couldn't get them up in time. . . . I got 'em . . . I got back to my outfit and a pretty, young, clean-shaven white lieutenant from Massachusetts went through the usual routine. He said, 'How many you get today, Sarge?' And I handed him the pigtails I had cut off and said: 'Two, sir; with pigtails.'" Sgt. Jigaboo paused here and looked at Freeman. "You know what he said?"

Freeman spoke quietly. "No, Sergeant."

"He put his arm on my shoulder and said: 'Good boy.' That's what he did." Sgt. Jigaboo laughed. "Until . . . I wrapped the pigtails around his neck and started pulling. . . .

"So, now you know. Sgt. Jigaboo is crazy. Oh, not crazy enough to be thrown out of the war completely, understand. Just crazy enough to be assigned training duty. 'Cause only sane people are allowed to fight America's wars. 'Cause America being the Home of the Brave, it don't count if they win a war using crazy people; like Sgt. Jigaboo. Don't matter if the war's insane, but anybody who wants to fight in it for America, got to have all his shit together. . . .

"They gave me a leave in the States and absolutely free consultation with a psychiatrist. I bought a new car and every night I went out and I drove and I drove and I drove—seemed like I didn't ever want to stop. I only slept during the day. Freeman, you know what the shrink said 'bout why I was doin' all that nighttime drivin'?"

"No, Sergeant."

"'Cause in my head I was still out on night patrol. I was still fighting the war. Ridin' around the streets of L.A. lookin' for Charlie." Sgt. Jigaboo laughed again. The laugh was even more harrowed and devoid of mirth than before. "But I couldn't find Charlie on the streets of L.A. anymore than I could find him in the jungles of 'Nam. So I got sent over here. And that's one part of the program, I mean, war, you're never going to have enough training for. . . ."

Then he became all military again. "But gentlemen, as far as the Army is concerned, this is all the training you need. Dismissed!"

My most lasting memory of the go-go school was when we were digging our holes for the last time, completely concealed by our piles of dirt. Hogbody rested for a few seconds before disappearing into his bottomless pit. "You know," he said. "My hydraulic valve is clogged up real bad."

Patterson wiped sweat off his brow. "What the hell you talking about?"

"Women, Superstud, *women*, ever hear of them? It's been almost two weeks."

"Hey, I remember them," Taylor said. "You mean those succulent creatures with smooth skin and curvaceous bodies and shorter vocal cords so their voices rise like *this*. I almost forgot about them!"

Hogbody looked thoughtful. "As soon as I get out of here I'm heading for Good Pork Betty's, the cleanest fornicatorium

144

this side of the Ganges."

"Amen, Brother Hog," Taylor said. "That was Whore House Charlie's favorite."

"What kind of man would paddle up a canal just to get laid?" Patterson asked.

"We all would," Hogbody answered. "Especially you, so shut up and dig. Maybe you'd like—"

Although I wasn't looking in Hogbody's direction, from the way he had broken off his sentence, I knew that something was up. I leaned on my entrenching tool and turned to find Sgt. Jigaboo looking down at us in our holes. It was the first time I had seen a genuine grin on his face. He seemed to be staring into me. "Find the end yet?" he asked.

"No, Sergeant," I said. "It seems to be bottomless."

His face lost its grin and he looked out over the landscape. "It is," he said.

14

GOOD PORK BETTY
23 January 1968

Hogbody's insight into the behavior patterns of American GI graduates of an a-go-go school course of two-week's duration, as well as his unshakeable belief in Patterson's willingness to participate with alacrity in those behavior patterns, proved astonishingly perceptive. Within 24 hours of our graduation, Patterson, Taylor, Hogbody and I were crammed into a small Thai vegetable boat paddling, with uncoordinated and often opposing strokes, up a canal on Bangkok's northern outskirts. The canal was surrounded and partly covered by overhanging trees and beyond the profuse vegetation ricefields stretched on both sides of the canal as far as a sweat-filled, sun-blinded eye could see.

People along the shore and on porches of houses-on-stilts waved and smiled as our boat passed unsteadily by. We paddled up to the porch of an unpretentious canal-side house. In addition to the boats belonging to the house, another boat tied along the porch indicated that at least one other customer was already inside. Two laughing teenage girls jumped out of the water onto the porch and wrapped their wet *phatoongs* tightly around them, enhancing even more the allure of their vivacious feminine forms. We clambered out of the boat and entered the house.

A corpulent, middle-aged woman with close-cropped hair and enormous breasts sat by an open window enjoying her favorite Thai snack—crickets washed down with Mekhong whiskey. Edible cricket season may have been over but, however she did it, Betty seldom ran out of her cherished delicacy.

Millions of crickets are caught in nets above village houses in places like Lopburi and Suphanburi and Kanchanaburi and sold to guys in Bangkok who fry them in oil outside the bars; and the bar girls love them. You wanted to do the nasty with a Thai bar girl in those days you didn't bring long-stemmed roses and chocolate-covered gummy bears. No fucking way. Crickets fried in oil.

So, anyway, here was Good Pork Betty sitting by an open window, her hair blown into unnatural shapes by the wind, popping these crickets into her mouth the way we eat pop-corn. Of course, a lot of crickets didn't make it into her mouth because of the fucking wind but Betty didn't seem to notice. But I sure as hell did because, in Southeast Asia, more fatalities had been caused by wind-driven crickets than by Vietcong satchel carriers. As always, Betty was biting the heads off the crickets and spitting them out before popping the rest into her mouth. So the floor was covered with cricket heads, wings, antennae, legs, all of which crackled, popped and snapped as we walked across the room. The whole room sounded like it was crackling and popping and snapping. She was wearing the largest pair of shorts and the most stretched-to-capacity T-shirt I'd ever seen. On the T-shirt, across her bulging breasts, were the words, 'Good Betty'.

"Hi, Betty," Taylor said cheerfully. "How's our girl?"

Betty opened her arms to embrace him and Taylor moved into them. Within seconds, his face and neck turned reddish-pink, then pinkish-red, and, finally, as Betty's enthusiasm was about to bring down the final curtain on his respiration, a deep and resplendent sunset purple. He was released from this crushing affection only after Hogbody showed impatience about getting on with the business at hand. As Betty's motto was business before pleasure, Taylor was released from her embrace—and saved from extinction.

Patterson turned to him. "Her T-shirt says 'Good Betty'; what happened to the 'pork'?"

Taylor held his reply until he once again felt air enter his lungs. He motioned for Betty to pull her shirt out from between her breasts. As she did so, the word 'pork' began to emerge.

The men of the unit had made the T-shirt for her and it was Betty's proudest possession. Betty had formerly been the respected proprietor of a medium-sized whorehouse in the northern city of Chiang Mai, but with the influx of tens of thousands of GIs and Air Force personnel into Bangkok, Betty decided to go where the action was. Her whorehouses were known to be among the most relaxing and least expensive in all of Bangkok and business for Betty was very good.

Of all the dozens of fornicatoriums which Taylor said once made up Whore House Charlie's empire, Good Pork Betty's was the only one which still had faded letters over the door: 'Brothelarium'. Taylor claimed Betty knew Whore House Charlie well and it was in fact Charlie who had set her up at the fornicatorium. It was a safe claim, however, as Betty spoke no known language, and the few words she did utter were always unintelligible.

According to Taylor, Whorehouse Charlie was precocious at an extremely early age. Legend had it that he had actually drawn up blueprints for his first brothel at the age of four. It was said that his father (whose talents also lay—no pun intended—in that direction) accompanied the child-genius on a tour of the brothels of Europe where Charlie was the sensation of the underworld and acclaimed by pimps, hookers, brothel owners, managers and madames, police on the take, as well as customers wherever he went. Charlie's entrepreneurial and organizational ability in the location, design and management of brothels, as well as his own striking improvisations, was clearly that of a genius. By the time Charlie was a young man he had been named a chevalier of the Order of the Moving Mattress and been named *Brothelmeister* for all of Europe. It was then that Charlie turned his attention to Asia where before long he had met one of Asia's brothel's most frequent customers, Taylor himself.

It was only natural that as Taylor's recollections of Whore House Charlie's miracles increased in number and in dimension, cynics began demanding proof. Taylor informed all who would listen that several thousand peasants in the impoverished Northeast region of Thailand could attest to dozens of miracles performed by Charlie. Taylor elaborated on only two: the 'Miracle of the Changed Climate' and the 'Miracle of Suddenly-appearing Worlds'.

He insisted that, in the Northeast, villagers still gathered at their headmens' huts to speak in awe of miracles in which Charlie actually changed weather conditions or in which entire rooms changed appearance at his command.

It was only on his ninth Singha beer while nearly asleep inside a booth of Jack's Off bar that Taylor at last revealed the truth of those two miracles. It seemed Whore House Charlie spent his leave time traveling in the remote villages in the Northeast looking for delectable young Thai village girls whom he could suitably impress with his 'miracles.' He would gather together as many of these girls as he could and then take them to a newly constructed hotel in a small Thai town where he would first explain that he was about to change the weather, as well as the setting of a room. He then led his retinue of giggling Thai rice-farmers, construction workers, and highway sweepers into a room of the hotel which he had rented for the purpose.

While the girls looked on, Charlie burned incense, did a ritual dance and mumbled mysterious, arcane words which he recited from a 'sacred book,' all to invoke the benediction of the 'Weather God of the North,' the god who could relieve the people of the frightening heat and humidity. While the girls were *not* looking on, Charlie clandestinely pushed the 'on' button of the air-conditioning unit, and lo and behold, to cries of amazement from farm girls completely unfamiliar with air-conditioners, the room *cooled*. The God of the North had *heard* and *obeyed*.

It was with lowered voice and a barely concealed look of triumph that Taylor admitted Charlie's 'mystic words' to have been from the *Soldier's Code of Conduct* and the 'sacred book' from which he chanted his words to have been from none other than the *Soldier's Guide*. Once the room had cooled, Charlie would again ask the astonished girls to repeat the magic words after him, sentence by profound sentence, and with the 'off' button quietly in place, the Weather God again heated up the room.

While still reeling from this miraculous performance, Charlie's suitably impressed flock was led into a small dark room completely bare of furniture and decoration, where a similar ritual with even more esoteric words (this time the 'Oath of Allegiance') was performed. With right hands raised, Charlie and the girls intoned the unorthodox liturgy. In this highly charged atmosphere, Charlie opened and closed the door of the room several times. Each time he did so, the 'ad-joining' room completely changed in appearance: couches changing positions, curtains changing colors, and chairs appearing and disappearing. As the farm girls had never before been inside an elevator, and failed to realize they were seeing *different* floors of the hotel, their belief in the 'Miracle of Suddenly-appearing Worlds' was as unshakable as their belief in the 'Miracle of the Changed Climate'.

Having attained divinity, Charlie would then lead his stupefied disciples back to his rented room where he bade his new converts to join in the baptismal ritual known as 'taking one's clothes off,' after which a jealous god, his sacerdotal functions completed, would presumably collect his well-earned if somewhat sensual reward.

Two of Betty's girls were occupied in setting one another's hair, a process interrupted by Patterson and Hogbody who chose the two as their companions. The four of them walked happily up the creaking staircase. Good Pork Betty placed her hands on her breasts as if to prevent their flopping about, and called loudly for another girl.

A beautiful 19-year-old girl entered the room from one of the many adjoining bedrooms. She placed her hands together before her face and *waiied* us. Her name was Sundaree and she spoke very little English. Ordinarily, Taylor would have insisted that such an innocent and young angelic type was obviously meant for him. But as his breathing had yet to return to normal, and as his role of Typhlophile at Large had somewhat reformed him, he decided to stay awhile and chat with Betty although they resorted to an involved and somewhat obscene sign language for communication. I thanked him for his magnanimity and took Sundaree by the hand.

Inside the bedroom I took off my clothes, checked the immediate area for water snakes and intricately fashioned cobwebs for poisonous spiders. Then I lay in my undershorts on a mattress on the floor covered only by a thin, well-worn blanket with a flower design more appropriate for a nursery. The room's decor consisted of a mirror, a shelf, and a table loaded with cheap perfumes and other bottles brimming with exotic potions, circumstantial but convincing evidence of someone's reprehensible abuse of PX privileges. There was no other furniture. The walls were covered from top to bottom with old newspaper and magazine pictures of Thai television stars, Thai movie stars, and pictures of former Miss Thailand's. The combination tin-and-wood ceiling had no holes but a long rectangular area different in color from the rest might once indeed have served clients as a brothelarium.

Sundaree entered the room with a rickety electric fan, a bowl, a bottle of water and a towel. She closed the wooden shutters, set up the fan to insure the maximum amount of breeze and bugs, and lay beside me. Just as I reached over to begin my sinful episode, she jumped up and ran to the row of cheap dresses hanging from the makeshift shelf. She began hanging dresses, blouses, and *phasins* around the room in front of small holes in the walls so that should any of her idle girlfriends enjoy the undeniable thrills of voyeurism, they were in for a disappointment. "No want them see," she said.

"OK," I said.

She slipped out of her *phasin* and bra, demurely wrapped a towel around her smooth, brown body, and finally slipped her pink-and-white panties off. As she lay beside me on the mattress, a light rain began tapping softly on the roof's rusted tin and rotten wood. An observant God was drumming his fingers, whether in disapproval or excitement I wasn't sure. I now had only a towel across my mid-section, which, due to my erection began rising; Sundaree's eyes got very large and as she drew back, I realized panic was setting in. I held her arm and smiled. "I got a feeling you're new at this business."

Her intense gaze never left the ever-rising towel. "I come yesterday," she said. "From Northeast."

"Yeah, well, I'm about to come from the southwest. Just relax."

Hogbody, in the room beside us, had apparently heard everything. "Hey," he yelled, as he banged on the wall, "is this a seminar on sex education or a whorehouse?"

"Give me a little slack, will you, Hog?" I said. 'This girl is new. She seems to think an erection is a miracle or something."

"In your case, it's probably true." I threw him a bird even though I knew he couldn't see me and then I returned to fondling Sundaree. As I began making my usual unorthodox advances toward a bed partner, I found that Sundaree was not at all the compliant and uncomplaining andromaniacal bedmate one expects to find in one of Whore House Charlie's brothelaria. There were certain movements and positions Sundaree definitely frowned upon and, as her English was limited, she would respond to such suggestions with a "no thank you," or else a "thank you." Not unlike the complicated circuits of on-off computer switches that reduce all information inside the computer to 'yes' or 'no' choices. Hence, by trial and error, I gradually learned the way to her heart and to other areas of her anatomy as well. It was very similar to the mazes I had played as a youngster in which one begins at the outside of the maze, at 'start,' and attempts to reach the center by finding the correct path. The process was full of dead ends ("no thank you") and proper passageways ("thank you") which eventually led to the goal. The trick to the maze, of course, was to *start at the center* and then work your way out. I soon found that was also the best way to handle Sundaree's temperamental sexual proclivities.

I rolled onto her and we began making love. She tolerated it, I enjoyed it; I tolerated it, she enjoyed it; third time lucky—we wiped each other out. Afterwards, I washed, put on my shorts and sat on the floor smoking a cigarette watching her wash herself with the water from the bottle.

No matter how many times I would experience a similar scene, I was always amazed and pleased by the absence of Puritan guilt in the Thai mindset or of any sordid atmosphere in Thai brothels. It would no doubt seem strange to anyone in the new millennium that I had managed to land in Bangkok in the early 60's as a virgin. But anyone who grew up in America during the Eisenhower Years—Duh!—will remember that if you even so much as smiled at a girl, she was likely to peg you as a pervert if not actually have you arrested. Everyone knew sex was a dirty thing practiced on moonless nights only by low-class trailer trash with strange-sounding names in Southern California brothels and West Texas bars. In Thailand I had come face to face with an attitude toward sex that was neither judgmental nor disparaging. I well understood exactly why the men of the *Bounty,* once enamored with Polynesian women, had mutinied against Captain Bligh. Christian Fletcher's revolt was not carried out primarily for the privilege of sexual abandonment but rather as a repudiation of Judeo-Christian mores. Fletcher's mutiny had been stirred not simply by fraternizing with gorgeous and erotic women, but by the discovery of a refreshing and reasonable attitude toward love and sex.

And to a perceptive observer, American men newly arrived in Bangkok ('still pissing Stateside water') were different in many ways from those of us who had been here for some time.

Whenever several of us would be discussing how much fun one of the bargirls was in bed and how much she charged, the newly arrived American would always wrinkle his brow, listen quietly and finally interject with: "I never pay for it."

And there it was: the American male ego; the American desire to be loved 'only for myself.' Which, of course, to the Thais made little or no sense because it was precisely the 'self' or 'ego' which had to be extinguished before escaping the cycle of rebirth and the attainment of Nirvana.

There were, of course, practical reasons why we 'paid for it.' Not least of which was that few Thai girls from good families in the 1960's were about to go out with foreign soldiers and, second, bargirls had to make a living like anyone else. A man living in Bangkok might actually have more fun and more real communication with a Thai bargirl than an American and his bar pickup in the States. But if the American didn't 'pay' for it, and we did, he was 'normal,' we were losers. The idea that nightlife in which money changes hands for sex must be sordid was ingrained in the American psyche and no doubt said something about American puritanical values but, not being an officer, I realized I could never hope to grasp the Big Picture.

My thoughts were interrupted by the rhythm of a brief downpour outside. Something about the sound of bugs tapping against the light bulb, the smell of stale beer and garlic and beetle nut and chilies, and the wall lizards scampering about trying to fuck each other—all that started to make me sleepy. Then she was again by my side on the mattress and I began fondling her. "You've got more benefits than a re-up bonus, you know that?"

She began playing with the minuscule amount of hair on my chest. "You like Thai girl?"

"I *love* Thai girl." As I started to take her bra off again, I heard something that sounded like chanting coming from another room. I listened for a few moments and remembered that I had spotted another customer's boat when I'd arrived. Sundaree smiled and pointed toward the opposite wall. She rose and walked to the wall and removed a polka-dot dress with wide-eyed bunnies she had hung near a small carrot-shaped hole. The sound increased. I walked over and quietly knelt beside the hole to look into the next room. I saw a decidedly bored Thai girl leaning on her elbow reading a Thai movie magazine. I moved my head slightly to see who her companion was and suddenly found my heart desperately trying to push past my Adam's apple. Blinky was lying on his elbows next to her on the mattress looking toward his waist. I could just barely make out the words: "Every day in every way it's getting harder and harder. Every day in every way it's getting harder and harder. Every day in every way—"

The accelerity with which I replaced the bunny dress over the carrot hole and with which I exited the room will, I'm sure, still be subject for discussion even after sex is dead; it will definitely long remain one of the mysteries of Sundaree's life. That I never told anyone about what I'd seen was due less to human compassion or fear of retaliation than to Sundaree's comment just before I bolted from the room. She placed one finger of her hand before her lips to indicate secrecy, and tapped the crotch of the panties she was wearing with her other hand, and in a tone which conveyed nearly unutterable sorrow said, "Baby him sleep; no can wake up."

What she said as well as the call for secrecy made me understand that, like *Noh* plays in Japanese paper-thin houses, what is espied from carrot-shaped holes in a Bangkok brothel is also to be held in the closest confidence and not to do so would be both a monstrous indiscretion and a venal sin.

We paddled away and waved goodbye to the girls on the porch. "You know, I feel kind of guilty," Patterson said.

"Guilty?" Hogbody asked.

"I mean hurting the American economy by spending dollars on the local market like that. And we were getting paid the whole time we were in there."

"Roy," Taylor said patiently, "if our president didn't want you to spend U.S. dollars in whorehouses overseas, or if he didn't want you to go to whorehouses on your lunch hour, don't you think he would have said so?"

Roy thought for a minute. "Well, he did say he wasn't gonna' send American boys over to Asia to do what Asian boys should do."

Taylor wiped sweat from his eyes. "Relax, Roy. I'm telling you our commander-in-chief doesn't give a shit if we visit Good Pork Betty's or not."

"Yeah, I guess you're right," Patterson said thoughtfully. "It does seem like he would have said something."

15

OPERATION CHAMELEON
2 February 1968

The decor of our room was never static. It was constantly undergoing changes, reflecting the perpetual turmoil of the march of events in the States, news from the war zone (which every day in every way was getting wider and wider) and the inside of our own heads. As friends in Hawaii insisted that I should remain up on the struggles taking place there, I duly placed about the room anything I was sent. Hence, our wall was now covered with no fewer than three anti-land developer stickers which read: 'Save Diamond Head—All of it.'

There was also a drawing of a piece of land sloping into a river entitled: 'Why GIs Don't Make Waves.' High up on dry land was a general, behind him with only his feet in the water was a lieutenant, behind him up to his waist in the water was a sergeant, and in the water up to his neck was a GI, which looked quite a bit like Taylor. Below a photograph of General Westmoreland a sentence with variously colored words and letters posed the question, 'Would you buy a used body bag from this man?' And beneath a photograph of a solemn-faced Richard Nixon, was the line: 'Ask not what Agent Orange can do for you, ask what you can do for Agent Orange.'

Taylor's latest decoration was a neatly printed sign taped

to the side of his wall locker:

GENERATIONS TO COME, IT MAY BE, WILL SCARCE BE-
LIEVE THAT SUCH A ONE AS THIS EVER IN FLESH AND
BLOOD WALKED UPON THIS EARTH.
ALBERT EINSTEIN ON MOHATMA GANDHI

ANYBODY WHO DOESN'T BELIEVE WHORE HOUSE
CHARLIE EXISTED HAS GOT HIS HEAD SO FAR UP HIS ASS
HE NEEDS A GLASS BELLY-BUTTON TO SEE OUT.
RICK TAYLOR ON WHORE HOUSE CHARLIE

Just as we were protected from actual battlefield situations by being in Bangkok, we were also protected from other excesses the war generated. Hence, no one at our unit was addicted to any hard drugs nor had a great desire to try any. Pep pills and marijuana, were, of course, something altogether different, somehow more fitting among genteel warriors at peace. Freeman had bought a supply of marijuana while he was visiting the northern city of Chiang Mai and was soon sharing it with us. He and Taylor each contributed their unique skills and talents in such situations. Freeman taught us to inhale a joint while holding it in our fist between the first finger and thumb. He had learned from the hilltribes that in this method the grass (or whatever) goes directly into the lungs without drying the throat. Taylor's contribution was the practice of burning strong-scented incense to cover the smell of the grass.

One afternoon, shortly after an inspection so disastrous that Bumbles's discrepancy book literally bulged with names, Wat entered our incense-laden room and ran over to Taylor who was now sprawled out on the bed with his eyes closed. He put his hands down hard on Taylor's head. Taylor was indignant. "Jesus, Wat. You're as bad as Dang. My spirit resides in my head, you know. You may have damaged my spirit. Don't you know Thai customs?"

Wat grinned from ear to ear. "You got more to worry about than spirit. Two girls ask your name. They pull up in blue Ford at gate. They talking goddamned Chinese."

Taylor sat up. "Oh, my God. It must be Ching Li and Mei Ling."

"Who?" I asked.

"They're from Taiwan. Their father works in a company here in Bangkok. I'm teaching them English." Taylor jumped up. "Quick! Operation Chameleon!"

Everyone began frantically changing the room from Thai decor to a Chinese decor. Wat removed a picture of a Thai movie star, I removed the pictures of the Thai king and queen, Freeman removed a Thai flag and calendar, and Taylor placed the Thai Buddha into his wall locker. He then began unfolding a Nationalist Chinese flag, large pictures of Chiang Kai-shek and Dr. Sun Yat-sen and taped them securely to the wall. Freeman carefully lifted an ivory statue of the Goddess of Mercy out of the wall locker and placed it in a place of prominence on top of a foot locker. A Chinese calendar with Chinese movie stars replaced the Thai one. Books on Chinese culture were scattered on the beds and piled reverently against the wall. Finally, we were finished, and Taylor looked around approvingly. "There. Now if this fucking place doesn't look like the headquarters of the Kuomintang, my name isn't Rick fucking Taylor."

Just after Wat exited, the two girls knocked and entered. Both of them were beautiful. I felt an erection growing, so I sat down on my bed and placed a book on Chinese history on my lap. "Hello, Rick," one of them said. "We're sorry to bother you."

"Not at all, Ching Li. Come in, come in. This is Freeze, a

161

friend of mine, and Pineapple, one of my roommates."

Mei Ling sat on the bed and Ching Li displayed her shapely legs in the room's only chair. "We're leaving for a short vacation to Taiwan so we have to cancel our class for a week. We just stopped by to tell you."

Freeman, beginning to get stoned, started to giggle. Taylor gave him a glance of disapproval which Freeman failed to notice. "Well," Taylor said with appropriate melancholy, "I'll certainly miss you both."

Ching Li began observing the decorations. "Why, Rick, your room is decorated in Chinese style."

Freeman giggled again as he passed me the joint.

Taylor spoke diffidently. "Well, you know how it is, Ching Li, I like Chinese culture a great deal. I've always admired the greatest of Chinese emperors."

Which was news to me because Taylor always said he admired the *worst* of the Chinese emperors because unlike the 'greatest' who were forever sending large armies (GIs) into battle, the 'worst' emperors always let the eunuchs run the empire while the emperors themselves became dissipated and indulgent and died in bed with beautiful concubines.

Ching Li smiled coyly and crossed her gorgeous jade-white legs. I studied her perfectly formed feminine knees and felt my erection raising learned reflections on Chinese historical patterns even higher. "I'm glad," she said. For a few moments, she and Taylor exchanged smiles and spoke a bit of mandarin. Taylor's mandarin always sounded to me like the tin roof of a village brothel flopping madly about in monsoon winds but the two Chinese girls seemed to lap it up. Finally, Ching Li stood up. "Well, our driver is waiting."

Freeman and I watched from the porch as Taylor escorted the girls to the gate. He waved goodbye and the car pulled out. He turned toward the building but as he started to approach a Thai

Army jeep appeared in the driveway and the horn began blowing. It was Watana and her husband. Taylor turned toward us and began making frantic gestures of changing his clothes. Freeman began giggling. "What's his problem, man?"

"Maybe he's hot."

As Taylor and the two Thais neared the building, I suddenly woke up. I slapped Freeman's shoulder. "Hey! I forgot. Watana and her husband are paying a courtesy call on Blinky. To thank him for the slot machine money. They're coming here first. Rick means Operation Chameleon! Let's go!"

A giggling and stoned Freeman helped me as much as he could in again trying to change the decor of the room, this time back to Thai. All Chinese paraphernalia was finally discarded, concealed or covered over by Thai paraphernalia just as the others walked in. During the exchange of pleasantries, all Freeman could do was giggle. "Far out!" he said, to no one in particular.

"Oh, Rick, your room is decorated like a Thai's! You're even burning incense!"

Taylor again spoke diffidently and from the heart. "Well, Watana," he said, "I guess the truth is my heart belongs to Thailand. I've always admired the greatest of the Siamese monarchs."

I began coughing on my joint while Freeman giggled hysterically. Taylor combed his hair. "I'm ready to see the Old Man," he said. Then he turned to me. "We're off to see Blinky. Want to come?"

"Sure, why not?" I looked at the sprawled out, giggling form of Freeman. "What about him?"

"He's happy here," Taylor said.

Watana stared at Freeman. "Why is Warren so happy, Rick?"

Taylor held the door open for her. "Oh, it's his day to laugh, Watana. He's an African tribesman; it's a custom of his tribe: They get hysterical when they reach puberty. Let's go."

We hadn't walked more than a few steps when I saw the

flashes of light coming from the window of the orderly room. I reacted immediately. I ran to the rail and shouted down to the small group of bargirls standing near the gate. I pointed to Corporal Comatose, the only one in Court Countdown who could read Morse Code, and shouted hysterically.

Unfortunately, the previous night, Corporal Comatose had gorged himself in his usual fashion, 'sticky' rice from the Northeast, hot rice wine, and cobra meat curry spiced with heaps of *ganja* (marijuana), all washed down with great amounts of Mekhong whiskey. Fortunately, the bargirls had had years of experience in waking even the most inebriated GI at closing time to send him home, and in a matter of seconds they had managed to shake Corporal Comatose awake. He sprang to life, faced the direction of the orderly room, and stood at attention. Once the flashes of light had stopped, he saluted, pivoted, and turned to face the bargirls. He saluted them and made his report. One of them yelled to us in English, "Surprise inspection. Five minutes."

We sat Watana and her husband on the steps, hurriedly excused ourselves, and dashed back into the room. With a minimal amount of help from Freeman, we began the operation. Wall and foot lockers were hastily thrown open and shelves rummaged for material. Within three minutes the ultimate metamorphosis was completed. The Thai calendar had been replaced by a picture of George Washington crossing the Delaware; The Thai Buddha was replaced by a medium-sized metal statue of an American soldier with his rifle—a la Fort Dix, 'Home of the Ultimate Weapon'; the Thai flag was replaced by a framed copy of the American constitution and a photograph of the Lincoln Memorial. An American flag fluttered near the door and books on American military strategies during World War II (the war that *did* in fact get better and better) appeared on shelves and boxes. A small cassette recorder blared out a tinny version of 'Battle Hymn of the Republic' to insure that even as Blinky and Bumbles strutted across the length of Court Countdown, they would know, beyond any shadow of a doubt, the extent and depth of the fanatical loyalty of their men.

16

THE BETEL NUT QUEEN
28 February 1968

As 'the folks back home' would learn several years later, not all Americans-in-uniform in the 1960s regarded Vietnamese as the main enemy, or even as *the* enemy. Notes of sympathy and even encouragement were sometimes left for Vietcong who spent their lives in tunnels below ground, and many black soldiers who didn't understand the need to shoot at their 'brown brothers' agreed with Mohammed Ali and felt that they also "had no quarrel with them 'Cong'." In time, the ultimate expression of alienation — the phenomenon of fragging — was picked up by the press. The American enlisted man's identification with and even admiration for the Asians he fought with, for or against had its corollary in his growing disenchantment with the military mentality of his own officers.

None of us in Thailand needed to worry about booby traps, sniper rounds, or incoming artillery, yet, even though stationed in paradise, the dislike for some of our own career officers and NCOs went far beyond the normal soldiers' right-to-gripe of previous American wars. And, despite Bumbles's tirades, there was not a communist dupe among us. In fact, none of us believed the words of officials of either Vietnam any more than we did the reports of American victories which followed every battle; and, certainly, none of us liked communism, as, for one thing, it immediately forced beautiful young Asian girls into re-education camps rather than allowing them to remain free and, in Taylor's words, "follow successful careers in bars and massage parlors if they so choose."

There was, we knew, one enemy camp centered in Hanoi in which skilled military and civilian leaders hypocritically, deceitfully, and dishonestly spoke of a quest for peace while carrying out a brutal war. The policies of this enemy camp caused untold misery and death to hundreds of thousands of civilians and *enlisted men.*

The second enemy camp was centered in Saigon. This camp was led by skilled military and civilian leaders who spoke hypocritically, deceitfully, and dishonestly of peace while brutally and viciously stifling dissent, and carrying out a brutal war. The policies of this enemy camp caused untold misery and death to hundreds of thousands of civilians and *enlisted men.*

The third enemy camp was centered in Washington, in a building known as the Pentagon, and in another building known as the White House. This camp was led by skilled military and civilian leaders who spoke hypocritically, deceitfully, and dishonestly of peace while carrying on one of the most devastating wars in history. The policies of this enemy camp caused untold misery and death to hundreds of thousands of civilians and *enlisted men.*

As far as Bangkok warriors were concerned, any leader who proposed policies which, in their implementation, endangered even one enlisted man of *any camp,* was *the enemy.* Hence, Taylor spoke for all of us when he readily and unashamedly stole a leaf from Marx's notebook in his declaration that "enlisted men of the world unite, you have nothing to save but your ass"; and from Mao's 'little red book' as well, in that, "enlisted men do not fight enlisted men."

An example of this 'diplomatic revolution' involving, on the one hand, Asians and American enlisted men, and, on the other hand, American officers, occurred the day Taylor and Patterson were once again late for work. Blinky had warned that if they were late to work again, he would have to punish them; in his words, it would "be time to Katy-bar-the-door." Word reached me while I was fighting the bugs in the messhall that they were late again. I rushed into Club Victory and over to Wat at the bar. "Wat! Rick and Roy! Have you seen them?"

He grinned and pointed to four GIs in fatigues sitting around a table. "They no can leave," he said. "They make too much money playing pinochle."

I walked to Taylor's table and stood behind him as he and three others played cards. "Hi."

Taylor's response, in the form of a grunt, was delivered with a distinct I-don't-want-to-be-bothered-now tone. I straddled a chair and leaned on the back of it. "When you get finished playing cards I think I know a couple of guys who want to play you for big stakes."

Taylor's eyes never left his cards. "Yeah? What stakes?"

"Your ass. Pearshape just called in from the compound to tell Blinky and Bumbles you two are late again and they went out to hang you when you do show up."

He carefully arranged his cards in their proper suits. "It just so happens, Pineapple, baby, that last night Pearshape himself gave us today off."

"It also just so happens, Rick, baby, that the computer decided this morning that we need five guys working in your section and we've only got three."

Taylor threw his cards down as if they'd suddenly become too hot to hold. "Computer!" He jumped up as if his chair had suddenly become too hot to sit in. "You're telling me I'm about to get dicked away because I'm disobeying the orders of a fucking *computer?*"

"I didn't make the rules, man. Save your pleas for the lifers."

"Well, no mechanical man is going to dick me away. He looked at the clock. "How long ago did they leave?"

"About three minutes."

He grabbed his hat and scooped up his money. 'Then we're not finished yet. Come on, Roy, let's move."

Patterson chugged the rest of his Singha beer and pulled his wrinkled hat out of his pocket. "I'm coming!"

The three of us ran out to the gate, past a snoring Corporal Comatose, and jumped into a taxi. Taylor leaned forward to speak to the driver. 'The lifers are trying to hang my ass. Head for the airport. Hurry!"

The driver was confused although his English wasn't bad because he'd been hanging around in front of our unit for years. "Lifers? Airport? How much you pay?"

"Anything!" Taylor said. "Anything! Just move!"

In a country which has all the rice it needs and the most beautiful women in the world, *anything* could only mean one thing: the most valuable commodity imaginable to any Thai driver. "Appen?"

"Yeah, yeah, apples. Next time the messhall has them, you get a fucking dozen."

The taxi moved out at incredible speed. A few minutes later, we spotted Bumbles's faded grey Chevrolet in front. 'There it is!" I said. "Let's duck. Maybe they won't see us go by."

Taylor shook his head. "No, that's no good. Even if they didn't see us, there's no way to get by Pearshape's office without *his* seeing us."

Pearshape was a man of mystery; probably to those he served under as well as to those who served under him. As he always seemed to be scratching his left shoulder with his right hand, his arm was invariably blocking his nametag, and none of us knew even his surname. There were two rumors about Pearshape, neither of which could be proved but, according to computer personnel during brief periods of truce, apparently based on fact. The first was that he had formerly been in line to command the unit but had been passed over because of a suggestion he had sent along to COMPAC, Commander, Pacific Region, to the effect that consideration should be given to developing a weapon which while annihilating enlisted men, would leave officers intact; a kind of ultimate chessboard solution for those forced to taint their hands with the very pawns they needed to win battles. This rumor concluded by saying that Pearshape's request was denied and he was considered unsuitable for command.

The second rumor also confirmed that he had been formerly in line to command the unit and had mooted the idea of eliminating the world's population of enlisted men by the special-effects weapon, but, according to this rumor, it was not any high-ranking officer which had turned down Pearshape's proposal, it was in fact a high-ranking computer.

Although we had no way of telling which version was the truth, or, at least, less false, as he was fond of sitting at his desk and staring through his window at the road leading to the compound, he was sure to spot us.

"So what do we do?" Patterson's tone showed clearly that he felt the hangman's noose slipping over his head.

"We do like the Thais do—we use a boat."

As soon as Bumbles's Chevrolet made a left, Taylor ordered the driver to stop beside a small canal which crossed under the highway at right angles and continued on into the countryside. We leapt from the taxi and made our way along the canal in the direction of the operations compound.

Although it was true that no one except Taylor remembered Whore House Charlie, it was equally true that there was certain archaeological and anthropological evidence for his existence in the form of a string of canalside whorehouses which, in sheer number alone, would put Playboy Clubs to shame. Circumstantial though the evidence might have been, someone of superhuman determination and imagination had located and standardized one of the most elaborate systems of brothels in modern history. And although Taylor had always stopped short of introducing a 'chariots-of-the-gods, being-from-another-planet' explanation, it was clear that he had not performed the task alone.

According to Taylor, he and Whore House Charlie used to paddle in the canals inside and on the outskirts of Bangkok looking for whorehouses which might, with vision and labor, be upgraded to brothelarium status; and one day they found that the canal we were now following passed, at its south end, less than fifteen yards from our work operations area. As the Army rulebooks say to use whatever the indigenous population can offer in order to combat the enemy, so Charlie and Taylor bought kites for the kids who lived along the canal. In return, whenever they spotted an officer's car, they flew the kites with olive-green tails. Some of the children actually began to play near the bridge so that they could be the first to spot a lifer's car. Taylor and Charlie began distributing prizes (usually messhall apples or cookies) to the kid who spotted the most lifers each month. And, it was a fact, that the only word they knew in English was 'lifer'.

Once an officer's car was spotted, the first in line would fly his kite with the olive-green tail. And the kids farther down the canal would spot that kite and then in turn fly theirs until finally the last few kites at the south end of the canal were visible to the Thai guards around our work area. They would then sound the warning. And since almost all inspections were held during the day, the number of successful surprise inspections had dropped by over ninety per cent.

The three of us came upon a wooden Thai house resting precariously on stilts above the water. An old bare-breasted Thai woman with leathery brown skin, close-cropped white hair and red betel-nut lips was sitting on the small porch overlooking the canal. A faded 'coca-cola' sign hung above a small table lined with vegetables and fruit. She was flying a kite.

Taylor pointed to the woman. "There she is!" he said proudly. "The Betel-nut Queen. That old woman sits on her porch all day and chews betel nut and sells vegetables. So she watches the bridge for officers's vehicles. She knows if they turned off the highway onto this road, they must be heading out to the house."

"Has she ever warned the house before this?" Patterson asked.

"Has she ever! I hope to shit in your messkit, she has. This old lady has saved my ass more times than I can remember."

The Betel-nut Queen waved heartily and sent a little naked boy across the porch to get Coca-cola. Taylor began speaking to her in Thai while pointing to the vegetable boats. The Betel-nut Queen grinned, and, holding her wrinkled breasts to prevent them from flopping, ran over and untied a boat partially full of fruit and vegetables. She paddled the boat over to the porch while she and Taylor spoke in Thai.

As the Betel-nut Queen chatted with Taylor, she would occasionally take in a bit of snuff, or at least attempt to, by means of a slender and unadorned U-shaped length of metal pipe. She would pack a bit of snuff in one end, and place that end in her mouth. She would then blow the snuff through the pipe and into one nostril at a time. Unfortunately, her hands—although a beautiful shade of brown and very expressive—were unsteady, and the snuff usually shot straight into one of her wide brown eyes, leaving her eye momentarily submerged in brown snuff, and her red, betel-nut lips mumbling in confusion.

The three of us took quick gulps of coke then got into the

boat and waved goodbye to the Betel-nut Queen. Taylor and I paddled at each end while Patterson was squeezed in the center with the vegetables. "What chance we got in making it?" Patterson asked.

Taylor continued to paddle furiously as he spoke. "Well, the canal runs almost straight toward the river and ends up just behind the compound. The road Blinky and Bumbles are on goes way out toward the airport before it swings back again. There's a chance that if we paddle like hell we can get to the compound before they do and sneak in the back way."

Taylor and I demonstrated difficulty coordinating with each other on the paddling and the boat began gliding erratically down the canal underneath the overhanging trees. Thais in other boats steered clear of it. A woman on the right bank, with her *phasin* wrapped around her, stood beside her large Thai-style fishing net which was dipped into the water. She belatedly realized the boat was heading directly for her net and managed to raise it just as we passed underneath, scraping the bank and losing some of our load. The water was full of Thai children swimming and grabbing the fruit.

Patterson began laughing. "I haven't had so much fun since granny got caught doing pushups in the pickle patch."

"You're splashin' my fucking fatigues," Taylor said. "And will somebody get these goddamn mangoes away from me?"

I looked at the bucolic scene around me. "Green rice fields, green trees, blue sky; a fellow could forget all about lifers and dickaways and PX's out here."

"Sure," Taylor said. "It's easy for you, shit-for-brains. It's my ass they're trying to hang, not yours."

Naked brown children dove in and swam around the boat, laughing and shouting. The kites with bright olive-green tails were up ahead as far as the eye could see. Taylor suddenly placed his paddle on the floor of the boat.

"What's the matter?" I asked.

"We're not going to make it. We can't paddle for shit."

Patterson pointed to the children. "I bet they know how to paddle."

Taylor spoke in Thai to one of the boys. "Can you paddle like hell?"

Within seconds the three of us were bunched together with the fruit and vegetables in the middle of the boat while one boy paddled at the stern and another at the bow. Taylor turned to me and studied me for a few moments, like a bargirl trying to decide if a new customer is likely to be a big spender. "One more thing we've got to do. You've got to get out."

"Get out! You want me to swim?"

He pointed to the bend up ahead. "We're getting near the road that turns off to the house now. Their Chevy should be the only one on it. When the canal veers near the road again, we're going to pull over and let you out."

"And then?"

"Lek, the little fellow, paddling up front, says his house is just around the bend. He and his older brother have three water buffalo. You are going with them to get the buffalo and see to it that they find a nice shady spot to relax in the middle of the road at the most narrow point. You are going to direct that operation which will successfully put the enemy out of action for awhile, 'neutralized' as officer training guides say. Then find a phone, get hold of Butterball and tell him to ask Lek and Corporal Napalm to misplace Blinky's badge for awhile. Bumbles's too. If you get through in time it'll give us a few more minutes to beat them out there. Any questions?"

"Yeah. You didn't have anything to do with planning the Charge of the Light Brigade, did you?"

"If this works," Patterson said, with new hope in his voice, "we should be promoted to generals."

Taylor's sweat-filled face broke into a grin. "I'll settle for an early out."

Taylor and I saluted and then exchanged late-show, military-type do-your-best-for-God-duty-country expressions that would have made John Wayne proud.

Lek and I jumped out onto the bank of the canal and ran along the elevated banks through the rice fields. We arrived at his house and he began talking rapidly to his mother who was in the midst of suckling a baby. She pointed and Lek and I ran in that direction.

Lek's brother was sitting on top of one of the buffalo while all three buffalo were chewing grass. They had good-sized horns but were lazy and gentle. Lek jumped onto one of the buffalo and as we all moved out Lek spoke rapidly in Thai to his brother. We reached the road and while Lek's brother and I sat the buffalo on the road under the shade, Lek borrowed pans, saluted and ran off down the road. His brother made himself comfortable and began whittling on a piece of wood. I crouched behind tall grass and trees. In the distance, I could hear Lek beating the pans to warn of the car's approach.

A minute later, Bumbles's car appeared and halted in front of the buffalo. He slowed his car and tapped on the horn. Nothing moved. The car's engine stopped. After a few seconds and another tap on the horn, he got out and walked over to Lek's brother. "Those your buffalo?" Bumbles asked. (His tone suggested they were double-parked.)

Lek's brother only smiled and continued whittling. Bumbles spoke firmly. "Now, look, I'm afraid I'm gonna have to order you to move those buffalo."

Blinky joined him in using broken English and sign language. He got an even bigger grin. Lek joined his brother in smiling at Bumbles and Blinky. More children began gathering.

Blinky took out his handkerchief and wiped his neck. "Can't we go around them, Sergeant?"

"We'll only end up in the ricefield, sir. If we can just get one of these things to move, we should be able to make it."

"Well, talk to him some more," Blinky said resignedly. He opened the car door and sat on the seat while more children gathered around to stare at him. Some children began running from the direction of the canal. One of them had a kite with an olive-green tail. As he passed, I motioned for him to continue on to Blinky and Bumbles. The boy sent the kite flying high and, with a big grin, handed it to Bumbles who was still trying to explain in broken English that there was a war on and they had to get through.

Bumbles hesitated but Lek put the kite string into his hand. As Bumbles held the kite, the children jumped up and down, laughing. Blinky got out of the car and again wiped the sweat from the back of his neck. He held out his hand. "Sergeant, will you give me that thing and try to coax one of those damned animals out of the road before we spend the rest of the day here?"

Bumbles handed the kite string to Blinky. "Yes, sir." He began talking softly to one of the water buffalo while prodding it with a small stick. It turned its head to look at Bumbles and Bumbles jumped backward to the great delight of the children. (*Another off-Broadway spectacular with an all-star cast of deranged foreigners.*)

I decided I had seen enough. I ran along the canal toward the highway, keeping plenty of bushes and trees between myself and the footlights. I flagged a taxi and reached an airport phone booth. On the second try I got Butterball on the phone. I started to speak, but he interrupted me. "They're here, baby, they're here. Operation Betel-nut Queen is a success. Come on in."

I slammed down the phone and jubilantly hailed a taxi. The taxi pulled up behind Bumbles's car. He and Blinky were sitting morosely in the front seat with both doors open. Lek and some of the children were still there. So were the buffalo. Lek's kite was still flying. I walked over to Blinky and saluted. "Afternoon, sir."

Blinky looked astonished. His widening eyes caused facial layers of fat to flee in all directions. "What are you doing here, Pineapple? Aren't you on break?"

"Gillis just called me on the field phone, sir. He said some new material just came in this morning by courier that he thought I should take a look at."

"Well," Blinky said dolefully. "these water buffalo are holding up the war effort. You speak some Thai don't you?"

"Just a little, sir."

"Well, try to explain to these kids that we've got to get through here even if it means running over a water buffalo or whatever the hell they are."

Bumbles spoke angrily. "Goddamn communist animals if you ask me, sir."

I turned back to Blinky. "I'll try, sir." After a minute of exaggerated gesturing and talking, I told Lek it was OK to move them. Lek held a brief conversation with some of the other children, then pulled in his kite and prodded the first buffalo with his stick. In a few seconds, they all rose and walked slowly off the road, with great dignity.

"Well, I'll be damned!" Blinky said. "What'd you tell him?"

"I just told him we wanted to use the road, sir."

"Well, I'll be damned!" He said again, as if there was a need to repeat the obvious.

"All right, Pineapple, pay your driver and hop in the back."

As Bumbles drove, Blinky turned around and stared at me for a few moments. Then a big smirk crossed his face. "Looks like your friends Taylor and Patterson didn't make it to work again today."

"Really, sir? I thought I saw them get on the bus."

"Well, if they're late this time I'm afraid we'll have to press charges." He paused to wipe his neck. "Sure are a lot of kites out today."

"Yes, sir," Bumbles said. "It's the national sport in Thailand. It's the season now, too."

Bumbles parked the car next to the house and the three of us stood in front of the Thai guard shack for our badges. Butterball was getting a coke out of the *klong* jar behind the shack. He saluted Blinky.

"Specialist Gillis," I asked. "Did we get that stuff in by courier, all right?"

"Sure did, Specialist," he answered. "It's already inside the house. I thought you ought to come out and take a look at it for yourself."

Blinky entered an office to talk to Pearshape while Bumbles stopped in the hallway to get some coffee. I went on through to the finance office. Taylor, Freeman and others in the room had huge grins on their faces. Bumbles finished getting his coffee and walked into the room. His eyes bulged and his coffee spilled as he saw Taylor and Patterson. He turned around and headed for Pearshape's office.

"So how'd it go?" I asked.

"Complete victory," Taylor said. "We came in the back way. Pearshape was using Blinky's office, so Roy and I went in to see him about getting an air-conditioner fixed. He was probably working on our court martial papers."

Patterson continued. "His eyes got real big like a Thai kid's when a foreigner says hello. And he looked out the window trying to spot a taxi."

Taylor began doing a little dance. "So our esteemed Commander-of-all-Computers is in there right now trying to explain to Blinky and Bumbles how we were here all the time and he just didn't see us."

I sat down in one of the swivel chairs. "That man is going to be a lieutenant for the rest of his days," I said.

Taylor stopped dancing, and a far-away look crossed his eyes. "Tomorrow," he said solemnly, "we will return to that canal and give out several Whorehouse Charlie Above-and-Beyond-the-Call-of-Duty-Awards, and a dozen apples to the Betel-nut Queen."

The actual awards ceremony I remember with difficulty because of the incredible heat and humidity made even more unbearable by Taylor's insistence that we wear our khakis throughout the presentation.

Taylor and Hogbody stood facing the Beetle Nut Queen who had planted herself between Lek and his brother. Taylor held a clipboard and notes and Hogbody held the awards. Both stood stiffly at attention as, in fact, we all did. Taylor began reading from his notes, only a part of which I remember: ". . . and did furthermore, at great risk to himself, volunteer unhesitatingly for combat duty. Lek and his brother not only fully participated in crucial elements of the operation but despite the danger to themselves improvised even in the face of the enemy."

Lek and his brother were both shirtless, but had managed to scare up clean shorts and bright yellow sandals for the ceremony. The Betel Nut Queen was dressed in her well-worn sarong and black sandals. Her bare breasts hung suspended like deflated beach balls. Taylor drew himself up to an even stiffer position of attention and concluded his speech: ". . . As a veteran of several campaigns against the enemy, I would like to add that I have seldom seen such courage and daring as was displayed by these two men. And it is with an enormous amount of pride that I now present these brave men with pure tin and aluminum Whore House Charlie Medals of Honor."

Taylor held out his hand to Hogbody who placed two medals in it. He then stepped forward to pin the medals on Lek and his brother, and then stepped back. They exchanged salutes smartly. The pure tin and aluminum Whore House Charlie Medals of Honor were engraved with a somber but baby-faced GI who, according to Taylor, bore close resemblance to Whore House Charlie as he solemnly pointed out the True Way. His finger was in fact pointing toward several sexy prostitutes in various stages of undress. Beneath the illustration were the words: 'Follow Me!'

We again stood rigidly at attention as Taylor began reading from his notes: "On the early afternoon of the 28th of February, in the Buddhist year two thousand, five hundred and eleven, one Thai woman known to her compatriots the length and breadth of this canal as the Betel Nut Queen, did, as she has done on several occasions before, join in battle with American enlisted men and did aid them in their ceaseless and righteous war against American military officers, that is, the Enemy."

During Taylor's address, several Thai children approached and stood listening quietly. The Betel Nut Queen also remained rigidly at attention, except when shooing away persistent flies, and in busily chewing betel nut, which occasionally spilled from her red lips. Taylor concluded his encomium: ". . . Despite the time, effort and danger involved in these missions, the Betel Nut Queen has time and time again sacrificed her own personal comfort for that of the American enlisted man. Her efforts have been far and above the call of duty and it is with an enormous amount of pride and respect that I now present, on behalf of the men of Court Countdown, a Golden Whore House Charlie Betel Nut Leaf Cluster Medal of Honor."

Taylor leaned forward, hesitated before her naked breasts, and finally pinned the medal on her sarong. He then stepped back and saluted. The Betel Nut Queen, obviously moved, also saluted. Soon everyone was saluting everyone.

The Golden Whore House Charlie Betel Nut Leaf Cluster

Medal of Honor was similar to Lek's medal of Charlie pointing in the direction of happy hookers, but in addition to being made of the least expensive gold available, instead of the words 'Follow Me!' at the bottom, inscribed were the words: 'Do it!' It was obvious with one glance at the incredible number of her grandchildren cavorting in the area, that when it came to doing it, Whore House Charlie and the Betel Nut Queen were of one mind.

17

AIDING THE ENEMY
1 March 1968

I suppose I should say something about the TET Offensive. But, to be truthful, the fact that the war was being bitterly fought had little effect on those of us who didn't even have television sets to keep up with it. It did, however, have a profound effect on Blinky and Bumbles who, in the face of at least temporary military setbacks strove mightily to believe that the war was getting better and better. Hence, they repeated the official line of the American military command in the war zone.

Avid readers (and creators) of Vietnam war stories will recall exactly what that line was. Whenever disastrous military reverses occurred in the war, statements were immediately issued by General Westmoreland and his staff that such enemy activity was a sign, nay, irrefutable evidence of a desperate, defeated enemy "betting his last chips" in a suicidal attempt at victory. And every action on the part of the enemy, no matter what the outcome in terms of American dead and wounded, was *exactly* what our military command *wanted* the enemy to do.

This is why, even in the midst of the TET Offensive, we knew deep down inside that should South Vietnam ever be conquered by the North, the supposed defeat of the South would be *exactly* the bait our generals wanted the enemy to take; the conclusive, sure-fire, incontestable confirmation that the enemy had bet his last chips in a desperate, suicidal attempt, thereby unwittingly fulfilling a brilliant American military strategy to make the enemy overconfident before the final counterattack which would lead us to the sacred light at the end of all tunnels, the triumph of His Work and the Forces of Good, and renewed faith in John Wayne and His Celluloid Macho Morality.

And by the end of the fourth day of TET, Blinky was able to tell an assistant C.Q with complete confidence, that every day in every way, the light at the tunnel was getting brighter and brighter.

Every GI, whether a finance clerk or assistant cook, well understood that just as the "enemy" had bet his "last chips," so too, in order to win the war, would General Westmoreland not hesitate to bet *his* "last chips." And every enlisted man knew instinctively what military officers meant by the euphemistic term, "last chips."

Westmoreland, of course, was to rise to even greater heights with his theory that the Russian military leaders must be extremely jealous of how much valuable experience American military men were getting in Vietnam which was a bit odd, as we never met a GI involved in the war who felt that stepping on land mines, fainting from heat strokes and shooting at empty branches was something to be jealous of. It was unfortunate that men like Hubert Humphrey who spoke of the war as our glorious adventure did not have such 'opportunities' as the average grunt in Vietnam.

After his retirement General Westmoreland would go on television to say that television contributed to the media distortion of the war with "compressed, dramatic film clips of . . . guns firing, men falling, helicopters crashing, buildings toppling, huts burning, refugees fleeing, women wailing."

Perhaps now the time has come for American newsmen to apologize for not spacing the scenes of destruction far enough apart to suit American officers. Perhaps during the next war there might be a regulation stating that during a one minute film clip, no more than 20 guns may be fired, no more than 10 men may fall, no more than five helicopters may crash, no more than three buildings may topple, no more than six huts may burn, no more than 12 refugees may flee, no more than four women may wail, and no more than two people will be allowed to die.

Yet the Vietnam War did in fact provide Americans with one consolation: that goal at the end of every war which has proved most elusive did not this time escape us. After every war, Americans (say other Americans) win the war but lose the peace. At last, as the near desperate desire of the Vietnamese for relations with America in the late 1970s was to prove, Americans had finally, after 200 years, lost a war but won the peace. Victory is ours.

Of course, in a certain sense, Blinky and Bumbles had been born a bit too soon. It is almost certain that America's favorite spectator sport—war—will be even more exciting in the future than it was in the '60s and '70s. In the future, mom and pop will have far more realistic methods and far more rewarding opportunities of watching the pageantry of young Americans at war—on pay cable television, on specially designed interactive computer web sites, via a video disk and on video-cassette recorders—without even one commercial break spoiling the show's continuity. And with the promised two-way TV of the future, American families can answer an announcer's questions by punching the appropriate response button which in turn will be picked up by (non-aligned) computers. ("Now that you've seen 45 uninterrupted minutes of men killing each other, if you were the American commander, which option would you choose—annihilate the gooks; annihilate your own enlisted men; declare time out for Happy Hour; inflate the body count and withdraw.")

But that's not all. The new method of a miniature picture simultaneously screened on a corner of a larger picture means that mom can keep up with her yoga lessons while dad doesn't miss as much as one mortar round of the war. And if it happens to be dad's bowling night, he can simply set his video-cassette to record every minute of every battle and go off to the lanes confident that win, lose, or draw, nobody's likely to be more well-informed than he is. And as the warriors of the future join battle on enormous screens and all war dead become more and more lifelike, there seems little doubt that widescreen, technicolor deaths on 84-inch screens will prove a major inducement for jobless recruits visiting their Army recruiting centers. And best of all, as Americans have learned nothing from Vietnam, and continue to gorge themselves on the black art of sophisticated gadgetry, rather than on understanding the aspirations of impoverished people, America's foreign policy failures of the future promise to be even more spectacular, more fulfilling, and more laden with entertainment-value than ever before.

The only immediate effect on those of us stationed at the court was that which involved a curtailment of overt criticism. Blinky and Bumbles had overheard Hogbody complaining to Noy the Laundry Girl about the military laundry service. This brought him a severe berating from both officers as, in their view, criticism of American military laundries would give comfort to the proprietors of laundry services throughout North Vietnam. Less than two hours later, one of Patterson's indiscreet comments about messhall food was also cause for a lecture as complaints about American military

messhalls obviously gave comfort to military messhall proprietors throughout North Vietnam. By that time, although as enlisted men we might not have been able to see the Big Picture,
we had seen enough of it to get the message. For the rest of our
tours of duty, none of us ever complained about a bad screw with
a Thai bargirl. We knew full well whom it would comfort.

18

WHORE HOUSE CHARLIE
11 April 1968

I suppose it is inevitable that when a great saint or prophet constantly expounds on the devout and noble qualities of his messiah certain innocent interpolations and inoffensive exaggerations slip in. It is also likely that, as the canons, tenets, doctrines, scriptures and apologetics of a religion increase in number and in complexity, less reverential followers, declared sceptics and implacable infidels may begin to question the faith's apparent contradictions which even the most learned missionary may find difficult to resolve.

That Taylor's god should eventually fall and he himself with it was not unexpected. But that it should happen in not one but two stages, seemed a cruel, agonizing and unusual punishment. The beginning of the end of Taylor's religion and of his role as apostle occurred inside the finance office at Operations and the final stage, in which the deification of Whore House Charlie was brought to its devastating conclusion, was reached, suitably enough, in a brothel.

Due to a misunderstanding, all of us were working the day the first stage of the fall occurred. Patterson had thought Hogbody was taking off and Hogbody thought it was my night to skip out and so on down the line. Freeman entered the room after having fed messhall bread to the fish in the nearby canals. Blinky had forbidden the feeding of Thai fish with American bread and, when the fish started dying like flies, so did Thai fishermen. But Freeman said it relaxed him.

"I got a good joke for you," he said, taking off his fatigue cap and shoving it into his pocket. "How do you catch an officer's wife?"

"The question," Hogbody said, "is not *how* but *why?*"

I decided to be kind. "I give up, Freeze, how do you catch an officer's wife?"

He was one big smile. "Hide in the bushes and make a noise like a PX."

Taylor looked up. "Jesus, Freeze, that joke was already old when Whore House Charlie ambushed Pearshape's computer."

Hogbody snorted. "Pearshape may be crazy but at least he exists. Whoever met Whore House Charlie?"

Other than the obvious fact that he was pear-shaped, little was known about Lieutenant Pearshape. He was seldom seen and when he was seen his preoccupied manner and distracted stare discouraged even the boldest GI from approaching him. He could sometimes be glimpsed just after sunset scurrying away in the van reserved for officers like a vespertine apparition in flight, and, less frequently, one might briefly spot him hurriedly entering or exiting the computer room. His motionless head and torso could also be seen sitting at the window of the computer room, partially concealed by the tinted, translucent glass, as he stared for hours toward the road which led away from the compound. Rumor-control had it that Pearshape's mind had been permanently scarred by the Whore House Charlie—Computer Showdown and he now sat out the rest of his tour-of-duty with large sunken eyes fixed in a vacuous stare looking at nothing.

It was also said that Agent Orange happened to be in the computer room at the time of the battle and she had had miscarriages for several years after. No one dared question Pearshape directly about the affair, and, of course, the miscarriages of Agent Orange could have been caused by other factors, such as being almost daily in the presence of enlisted men.

Although there were several versions of the battle between Whore House Charlie and the computer, the one generally accepted portrayed Charlie as the aggressor and both Charlie and the computer as the losers. Like many men of genius, Charlie had built his empire too fast, and had badly overextended himself.

Elaborate brothelariums in remote parts of the country were begging for business, while at smaller ones in central locations the lines of GIs waiting to enter stretched for blocks. Young women were recruited so fast that even Charlie was unable to rate them in terms of performance and V.D. probability factor. Reports of inaccurate V.D. probability ratings began spreading faster than the diseases themselves.

Thus Charlie realized that the only way to maintain and expand his empire was by computerization. One night, during the midnight shift, Charlie quickly and quietly opened the door of the computer room and, with magnet in hand, approached the computer. His idea seemed to be to use his magnet to alter the direction of the tape's magnetic particles and then feed the machine coded information on his brothelariums so that he could keep up to date on all aspects of his empire.

For whatever moral or technological reason, it is said the computer baulked at Charlie's program and adamantly refused to have anything to do with the scheme, despite Charlie's promise of an unlimited supply of apples. Although Charlie was defeated in the test of wills, a defeat which eventually led to the ruin of his empire, the computer did not emerge unscathed. It seems that, during the scuffle, Charlie managed to get behind the computer and was successful in his attempt to insert the magnet directly into the machine's rear aperture. The terrified howling of Agent Orange, the agitated whirring of the computer, and the profane bellowing of Charlie himself brought Pearshape, both guards and computer personnel in immediately.

There the story ends and it remains largely in the realm of myth, conjecture and legend. However, according to computer personnel with whom we fraternized during brief and tenuous truces, it was true that whenever anyone started to walk behind the computer, the machine immediately went haywire, its light glowing, its parts groaning, and its high-speed calculations totally haywire until the person involved moved away from its backside. Thus, if Charlie's cause could not prevail, he at least left a permanent mark on the exterminator of his once massive empire.

"Damn it!" Hogbody shouted. "You and your Whore House Charlie. I don't know if I believe there ever was such a guy."

Taylor had explained that Whore House Charlie could best be compared with the legendary Yellow Emperor of China or some such semi-mythological being who was said to have done such wondrous things that not everyone can believe. But, according to Taylor, ancient Chinese emperors used to choose the next ruler based on ability, character and traditional values; rather than on blood relation or friendship. And so it came to pass that Charlie had chosen him to carry on and even expand his string of whorehouses cum brothelaria. Taylor let it be known that he considered it a great honor and a great responsibility. He was, then, Whore House Charlie's St. Paul or Mencius.

Hogbody remained on the attack. "So, where is the great, honorable Whore House Charlie now?"

Rick was quiet for a minute. He pushed down on a stapler and held it. "He's dead."

"Dead!" I said along with everyone else.

"How'd he die?" A GI new to the unit asked.

Rick leaned back and his green eyes clouded over with poignant, and, possibly, prefabricated memories. He heaved a this-is-gonna'-take-a-lot-out-of-me sigh. "Well, it was many, many years ago. You know all those fortune tellers around the Weekend Market area? Charlie and a lovely lady friend of his went to one. The guy looked at Charlie's lifeline as well, and told him that he would die soon because his lifeline was so short." Taylor slowly sipped his coffee.

"So?" The new man asked.

Rick gave him a don't-be-so-impatient-you-damn-green-behind-the-ears-new-recruit stare and continued. "So, Charlie came back to the barracks and managed to get a bayonet from Supply and tried to cut into his lifeline and make it longer. But I guess because of the great exertions in his line of work, because of his great strain that clods such as you and I could never understand, Charlie wasn't so well coordinated." Rick theatrically thrust one fist into his other palm. "And the knife slipped and he accidentally cut his wrist instead and he bled to death . . . and the prophesy was fulfilled."

Everybody looked at everybody else. Nobody said a word. Taylor made it to the door before we grabbed him. "No, no!" he yelled. "I swear it's true. On my word as an enlisted man."

But four pairs of hands picked him up and carried him out to the *klong* at the back of the house where Lek, sporting a huge grin, opened the gate for us.

"No, Lek!" Taylor yelled. "Don't let the American imperialists do this to me!"

"You only American imperialist I know," Lek said.

"You know the punishment for lying to the boys!" Hogbody growled as he started to swing him. "One!"

"No! You're making a mistake. I swear!"

193

"Two!"

"No! My Christian brothers! How can you doubt the word of a disciple?"

As we counted 'three' we let him go and he sailed out into the weeds of the canal. It was an overcast night and he splashed into a circle of darkness. At first it looked like he was rising straight out of the water. I got the crazy idea that maybe he really could walk on water. The spell of the epiphany was broken when I saw the something-has-got-my-ass-in-a-bind look on his face. A pair of horns and a pair of big sleepy eyes rose below him. He had landed on a water buffalo. More of them started raising their eyes above water level. We could hear some Thai children laughing in the darkness on the other side of the canal. The buffalo he was on began to climb up out of the bank. Taylor jumped off and started walking toward the main road to catch a Thai bus into town.

"Hey, apostle, don't forget to wring out your hat!" I yelled after him.

"Whore House Charlie will avenge me for this!" he said.

19

A MINOR CHARACTER MAKES A MAJOR MISTAKE
6 May 1968

During the American involvement in Vietnam, should anyone have taken a tram along San Francisco's Market Street, he or she would have seen a narrow, rectangular sign inside the car, affixed just above one of the windows. The sign depicted a Vietnam scene with a weary but still proud American GI holding his M-14. Under the scene were the words, 'Buy U.S. Savings Bonds—He Does.'

One of these signs had mysteriously found its way to the men's room of our court with the words written across it, 'He does because the lifers hold back his promotions if he doesn't.' It was, in fact, Taylor who had placed the altered sign in the men's room and, as he was one of the few defiant enough to resist pressure to purchase savings bonds, he was already considered a traitor in the eyes of patriotic Americans like Bumbles and Blinky. According to Bumbles, those people who refused to buy savings bonds did "more harm to our country than communist stupeedos and congressional conspirators put together." Not to mention the harm done to Blinky's image as he and commanding officers all over the Asian region competed for one hundred per cent participation in savings bond drives for their men.

I have already described how Taylor had unintentionally played into the hands of the communist conspiracy by mooting the idea of replacing America's national anthem with one in which GIs might participate. Blinky was also aware that Taylor had taken *film* courses and actually spoke the *Chinese* language, the language of those who were at that very moment aiding and abetting the enemy. While he did not publicly claim that actors and foreign-language learners were outright turncoats, it was only natural that he might pause to consider if Taylor might also be abetting against us. It was obvious to Blinky that the actions of members of both groups deserved constant attention and rigorous scrutiny. In addition to all the above treasonable activities, Taylor steadfastly refused to buy American savings bonds and instead invested his money at long range in something called options, namely puts, calls, straps, straddles and warrants. No matter how he tried, Bumbles could find no Army regulation against an enlisted man purchasing stock options rather than bonds but it was no secret that Taylor was, in Bumbles's words, "skating on thin ice."

The ice broke the day Blinky learned something that horrified him to such an extent that he shut himself up in his office and refused to receive any calls, although, with the exception of Lachrymary Mary's lamentations, he seldom received any. When he had recovered sufficiently, he demanded that Specialist Taylor "be brought" before him without delay. Even during the worst of times, a time of peace, a commanding officer has the right to expect that those who serve under him act according to the accepted norms of the American way of life. During wartime, it was unthinkable that any American— even an enlisted man—could be disloyal. Taylor had been summoned in the middle of a messhall meal by both the C.Q. and his assistant. Although they denied any knowledge of why he was being summoned, they knew from Blinky's explicit instructions that Taylor was some kind of traitor, and they made it clear that any sudden move would be Taylor's last. Followed closely by the C.Q. and his assistant, Taylor exited the messhall, picked up an empty apple carton, and strode off in the direction of Blinky's office. Half an hour later, he returned to a nearly empty messhall and asked for a beer, "large, cold and fast." As he explained it, the charge against him was extremely serious, and Blinky had been completely justified in being beside himself with anger.

It seems that word had reached Blinky that, while the vast majority of enlisted men were unquestionably loyal Americans who, in their off-duty hours, played poker with other unquestionably loyal Americans, Taylor and a few others, however, had been seen playing *pinochle,* a far less simple, less straightforward, less *American* game, one which, to Blinky's knowledge, was by unwritten law, unchangeable custom and unspoken consent reserved for officers and civilians. (Pinochle, Blinky knew, was a corruption of the French binode—'binocular'—and everybody knew whose side the French were on.)

After a friendly, open, man-to-man talk best described as a threatening, closed, superior-to-inferior lecture, Taylor had seen the errors of his way, and had given his word that neither he nor any other enlisted man in the Asian region would play pinochle again; at least not while there was a war on. Blinky seemed genuinely pleased that, just before Taylor left the office, without any prompting whatever, Taylor said that, in his opinion, every day in every way the war was getting better and better. It was probably several minutes after Taylor's departure that Blinky remembered Taylor had not said *for whom* he thought the war was getting better and better.

As we exited the messhall, we all picked up empty boxes and

began carrying them. Almost all the GIs we passed were also carrying boxes. "This is fucking ridiculous," Taylor said.

"What is?" asked Patterson.

"Everybody carrying a fucking box to avoid saluting."

"You started it," Patterson said.

"Yeah, but now Blinky will catch on and write a fucking regulation banning all boxes."

We arrived at Club Victory and entered. Four of us started playing poker at one of the tables. Patterson was quiet for a while, just observing the game, then he spoke to Taylor. "Hey, Rick, why the hell does everything exciting happen to you? You get the nicest looking girls at Good Pork Betty's and you get to help Doc Spitz, and you get the most beautiful girl in Thailand as your girlfriend. And Whore House Charlie chose you to carry on his work."

Taylor put a hand on Patterson's shoulder. "Listen, Roy, why don't you just pretend this is some sort of film, OK? And in every film there has to be a minor character to act as a kind of foil for the major characters, get it? Even the best comedian needs a straight man otherwise there's nobody to bounce gags off of. So, you see, it's not as if you're not important."

Freeman continued the patronizing tone. "Sure, minor characters have to be real people, too. They get their own personality, their own hang-ups, their own failures, their own pain, their own troubles, their own calamities, their own anxieties and they can even have their own subplot right, Rick?"

Taylor placed his face even closer to Roy's. "Yep. But their subplots must never, never become more important than the main plot. And no minor character should start trying to be major. You're not trying to subvert the subplot are you, Roy?"

"No, I ain't subvertin' no goddamn subplot," Roy said. "I—"

"I'll bet he is," Freeman said to Taylor, "I knew he was a subplot subverter the minute I saw him."

Patterson was getting red in the face. "I never even—"

Taylor interrupted: "A goddamn communist subplotter plotting fucking subs all over the place."

Hogbody joined in. "A subplotting, subverting son-of-a-bitch when all the time there's a war on."

"For Christ's sake," Patterson said, "Will you assholes play cards?"

"So you wanted a major fucking subplot, did you?" asked Taylor.

"I never subverted any fucking plotter," yelled Patterson.

"No, you just plotted subverts, you prick," Rick said. "We"ll teach you to plot subs around here, you goddamn communist stupeedo. Meeting of the Tennis Elbow Club!"

"Fuck you assholes," Patterson began. "I'm not—"

His protests were drowned out by accusations, shouts and the sounds of tables and chairs being moved to form the usual courtroom. He was shoved into the center chair and guarded by Hogbody and Butterball. Wat brought Taylor the black book. I insured that Lincoln again assumed his place of honor.

Taylor began, as always, in a solemn and dignified voice: "Hear ye, hear ye, hear ye. The 17th meeting of the Tennis Elbow Club is now in session. Specialist 4th-Class Roy Patterson, olive-green college dropout, known participator in PX privileges, frequent customer at Good Pork Betty's Fornicatorium, debauched devotee of Happy Hour, the charge against you is that you did willfully and intentionally attempt to"—and here he paused again for effect—"subvert the subplot." There were murmurs of shock by all present. "How do you plead?"

"Fuck you and the horse you rode in on," Patterson said.

A wave of indignation and anger swept through the group. Taylor continued. "Before passing sentence, in the interest of partiality and injustice—excuse me, I mean, impartiality and justice—I should like to hear from at least one witness. Hostile, of course." He glanced about the room. "Wat, step over here please."

As Wat walked quickly and obediently over to Taylor, Taylor grabbed a book from a pile of books and magazines on his table. He held up De Tocqueville's *Democracy* in *America*. "Place your left hand on the book and raise your right hand." Wat complied. "You do solemnly swear that the evidence you shall give in this court shall be the truth, the whole truth, and nothing but the truth, or at least that it shall truthfully aid in incriminating the accused. So help you God."

Wat spoke solemnly. "No sweat."

"Do you also solemnly swear that every day in every way the war is getting better and better?"

"I do."

"Be seated. Do you recognize the accused and if so please state as whom."

"What you say?"

"Roy is the guy accused, right?"

"OK."

"Fine. Do you agree that the accused did in fact do what this honorable court is about to pronounce that he did?"

"What you say?"

"Did Roy do what I'm about to say that he said?"

"Oh. That for sure. I see him do it. Many times."

Patterson fumed. "You assholes will pay for this."

"In the absence of good sense on your part, I shall overlook that remark and appoint you a lawyer. Wat!"

Wat spoke up immediately: "Him guilty!"

Patterson tried to rise but was held down by Hogbody and Butterball. "Yes, thank you, counsel," Taylor answered. "But as this is a military trial, we are all already aware that the accused is guilty. The question is: is he guilty of trying to subvert the subplot or has he in fact plotted subverts? If you would advise your client to throw himself on the mercy of the court, I might find him guilty of the lesser charge of plotting subverts."

Patterson was becoming still more angry. Like a bargirl accused of stealing money *and* giving a bad screw. I leaned forward in my seat and whispered to Freeman. "You know, Freeze, I'm not certain that a witness for the prosecution should be allowed to serve as a defense counsel for the accused. I mean, even in a military court, it seems highly irregular."

Freeman nodded thoughtfully and leaned toward Taylor. He began whispering. He then listened attentively to Taylor's whispered reply and again leaned over to me. He continued to speak *sotto voce*. "The court wants to know if it's your intention to be charged with aiding and abetting the accused."

"That wasn't my intention, no. I just—"

Freeman placed one hand on my knee. "Then the court says for you to shut up your wise-ass mouth unless you want a Singha beer can shoved up the mouth of your wise ass."

I nodded. Freeman made the thumbs-up signal for Taylor to continue. "Specialist Freeman, you are the court-appointed expert witness in this trial, hostile, of course."

"I would be happy to serve as an expert witness for this honorable court."

"Would you state your qualifications for serving as a witness in a military court?"

"I have appeared as witness at several trials of the Tennis Elbow Club and have never found anything favorable to say of anyone accused by the court."

"Then you are obviously very familiar with procedures in a military court and this court wishes to commend you for your loyal service."

"I'm always happy to dick GIs away."

Patterson's face reddened to an even angrier shade. "You can't *appoint* a witness, you asshole!"

Taylor smiled sweetly. "If courts can appoint lawyers, they can appoint witnesses. And this court will not tolerate your badgering of witnesses, appointed or otherwise."

"You'll all pay for this!"

Do I hear any more bids?" Taylor asked. "Going once! Going twice!" He banged the table with his improvised beer can gavel. "Gone! This court finds the accused guilty of plotting subverts as charged. Beer is on Roy." There was applause by all except Roy who, for several hours, almost continuously cast the bird to everyone in the room.

20

IS THERE ANYONE DOWN RANGE?
18 June 1968

One month later, Taylor and I were sitting on the edge of the firing range in Thonburi, practically on the bank of the *Menam Chao Praya,* Lord of the Rivers. After each group fired, or rather, missed, we changed the targets but if it hadn't been for regulations, it seldom would have been necessary to change targets. During firings, we sat on the ground with our backs against a crumbling, brick wall which shimmered in the late afternoon heat as it stretched behind the range to the other side. The river rolled leisurely under a bright blue cloud-streaked sky, from its origin far above the old capital of Ayuthya, to its inevitable merger with the Gulf of Thailand at Paknam. Its muddy brown water carried patches of green weeds, flotsam, ferries, naval craft, heavily laden rice barges, heavily laden tourist boats and fast moving vegetable boats skillfully paddled by Thais every bit as colorfully dressed as their postcard counterparts.

Across the river, somewhere to the north of Bangkok, a solitary smokestack belched out a horizontal stream of dark brown smoke which paralleled and paced the river. The thin brown stream of pollution floated leisurely over sprawling green trees, coconut palms, and picturesque, ramshackle tin-roofed wooden houses, leaning precariously out over the water. The staccato sounds of boat engines rose and fell like the water's swells and were themselves punctuated by persistent and inaccurate volleys of fire from dozens of M-14 rifles.

Taylor was in an angry mood and it wasn't simply the product of the constant, enervating heat and humidity. We were involved in this firing session because we hadn't qualified during the last firing session and, as we knew we hadn't qualified in this firing session, we'd also be back for the next qualifying session; and the next.

Taylor threw a piece of one of the wall's bricks into the river, "Damn! Why is it I can shoot rubber bands perfectly straight but I can't shoot the fucking rifle for shit?"

I wiped sweat off my eyelids and eyebrows and watched a mammoth orange-and-blue butterfly detour around us. "If the 'Cong would only fight with rubber bands, you'd become the John Wayne of the war."

The voice on the megaphone spoke up, irritating, metallic and perfunctory. "Load your weapons . . . release safeties."

Taylor suddenly stood up and stared for a few moments toward the other side of the firing range, where a few minuscule, well-manicured plots of flowers and eroded, desolate brick segments of the wall separated the range from the surrounding jungle. "Look!"

I thought he was only looking at the temple roof in the distance. "I know," I said. "It looks like the temple's on fire. It's only the sun's reflection."

The megaphone voice drowned out the sounds of boat engines. "Is there anyone down range?"

"No!" Taylor shouted. "I mean somebody's out there behind the targets! Oh, Christ, it's Preyapan!"

He began running. I got up on one knee. The glare of the late afternoon light made it difficult to see across the firing range to the opposite side of the clearing. But, as I squinted and shaded my eyes, I saw her, a slight figure in a light blue blouse draped over a dark blue *phasin* with red-orange stripes. She wore a straw hat with a thin blue band and sandals. She must have cut her hair shorter because of the heat, but it still hung forward on both sides of her shoulders ending just above her waist.

Preyapan walked on a narrow path which was parallel to and just behind the targets, slowly but not without confidence, as the chaplain might have walked when he crossed the minefield. Her form appeared like an incorporeal illusion suddenly materializing in the shimmering heat, and presented a fleeting scene of unutterable beauty too delicate, too ethereal and too intense to be captured on any film, black-and-white or color, fast speed or slow, dense grain or thin, wide gage or narrow. It was an image, exquisite, illusory, enchanting, dreamlike and intangible, which would last for a few quick seconds and in which light, movement, setting and expression all conspired to create brief but vivid magic and which, but moments later, would again become merely the sum of its parts.

Against the backdrop of an ancient, crenellated brick wall, partly distorted and destroyed by encroaching jungle growth, she continued toward us, a spectral figure moving silently across a phantasmagorical setting and tropical background. The image would vanish in seconds but remain forever in my memory. But Preyapan was not vanishing, only stopping in place in response to Taylor shouting her name. His words were distorted and destroyed by the metallic, discordant, perfunctory question: "Is there anyone down range?"

Although only a few seconds had passed since he had spotted Preyapan, it seemed like I had been rooted to the spot for hours. I ran toward the firing line. As I did, the voice repeated for the obligatory third and last time: "Is there anyone down range?"

"Yes!" I screamed and waved as I ran. "Yes, yes, don't fire!

Somebody *is* down range!"

The voice continued unperturbed. "Ready on the firing line. . . ."

In the pause I fell to the ground and spun to face toward Taylor. I saw his figure still approaching the stationary human target in what seemed like a slow-motion run. The word sounded like a thunderbolt in an echo chamber: "Fire!"

Taylor hit Preyapan's waist and crashed with her to the ground. I heard a lone shot on the word 'FIRE' then a long volley, then two shots almost simultaneously then silence.

Finally, Taylor got up and carried Preyapan in his arms. I got up on my knees and watched them come closer. Preyapan was holding Taylor around his neck and her face rested against his chest. When they were about thirty feet away I heard her crying. "She's all right," Taylor said hoarsely. "Just scared as hell. She thought she'd try to find us."

I made an effort to stop my legs from trembling. "Jesus, take her home will you? I'll change the targets. If I can stop shaking."

The megaphone voice spoke up again, with considerable suspicion and a trace of concern. "Target changer number two, is there someone down range?"

"No," I yelled. "There's someone up your ass, you blind son-of-a-bitch!"

21

TREASON UNCOVERED
5 July 1968

It was a day which found Bumbles in one of his most depressed moods. He had learned (through the usual Thai bargirl grapevine) of something which to him was a tragic mistake for America. He had heard from Lek who worked in the Amor Bar, who had heard a rumor from Noy who worked in the Roma Bar, who had got it from a mama-san in a now off-limits Sukhumvit Road bar that, among other new weapons, the American military was trying to develop a technological marvel known as a 'smart bomb.' (Although the American military was determined to create a 'smart bomb,' one which could guide itself unerringly to a target, it seemed to have no interest in fighting a 'smart war', one in which Americans might justifiably and profitably be involved.) A great deal of American money and effort was being expended to produce many new and incredibly destructive weapons systems of which military officers could be proud.

However, in view of the enormous expense and sophistication of modern weapons, such as the soon-to-arrive 'smart' bomb, it was Bumbles' considered opinion that "dumb, commie queers" should not be allowed to be destroyed by bombs smarter than they were. It seemed to Bumbles that "dumb, commie faggots" didn't deserve the benefits of American technology like smart bombs. *That* kind of know-how should be kept on ice for the Germans in the next war. The Germans at least fought wars "the way wars were meant to be fought," with flame-throwers and tanks, rather than by setting "unmanly bamboo traps that can't even distinguish whose balls they're grabbing for."

Bumbles was heard to remark that it would be "criminal" to unleash an intelligent weapons system against "gook stupeedos with a Freudian pyjama mentality" and that he personally would be insulted if some "queer, commie gooks" ever unleashed an unsophisticated weapons system against him or any of his men. Amen.

But not long afterward, during a late evening session at Jack's Off Bar, Dang, Taylor, Hogbody and I worked out the solution to Bumbles's problem. We decided that intelligence tests would be given by the 'United Nations Council on Understanding the Holocaust' (UNCOUTH) to everyone involved in the war zone. Those with high intelligence quotients would be legitimate targets of sophisticated weapons such as the 'smart' bomb. Those dummies with lower IQs would be regarded as out-of-bounds to any weapons system costing over five million dollars. Of course, in order to avoid accidents, people involved in war would have to be regrouped into those of higher intelligence and those of lower intelligence. This 'Assembly Distinguishing Inferiors or Superiors' (ADIOS) would then group those 'Individuals Deemed Incapable of Technological Sophistication' (IDIOTS) in one area, and those 'Granted Oblivion Through Carnage, Holocaust and Armageddon' (GOTCHA) would be resettled elsewhere. In this way, every man, woman and child involved — whether as destructor or destructee — could relax in the knowledge that the next holocaust would assure justice for all, which, I need not remind the astute reader, is what wars are all about.

The proposal we typed up on blank stationery, stamped 'Top Secret–Smart–Sensitive–Delivery During Waking Hours–Personal–For Addressee's Eyes Only' and sent off to Bumbles. There was, of course, no overt reaction. At first, we thought he must have seen through the proposal and realized that he was being had, but then we began to understand the more likely reason Bumbles would never agree to implement such a plan. And that was, that if IQ tests were given, the results might show that Bumbles himself was *unworthy of being killed at all.*

It was also one of Taylor's bad days. He had been teaching for a few days a week at an English school where things began to sour. From the beginning, he sensed that the students didn't know how to place him. All of Thai society looks up to a teacher and down on a soldier. Here was a well-educated American GI serving as their teacher. Thai-style psychiatrists with offices near the school were doing a booming business.

Then came further trouble in the form of a dipsomaniacal Butterball who semi-streaked from one end of the school's garden to the other, underpants, ammunition belt, helmet liner and canteen all that separated him from gross indecency. The final blow was delivered by a five-foot five-inch beauty with a cleavage of enormous proportions, who worked behind the bar of an R&R bar on Petchaburi Road. She appeared one day in the doorway of Taylor's classroom and made it crystal clear that she was waiting for the teacher who was also her boyfriend. Although Taylor had long before taken her for a short time once or twice, it was a very drunk Butterball who had given her Taylor's teaching address.

To be fair to the Thai students, it was not that they felt so strongly about a GI-teacher associating with bargirls, although that indeed crowded the edge; it was that Taylor's 'girlfriend' was a *Chinese* bargirl, and, after all, if 'Mr. Rick' was going to have a bargirl girlfriend, why hadn't he chosen a

Thai girl? After a particularly astounding Petchaburi Road drunk during which Butterball and Taylor began speaking to each other again, Taylor resigned from the school for reasons of ill-health.

What we should have foreseen was that with both Taylor and Bumbles in angry moods, a collision course was inevitable. Taylor certainly must have known it wasn't likely to be a pleasant day as, once again, he had found his socks balled up inside his shoes on the front porch.

The day began just like any other day. In the morning, on the way to the messhall, we fought through an ambush and blasted several Thai children/VC out of palm and jackfruit trees over the fence. In the afternoon, several of us were working at the site ensuring that no American in Vietnam was overpaid or underpaid, paid late or paid early, so that both American soldiers and Vietnamese black marketeers would continue to have full confidence in the American financial structure during the war.

Butterball entered with a coke in his hand. "A Rambler station wagon with a luggage rack just pulled up outside," he said. "You know what kind of person drives a Rambler station wagon with a luggage rack?"

Freeman jumped up immediately and ran through the room. "Lifer in the compound! Lifer in the compound! All hands to battle stations!"

Moments later Bumbles walked in scowling, his hollow cheeks sucked so far in that they may have been stuck together. He began his usual routine of pretending that there were papers on his desk urgently needing his signature. He brushed several rubber bands off his chair, the remnants of Patterson's latest assassination practice session. "Why are there always rubber bands on my chair and desk?" Only Agent Orange seemed to notice his rhetorical question. Then he sat down, and looked around the room. The gaze from his brown eyes slithered contemptuously down his nose to confront each of us in turn. "All right, gentlemen. In a few days some GS13s and a general will be coming through and let me tell you they are very sharp people. I want all your pay vouchers and charts all set for inspection. Believe me, this general is a no-nonsense officer who expects and will get zero defects. And whoever makes the general's coffee, remember, he likes it black with lots of cream and sugar . . . I mean *white* with lots of cream or sugar. Anyway, don't forget." As before, only Agent Orange seemed to show any interest in Bumbles' remarks.

A few minutes later, after we'd all returned to doing our work, Taylor silently handed me his request-for-extension form. I put it with my own and took them to Bumbles. I handed them to him. "Here are a couple of request-for-extension forms for your signature when you get a chance, sir." He looked them over and then put mine down on the desk. He grabbed Taylor's with both wiry hands and ripped it in half. As he threw it away Taylor walked to the side of Bumbles's desk and the two of them stared at each other.

Taylor spoke softly. "You didn't have to tear it up, Sergeant."

Bumbles turned to me as if Taylor weren't there. "One of the forms wasn't filled out properly."

Taylor turned and spoke to me as if Bumbles weren't there. "Yeah, right, but I mean he didn't have to tear it up, right? He could have handed it back and said it wasn't right or else just thrown it away. Why'd he have to tear it up?"

I stood there as if I were a Red Cross, United Nations team neutral observer, which was a lie because I'd already become a lamp. "Rick—" I said.

Bumbles interjected, still looking at me. "It will have to be done over, anyway."

Taylor looked at me wonderingly. "So he really hates me that much."

Bumbles spoke to me again as if Taylor weren't there. "I will

211

not grant an extension-of-stay to any member of this command who might identify too much with the country in which they're stationed."

Taylor finally turned back to Bumbles. "You mean unless you ship me out right away, I might marry a Thai girl, is that about it, Sergeant?"

Mercifully, Bumbles now acknowledged Taylor's presence. "Taylor, goddamn it, you're not very good at your job as it is. You haven't got the time to be sniffin' out local pussy. I want to inspect all of last month's vouchers that you've worked on before the general gets here. And you'll find out what a no-nonsense general expects from a team. Is that understood?"

Taylor walked slowly to his desk and sat down. He turned and looked right at Bumbles. "I understand, Sergeant. I already know what a 'no-nonsense general' is. He's a person with no sense of humor and a poorly developed personality; the kind of guy who gets a feeling of satisfaction from knowing that everybody who has anything to do with him refers to him as a 'no-nonsense general'. That's like taking a trip for him; better than grass. But don't you worry, Sergeant. We already know how many lumps of sugar he likes in his coffee and what kind of cigars he smokes."

Bumbles jumped up and slammed his chair into his desk. "Taylor, I've had just about enough out of you!" Bumbles was becoming furious, his sunken cheeks now rubescent and palpitating. "There is a war on, soldier."

"I suppose filing cards on how visiting generals like their coffee and what brand of cigarettes they smoke has something to do with winning a *war?*"

"Yes, it does!" Bumbles shouted. "We've got a job to do and we expect zero defects!"

Now Taylor jumped up. "You keep talking about zero defects when the whole fucking army is making the biggest defect in its history by fighting the wrong war in the wrong place against the wrong people." Then he began laughing. "We're part of one of the greatest mistakes in American military history and you're talking about zero defects!"

Spittle began to form at the edge of Bumbles's lips. "Your job is to process material for the computer not make foreign policy."

Taylor continued shouting. "Fuck the computer! The more I can work the computer, the less human I become. In old China etiquette in human relations meant everything; inventions were treated like toys. You'd have been the misfit there, not me."

Bumbles smirked and shouted at the same time. "Well, we're not in old China now. But if I hear one more word out of you, you'll wish you *was* back in China. Any place but here and now."

Taylor stared at Bumbles for a long moment. Then he looked slowly around the room at the rest of us. I placed a finger in front of my lips as a sign to shush him. Agent Orange, lacking our memetic ability, crouched low against the floor and whined softly.

Taylor sat down and slowly picked up papers and charts that had fallen to the floor. He faced Bumbles and gave him a slight smile. Then he spoke in a calm, even voice: "Sergeant Boogle, if I *were* back in old China, and if I outranked you, I would send you on a trip to what was known as the Silkworm Chamber, which is where men were castrated. It was so called because silkworms hatching and recently-castrated men both need a heated room in order to live. I would then relegate you to the position of inspector of the imperial stud so that for the rest of your life you would have to inspect what you yourself no longer possessed."

Bumbles began trembling from anger. "Soldier," he said softly, "one more word out of you and you'll be in the stockade with a broken arm. *And* facing a charge of disaffection."

Taylor spoke more to himself than to Bumbles. "I remember the ancient Chinese poem of the old man with a broken arm.

When he was young, in order to get out of going to war, he took a boulder and broke his arm. Many years later he said that his arm still ached, but all the men who went off to the war had died."

Bumbles was genuinely astonished at this collaboration with Tang dynasty cowardice. "Soldier, are you saying that you'd willingly and deliberately break your arm to stay out of the war?"

Taylor was equally astonished at Bumbles's astonishment. "Break my arm? Sergeant, I'd crush my balls!"

Bumbles's face visibly whitened. He grabbed his hat from the rack and stalked out the door. Patterson followed him out.

"You think he went in to report you?" Freeman asked.

"No," Taylor said. "I think he went to put me in for a promotion."

"Sometimes I think Bumbles really thinks this unit is helping to win the war," I said.

"This unit has done as much for the war effort as body stockings have for finger fucking," Taylor said.

Patterson returned looking serious. "I think Bumbles is really pissed off, Rick."

"Where is he now?"

"He's sitting in the latrine."

"Oh, yeah? Well, come on, we'll have to cheer him up a bit."

"What are you going to do?" Freeman asked.

"You'll see. Come on. You too, Pineapple. Bring some matches."

The latrine in the back of our operations compound was a well-isolated room with a long wooden bench running from one wall to the other and around the corner to a third wall, shaped quite a bit like a horseshoe. Water flowed underneath the holes in the bench. The dividers between the holes were only neck high. Bumbles was sitting with his trousers down on one of the holes along the far wall. When he saw us coming he picked up an old newspaper, obviously used to hit mosquitoes and other bugs, and opened it up in front of him so that he could ignore us.

Taylor whispered. "Good. Now it's easy. Come on over and sit down."

The four of us, Taylor, Freeman, Patterson and myself, dropped our trousers and sat on four holes of the bench beneath the room's only lightbulb facing the room's only urinal. The dim bulb was surrounded by the inevitable horde of mosquitoes; and above the urinal was the same grey-black area of dirty fingerprints, found over nearly all urinals, historical remains of male *homo sapiens* leaning against a wall while taking a piss.

Across the top of the area someone had written 'The Army is like a rubber—it gives a guy the feeling of security while he's being screwed.' Beside a roll of toilet paper someone had written: 'Film for your Brownie.' Above the urinal was an Army poster with a picture of a soldier handling classified documents. Its *double entendre* read: 'The future of America is in your hands.' Other graffiti included 'Will the last GI out of the war please turn off the light at the end of the tunnel?' and 'Flush hard, it's a long way to the messhall.'

Taylor picked up a few of the other newspapers lying around with dead, squashed insects on them and rolled them together into one large ball. He took Freeman's matches. He then looked to make sure Bumbles was still engrossed in his own paper, then he lit his ball of crumpled paper and dropped it into the hole he was sitting on. It got caught in the slow current of the water and started flowing toward the other wall where Bumbles was. The flames started to shoot up as they passed under other holes but the dividers hid them from Bumbles. Patterson, Freeman and I followed Taylor's lead and pulled up our trousers.

We walked out to the guard shack. As usual, Corporal Napalm was on duty. He was in his usual precarious position leaning well back in his chair, spit-shined boots propped up on the counter, a pornographic paperback novel in his hand, a forty-five at his hip, and a persistent erection raising a bulge in his fatigue trousers. Taylor leaned an elbow on the counter. "Hey, Napalm, you hear any screams around here lately?"

Palmer looked at Taylor as if he was mentally disturbed. "Screams? You must be dreamin'." He immediately returned his attention to his latest acquisition from the dayroom library: *Hot Lust Rewarded*.

Taylor nodded: "Could be," he said. "Guess you're right. Come on, guys, let's go back in."

Bumbles's scream was loud and sudden! "Aaaaahhh!"

Corporal Napalm's jaw, both handsome and jutting, dropped unceremoniously, and he tumbled over in his chair, *Hot Lust Rewarded* spilling out onto the floor to land directly in front of Agent Orange.

22

FLIGHT 1203
11 August 1968

In mixed motives involving a genuine desire to assist blind children, and also involving a genuine desire for Preyapan, Taylor began spending vast sums of money on taxis between our unit and the School for the Blind. In equally mixed motives of encouraging others to "help the poor kids" and of paying only one-third of expensive taxi fares rather than entire fares, Taylor encouraged Hogbody and me to get involved as well.

We would start the classes off with somewhat unorthodox teaching techniques. In the shade of banyan trees, we taught partly blind children able to see shadows how to shoot rubber bands at Blinky's photograph which Taylor taped to a banyan tree. We wrapped the rubber bands around their little hands and helped them point in the direction of the tree. Sometimes they missed completely and Taylor would forget himself ("What, are you blind!?"). But as often as not they would aim well and their little rubber missiles would land squarely on Blinky's military-bearing scowl. No one was happier than Taylor. We would then distribute some toys, play a few games, and before entering a classroom to teach, chat with Watana about just about anything we liked.

On the day I remember most vividly, it was not Watana who

joined us on the porch for tea, fruit and a chat, but her husband. He sat his wiry frame slowly into a rattan chair and, with a slight smile, said his wife had gone to town for awhile. His large black eyes peered at us from hollows set within his dark brown face and he looked at us with fatherly concern, as if we were new recruits attending his retirement ceremony.

Preyapan translated as he spoke of how he first met his wife at a village fair, her parents' objections over their marriage and subsequent approval, the origin of the school, Watana's brother's death in a plane crash, and his own retirement from the Thai army. His description of his career and the anecdotes were full of humor and warmth. It was only when the sun began to set that he remembered the time. In fact, he spoke more that afternoon than on all of our previous meetings put together. When he was silent for awhile, Preyapan rose and spoke in Thai. He then rose, took her arm, and they entered the house together, as if approaching a ballroom floor to dance.

Once inside the classrooms, Hogbody and I finished first, and sat at desks at the back of Taylor's room while he finished reading stories in English to some of the older children. They took down what he said by tapping away with small instruments to punch small holes in their paper, and checked their work by feeling the series of holes with their fingertips. Punctuation had to be read as well as words. Taylor walked back and forth reading from a book: ". . . and the rabbit said comma quotation mark I am afraid period quotation mark Mr. Bear looked surprised period quotation mark why should you be afraid question mark quotation mark space quotation mark Don't you know there is a pot of gold at the end of the rainbow question mark quotation mark new paragraph."

He would then pause for students to check their work. While they were checking them sometimes he would talk to them as if he were a drill sergeant, and they were the trainees.

"You know what you guys sound like with your tapping?" he asked. "A banquet of hungover woodpeckers, that's what. And there isn't any pot of gold at the end of the rainbow, trainees, only beautiful Thai girls. But that's enough."

A child held up his hand. "Mr. Rick."

"Yes?"

"Is Preyapan beautiful?"

Taylor pretended to be in shock. "Is Preyapan beautiful? She's the most beautiful girl in the world."

"That's what you said about the last girl you met on the construction crew in the court," I said. "And the girl in the messhall, and—"

Taylor shook a fist at me. "Well, this time Pineapple, my lad, it's for real."

Then he turned to the students. "OK, let's continue. New paragraph The rabbit said—"

I spoke to Hogbody but for Taylor's benefit. "If Rick likes Preyapan so much, I wonder why he switched to the day shift when it's not so easy to see her."

Taylor turned to me and raised his voice. "You want to know why I've been switched to days? I'll tell you why. Because way back in that lifer complex known as the Pentagon, nobody, as usual, had much of anything to do."

While Taylor yelled at me he failed to realize that the children were tapping out his words, thinking them part of the exercise. As he talked faster, their tapping also speeded up.

"And somebody got tired of throwing darts at a map to see where to bomb next. So all the lifers decided on a records check to see what we're doing and some no-nonsense general said: 'Hey! Look at this guy's record (meaning me). He got to learn Thai which is what he *wanted* to learn and he was sent to Asia where he may be able to talk to the people and now he's in love with a beautiful Thai girl and teaching English after work. For

God's sake! he might actually be happy!' 'Happy!' All the other generals shouted.'We can't have a man in our Army *happy!* What would it do to morale? It might spread! We'd better dick him away fast.' So the no-nonsense general said: 'Let's switch him to a different work shift every month. That way, as soon as he gets a few English classes together, he'll have to quit and start all over again at–'"

A child interrupted him. "Mr. Rick?"

Taylor suddenly broke off his acerbic tirade and again took in his surroundings. "What?"

"What does 'dick him away fast' mean?"

To see Taylor completely at a loss for words would alone have made the day memorable. But it was his second bout of silence which was to change the memory of the day from a pleasant one to one of sorrow.

Later in the evening, after the children had been put to bed, Hogbody and I sat on the porch, slapping at mosquitoes and eating lamsat and other Thai fruit. It was our usual ritual while waiting for Taylor to conclude his amorous dialogues with Preyapan in the kitchen. Preyapan's soft but despairing sobbing had been audible for over fifteen minutes, and we assumed that the lovers were having their first quarrel. For one brought up during the 1950s, the subject of undying love and tragic affairs of the heart naturally brought the Everly Brothers and their golden hits of that era into the discussion. This led somehow to specifics and then finally to minutiae. Hogbody, who was generally acknowledged to be a cognoscente on such matters, remembered the ill-fated flight in their 'Ebony Eyes' hit to have been number ten-oh-three, while I remained adamant (and correct) that it was twelve-oh-three. In this way, the discussion was rapidly approaching the level of a scuffle when Taylor finally came out onto the porch.

We walked in the darkness along the dirt road in a silence

punctuated only by Taylor's profanity, which he expressed with genuine fury. We were nearing a main road when he was finally able to convey the message. He threw the last of the small cherry-sized fruit at some bushes as he spoke. "Son of a bitch!" he said bitterly.

"Who?" Hogbody asked.

"God, that's who. The one with his head so far up his ass he needs a glass belly-button to see out."

Although there had always been more than a few cc's of bad blood between Taylor and his Maker, this was the first time he had indulged in sustained and serious blasphemy. His embittered expletives and nearly cracking voice finally revealed that Watana "had gone to town for awhile" to a hospital bed, until her malignant and inoperable cancer ended her pain forever.

23

SHAKING THE DUST OFF
22 September 1968

I cannot remember serving as assistant charge-of-quarters without some disaster or at least interesting event occurring during my 24-hour term of office. Blinky had informed Taylor through the previous assistant charge-of-quarters that he would like to see him, *at his convenience,* about a matter of importance. In other words, Taylor was about to be impressed with the grave dangers posed to the American way of life when a GI requests permission to marry an Asian girl.

When I entered Club Victory he was sitting at the table with Preyapan, Hogbody, Patterson and Butterball. The atmosphere was funereal and, as I was the messenger from the throne, I felt that somehow my hands were tainted. I walked to the table and draped my cap over Rick's beer can as if it were a *lettre de cachet.* "He's ready for you," I said.

Taylor rose, finished his beer and turned to other tables in the now quiet club. "Gentlemen, my time has come. I bid you farewell." He kissed Preyapan and headed for the door.

Butterball called after him. "Don't let him give you any"—he looked toward Preyapan, then again at Taylor—"Nonsense."

Taylor smiled and again started for the door.

Preyapan spoke. "Rick." Taylor turned.

"Don't let him give you any shit, either."

Butterball hugged Preyapan as we all laughed. "Now you're really one of the boys," Butterball said. "A Bangkok Warrior."

"Come on, Pineapple," Taylor said, "let's find out why I shouldn't marry a slope."

Blinky was sitting at his desk. Bumbles's chair was empty as it was his day to avoid paying taxes by flying over Vietnam. As we entered Taylor walked to the front of Blinky's desk and saluted. "Specialist Rick Taylor reporting as ordered, sir."

I took my place at the desk across the room where I had been working on some papers for Blinky. I was hoping he would ask me to leave but apparently he wanted me to share in the benefit of his wisdom as well. Blinky spoke in an I-don't-quite-know-how-to-say-this voice. "Oh, yes, Taylor, sit down."

He put some papers in a drawer and then folded his pudgy hands on his desk. "I have your application, Specialist."

"Yes, sir," Taylor said.

Blinky had obviously decided to meet Taylor's *lese majeste* head on. "So you've decided to marry a . . . *Thai* girl, is that right, Specialist?"

Taylor answered in kind. "Yes . . . *sir.*"

Blinky gave Taylor a hard look and jutted out his jaw but when even that didn't seem to be subduing Taylor's contumacy, he looked out the window and began smoothing his shorter-than-regulation haircut. Blinky spoke in a voice that suggested that exogamy was a treasonable activity. "Taylor," he asked, "why do you think our boys marry *Thai* girls?"

"Well, sir, I can only speak for myself. I find Thai girls feminine, intelligent, charming and, well, sir, I just think they're great."

Blinky began nodding with a so-you-really-think so nod. "Well, Taylor, you know I can't stop anybody from marrying a Thai girl or any other kind of girl if that's what they want to do. But I can try to help them realize what they're doing." When Blinky didn't get his expected 'Yes, sir,' he blinked a few times, ran his hand over his thinning hair, and continued. "Now, when you get back to the States and you see a really attractive American girl, well, you'll kind of look at her and then down at your wife and back at the girl and only you will know if you've made a mistake or not."

As Blinky spoke, two Thai girls were on a construction crew building a brick patio near the swimming pool. They were typical construction workers with blue jackets and sarongs, wide-brimmed straw hats and scarves around their lips and chins to protect them from the sun. They had very dark complexions and even with their lips covered their eyes beamed their smiles. They saw me looking at them and they began to smile even more. From where Blinky sat, he couldn't see them.

"Sir," Taylor began, "my girl is in the enlisted men's club. I could bring her in if you'd like to talk to her."

Blinky spoke quickly. "No, no. I don't want to talk to her."

After a moment of intense blinking he continued. "What do you know of her past, Taylor? A lot of these girls have records of prostitution, you know."

"Sir, my girl is almost totally blind, so I'm quite sure she isn't a local punchboard but it wouldn't really bother me if she were."

Blinky puckered his lips and blinked several times while pondering how best to proceed. "We may be a young country, Specialist Taylor, and not everybody likes our politics but one thing they sure do like is our women." He then managed a fatherly, conspiratorial grin. "Maybe I should bring over a boatload of American girls. I guess that would solve the problem, don't you think?"

"Well, sir," Taylor said, "we can run the idea up a flagpole and see who salutes it."

Blinky became all military again. "How's that again, Specialist?"

"Sir, I think a lot of fellows who have been stationed here prefer Asian women to American women."

"What is so wrong with American women, Specialist?" Blinky's tone was now that of one who has detected treason.

"Not a thing, sir. I just like girls that are graceful, petite and feminine. I like long black hair, succulent brown skin, high cheekbones and a big smile. Girls with a sense of humor, a Buddhist outlook on life and an attitude that says 'life is meant to be enjoyed'. And American girls. . . ."

"Yes, Specialist?"

"Well, sir, they're so big and masculine compared to Asian girls, if I walked down the street holding hands with one, I'd feel a bit like a homosexual, you know what I mean, sir?"

Blinky both winced and reddened at the term, "homosexual," then began blinking and drumming his fingers on *The Power Of Positive Thinking.* He glanced toward me, but, fortunately, early in the conversation, I had already transformed into a particularly unobtrusive not to mention loyal, made-in-the-USA goose-feather quill pen just like the one George Washington used to use. He turned again to Taylor. "In your opinion, Specialist, how do you think I can best prevent contacts and marriages between my boys and Thai girls?"

"I wouldn't know, sir."

"What religion are you, son?"

"I'm not any religion, sir."

"And your girl?"

"She's Buddhist, sir."

Blinky nodded again. Each nod became sadder and slower.

Then he spoke in a low, conspiratorial voice. "I can't talk you out of it, can I, son?"

Taylor was almost shouting. "No, sir!"

"Do you know of anyone else planning to marry a Thai, Specialist!"

"No, sir, I don't."

Blinky swivelled slightly in his chair, and addressed the window. "You, uh, realize, Specialist," he said, choosing his words carefully, "that this charge of 'disaffection' which you're facing is extremely serious. . . . Now if you were to be . . . cooperative on this matter . . . I mean, just think it over a bit more carefully, Sgt. Boogle and I might be able to reconsider our plans for prosecuting you."

Taylor didn't move. He stared straight ahead at Blinky.

Finally, Blinky spoke again. "You know, Taylor, I just can't figure it out. None of my officers want to marry Thai girls. Why is it only *enlisted men* give me this kind of trouble?"

Taylor's expression grew extremely thoughtful. "I think, sir. . . ."

"Well, go on, soldier, you can speak your mind." We had entered the third movement of Blinky's symphony. But I had a feeling that the crescendo was going to come early.

"I think, sir, " Taylor said, "it's because most enlisted men enjoy sex at least a few times a week; and most officers only take it out once a month and shake the dust off it."

Blinky stared at Taylor for a few moments without moving. Then he began blinking furiously and jutted out his jaw. "That's all, Taylor!"

"Yes, sir!" Taylor saluted at attention, pivoted and walked out.

Despite the fact that the door had an 'Air-conditioned Close Door!' sign on it, he neglected to close it. Blinky, in ill humor, rose, slammed the door, and returned to his seat. After a few moments of angrily staring into space, he turned his head slowly to look up at the wall. Just before I transformed into a Betsy Ross-style, Fort McHenry American flag I saw two Thai wall lizards going at it. Blinky angrily dug a handful of paperclips from a dish and threw them at the raunchy reptilians daring to copulate on his wall. The lizards scattered off.

If he wasn't getting any, nobody was.

24

THE LIFERS ARE COMING
19 October 1968

Although it often appeared that military officers disliked Taylor more than any other enlisted man in the unit, it soon became evident that Freeman was far more trouble-prone than Taylor, and that his very presence was usually more than enough to enrage his 'superiors'.

To be sure, Taylor was hated; he was the unit's heresiarch, and had, lest we forget, mooted the idea of a change in our national anthem, which if accepted, would have allowed even enlisted men to participate in what was obviously meant to be a prerogative of those in command. But Taylor was most despicable because, of all of us in the unit, Taylor was the most likely to do precisely what people like Blinky and Bumbles long ago realized (but never admitted) they could never do—Taylor could, if he chose, *make it on the Outside.*

Freeman, on the other hand, might very well make it on the outside but, being less educated than Taylor, less goal-oriented, and being a black man in a white man's world, he also might not. In that sense, then, lifers should have found if not a warm spot in their purple hearts, at least an innate empathy with him. That they did not can be attributed to Freeman's own brand of success which at least equaled Taylor's ability to

Make It on the Outside: Freeman was *liked*.

More than anyone else, people spoke well of him. He was, furthermore, without benefit of regulation, uniform, or code of conduct, *respected*. Blinky and Bumbles seemed instinctively to realize that Freeman had, among his peers, what self-help books call the 'likeability factor,' perhaps even a charisma, which explains why he collected extra details the way lifers at war collect medals and lifers at peace collect benefits. In a world where the pecking order depended on rank rather than personal magnetism, Freeman was a subversive.

One afternoon in early February, Freeman had been sent out of the operations compound to pick up several bottles of coca-cola. As there was no vending machine in the compound, soft drinks in bottles were piled inside a *klong* jar behind the Thai guard shack. Huge blocks of ice ensured that the coke was cold and, in fact, the arrangement served as a kind of local swimming pool for various insects in the area.

Lek filled Freeman's arms with as many bottles of coke as he could carry and Freeman started walking back into the compound. It was then that he saw the tell-tale cloud of dust on the road moving closer and closer. Well-trained soldier that he was, he instantly and instinctively began running toward the compound announcing for all to hear that the lifers were coming.

Although Lek tried to tell him differently, Freeman could hear nothing above his own shouts and inner fears, and he relentlessly pursued his mission to its disastrous conclusion. Had he proceeded directly to the guard shack to get the coke, he undoubtedly would have noticed the high-flying kite with the olive-green tail, and he would have seen Blinky and Bumbles arrive at the compound. However, as Freeman felt a definite fullness of the bladder, he entered the latrine and began a lengthy cervisial discharge. While sitting on the wooden bench his interest was directed to and perhaps stimulated by one of Corporal Napalm's most recent library additions, entitled, *Red Hot and Willing,* a serendipitous discovery which delayed him long enough to set the stage for the calamity which followed.

By the time Freeman had finished perusing the most prurient passages, and had again resumed his mission, Blinky and Bumbles had already entered the house. Blinky was in the midst of pinning new stripes on Hogbody's sleeves and simultaneously delivering a short but incomprehensible speech on why it pays to stay in the Army, how difficult it was to Make it on the Outside, and how the Army takes care of its own.

His second head, in the form of Bumbles, was peering over his shoulders. And in the same remarkable fashion as always, without even being able to see Blinky's face, Bumbles's expressions matched his superior's exactly, as they passed through their various theatricals, giving conclusive evidence, if any was needed, that rather than two separate beings, it was in fact a bicephalic monster which commanded our unit.

As Freeman began banging on the side of the operations room, Blinky was just in the process of stapling temporary Spec-6 patches on Hogbody's khaki sleeves. He paused as Freeman's first clamorous shouts sounded. "Lifer alert! The lifers are coming! The lifers are coming!" During the few seconds of silence that followed, as was always the case during such pregnant moments, we put our anticryptic ability to good use, and before you could say, 'Freeman's ass is grass,' everyone not immediately involved in Hogbody's promotion had transformed into desks, chairs, telephones, notepads, lamps, water coolers and even waste-baskets. It was Hogbody and two military officers.

After the three-second eternity, like a man clamoring for his own destruction, Freeman again pounded on the wall and shouted several more warnings couched in phrases decidedly unfavorable to military officers. Once the noise had stopped, Blinky leaned forward and continued to staple Hogbody's new stripes.

Yet, to those of us close enough to see it, there was something about the way he closed down on the stapler that suggested that the act of stapling, which until a minute ago was an innocent one, had now become something closely resembling behavior displacement.

Still, much to his credit, Blinky managed a smile. "You don't object to my pinning your new E-6 stripes on you temporarily with the stapler, do you, Specialist Branch?"

Hogbody returned the smile. "No, sir!"

Freeman then nicely sewed up his own dissolution by tearing into the room with just enough breath left to say, "The lifers are coming! Lifer—"

I was standing between Blinky on the one side and Freeman on the other, but, as I had in fact transformed into a water cooler containing pure Colonial brand water, I had no doubt that they could see each other plainly. Although no one moved, Blinky almost imperceptibly turned his head toward Freeman with a thin smile that suggested that the punishment to come would be tempered by fatherly forgiveness, but would be incredibly brutal and irrevocably final nonetheless.

Freeman moved slowly, almost funereally to his desk, which was certainly in keeping with the corpse he now was. He leaned forward and moved his arms slowly outward to allow the coke bottles to drop safely onto his desk, first one arm, then the other. He then lined up the bottles near the wall, opened his logbook and began working.

Blinky and Hogbody exchanged salutes and Blinky headed for the door. "All right, men," Blinky said pleasantly. "Let's get back to work for the boys in the war. They deserve the right amount of pay and they deserve it on time. A correct pay check can make all the difference."

Just as he reached the door he stopped suddenly as if struck by a sudden, relatively insignificant, afterthought. He turned slowly to Freeman and spoke warmhearted words in a cold-blooded manner. "Oh, Specialist Freeman."

Freeman rose and stood at attention. "Yes, sir."

"Do you think you could be in my office at eight o'clock tomorrow morning?"

"Yes, sir."

"Splendid."

Lighthearted pleasantries completed for the day, Blinky turned and went out the door followed by Bumbles who, unable to carry off the facade of joviality, had abandoned his mimicry of Blinky's expressions to give Freeman his best rocket's red glare.

After they left, Freeman brushed off all congratulatory remarks and attempted handshakes with various obscenities. He grabbed some rubber bands and began shooting them at Bumbles's chair from various angles practicing, as he said, for the planned assassination—one rubber band right through Bumbles's heart.

Fat Eddy got up and walked over to a small cigar box which had been painted in several shades of olive green. He dipped his hand in and pulled out a rolled-up piece of paper. "We'll all feel better if we get our daily bennie from the lifer bennie box," he said.

Our lifer bennie box had been set up as a kind of container of fortune cookies without the cookies. Whenever things got too bad, we would blindly select a neatly folded piece of paper to remind us of the blessings of being in the military. Fat Eddy looked at his paper. "'Congratulations! You've been transferred to the war'!"

We all cheered his good fortune and lined up to draw our own daily bennies. "My turn," Freeman said. "I get, let's see, 'Marriage to a vanilla-skinned round-eye'!" More cheers.

We continued to cheer after each drawing. Hogbody got 'Dicked away'! Taylor got 'Court-martial'! Butterball got 'One-year extension of enlistment'! And I got 'Permission to buy US savings bonds to help the war'!

Taylor then called out our military salute to which we responded simultaneously. "Morale check!"

"Fuck the Army!"

"Attitude check!"

"Fuck the Army!"

"Esprit de corps check!"

"Fuck the Army!"

It was later established that the vehicle which had misled Freeman into believing that officers were approaching was in fact a taxi bearing a still inebriated and very tardy Patterson out to the compound. He had been sober enough to salute Blinky's car as it passed him on the road, but he never did understand why, as soon as he entered the operations room, Freeman found it necessary to repeatedly, determinedly, and, until subdued by others, very nearly successfully, attempt to chop his balls off with the paper cutter.

25

BINGO!
20 November 1968

Although it would be a monstrous untruth to suggest that any of us ever completely understood Blinky or Bumbles (for that would imply that enlisted men understood those who understood the Big Picture), there was one time every three months when I felt I came closest to perceiving what it was that separated a man like Blinky from the men he commanded. It was when I was serving as assistant charge of quarters from 6 p.m. until 6 p.m. the following night that I felt I most understood what made Blinky tick.

It first happened one night about 6:30 when Hogbody, serving as C.Q., had gone to the enlisted men's club for a drink under cover of "checking the perimeter." I sat at Bumbles's desk and, like a small boy wondering what it would be like to sit in the pilot's seat, found it impossible to take my mind and eyes off Blinky's desk. Finally, I could bear it no longer and I got up, walked stealthily across the office, and reverently sat in His Chair. I placed my hand on *The Power of Positive Thinking,* first cautiously, then firmly, and swivelled the chair toward the large window overlooking the court. I leaned back in the chair, put my feet up on the desk and observed the scene below.

Almost immediately, an overwhelming and riveting rushing sensation of power and privilege filled my head and, like Alice, I seemed to be growing taller. The floating merged into soaring, and finally into an astrally projected out-of-body experience. In a world far below, enlisted men were going about their mundane, irrelevant, and often carnal pursuits: heading for Club Victory in search of bibitory pleasure, lining up at the messhall to fulfill immediate gastral needs, walking out of the court in rumpled civilian dress to a waiting taxi which would take them speedily downtown to a waiting prostitute. Others were cavorting in the pool, tirelessly tossing horseshoes around stakes, struggling to place a basketball through hoops or lining up in an untidy and unruly formation before piling onto the bus leaving for the operations compound. From morning to evening, from the first matutinal condemnation of malingerers to the last burst of crepuscular invective, Blinky had an unobstructed, unimpeded, unhindered and Olympian view of every movement of his men; a gigantic, ill-natured, vindictive lizard with waiting tongue and insatiable appetite ceaselessly observing unsuspecting, unaware and inescapably doomed insects; a *deus ex machina* that could at any moment, without warning, interfere in and completely alter the lives of those below, like a sex-starved poltergeist at a nudist camp wedding.

As I soared heavenward up the chain of command, the feeling of power increasing with each new rank, the door opened and Hogbody walked in. His words were: "Hi, ya, Pineapple."

By then, my normal personality had been completely submerged and I was in fact possessed by another, a kind of composite of a military officer. And my new surly no-nonsense personality tolerated no such familiar forms of address from an enlisted man. I only know the deep, strident, stentorian voice which bellowed from my lips was not mine: "Soldier, you get your goddam hands out of your pockets and stop walking like you've got a corn cob up your ass. And the next time you forget to salute I'll slap an article 15 on you so fast it'll make your head spin."

Although Hogbody was momentarily taken aback, he quickly recovered. His left hand on my collar and his right hand doubled up in a fist served admirably as an exorcist's incantation, and before I could even say, "joke, Hog, joke," I felt myself coming rapidly out of the trance.

By 8:30 anyone not intending to go downtown for the night had drifted over to the orderly room to keep us company. Freeman lay stretched out on the C.Q. cot reading a cheap spy novel; Hogbody was at Blinky's desk typing taunting, derisive letters to his Stateside creditors; Butterball was completely absorbed in designing and constructing the world's first totally obscene puzzle set in which, once all pieces were joined properly, male and female genitalia copulated.

Patterson entered the room in wrinkled civilian clothes. Tiny flakes of pink toilet paper covered his neck as evidence that too much drink leads to a shaky shaving arm. He walked over to the 'sign out' book and picked up the pencil.

"What do you think you're doing, buddy boy?" I asked.

"What's it look like I'm doing, Pineapple? I'm signing out to go downtown."

"Why not stick around? What does Bangkok nightlife have that we don't?"

"Tits."

"Oh, come on, Roy. Hog and I got 24-hour CQ. The least you can do is keep us company."

Patterson was still in an irritable mood from having once again been placed on trial and found guilty of another questionable offence. While drinking and talking in the Club, Roy had, according to Taylor, split an infinitive. It was immediately decided by all present that, intended or not, it was a serious offense as poor grammar could lead to poor communication which could result in confusion in the face of the enemy, i.e., American military officers. Roy once again found himself the accused in an enlisted men's trial held according to time-tested military legal procedures specifically designed to dick away the accused.

Although Wat, his duly appointed lawyer, found Roy guilty as charged with no mitigating circumstances or grounds for leniency whatsoever, the prosecution decided to accept the plea that Roy had in fact merely infinited splits. Split-infiniting was considered to be a lesser offence than the splitting of infinitives, and less likely to aid the enemy. Hence, Roy was ordered to buy beer for everyone for merely one hour, rather than for one day, and it was magnanimously decided that the trial would not be recorded, as Roy's record was already blemished enough. Roy had taken it all in his usual good-natured stride, and once he had promised to stop attempting to strangle Taylor and Freeman, he was released from his supine position on the floor, where he had been heavily restrained during the trial.

He turned to glare at me and then drew a line through his name in the book. "OK, Pineapple, you win. I'll have one beer in the Club and then come up. That satisfy you?"

I shot a rubber band in his direction. "That's mighty enlisted of you."

The field phone buzzed. I answered it. "Orderly Room. Specialist Fourth Class—"

Pearshape's excited voice interrupted me. "Yes, Lieutenant, what can I do for you? . . . You can't find Corporal Palmer. . . . Sure, I'll write it up in the report, Lieutenant. . . . Of course he should be at work on time. . . . Yes, Lieutenant, there certainly is a war on. . . . Right, Lieutenant. Goodbye."

"That Bumbles?" Butterball asked.

"Pearshape. Napalm is late for work. Butterball, how about checking the idiot's room for me. If he's asleep tell him to get his ass out to work. I'll keep it off the record."

Napalm was one of those who had fallen for lifer arguments and re-uped. He was drafted into the Army and, throughout basic training, hated everything military and lived only for the day when he could have his discharge papers. But Blinky had sent him to 'career specialists' in the personnel office who showed him horror films of unemployment lines in America's cities and suburbs, and inundated him with statistics on how only the most technically knowledgeable specialists had any hope for getting jobs on the Outside, and how difficult it was for the average man of average ability to make a decent living in today's America. No insidious communist propaganda film or cleverly prepared communist lecture ever more brilliantly and more successfully exposed and condemned the worst aspects of American capitalism.

Finally, Napalm was convinced. He had been persuaded to stay in the military because the very country he had sworn to defend was, according to Army specialists, impossible to live in. They should know.

Thus, after several sessions with re-enlistment officers specially trained for their work, one more American, who had once believed in capitalism and individual initiative, was as alienated from the American way of life as any communist party cadre.

Through one unfortunate and unforgettable incident, everyone at Court Countdown had learned that just as Taylor was helplessly addicted to Thai women, so Corporal Napalm was completely enslaved by his pornographic habits. The one occasion in which he had been denied his lascivious literature he had gone berserk. Since that time, it was standard operating procedure to send out a supply of pornographic books to Corporal Napalm whenever he requested them.

One evening about nine o'clock, he had called into the orderly room and asked that the recently arrived shipment of pornography be sent out to the guard shack.

Hogbody was on C.Q. in the midst of reading Napalm's latest library addition: *Flora Fleshes it Out*. Hogbody taunted Corporal Napalm over the phone by assuring him that, not only was he not sending anything out for several hours, but that he was ripping out and destroying all of the best passages, parts of which he read over the phone. Terrified and incensed by the destruction of his prurient reading material, and already shaking violently from the effect of being denied his pornographic fix, Corporal Napalm began shouting and swearing into the phone. He finally drew his .45 and fired several times in the air, setting off a chain reaction among the Thai guards around the compound and out by the main road who began firing at anything that moved, although, in fact, nothing was.

Inside the compound, it was naturally assumed that an enemy attack was in full swing. Within minutes of the first volley of shots, several burn bags crammed with 'confidential,' 'secret,' 'top secret-cryptographic' and 'sacred' material relating to American troops in Vietnam and their military-payment-certificate paychecks were already in flames or in shreds. In the computer room, panic and pandemonium reigned supreme. As Agent Orange did her best to shelter her pups beside the computer, computer personnel insured that hours of irreplaceable computer tapes went up in smoke, denying the attacking enemy any chance to learn the secrets of America's system of MPC payments to its men in the field.

Unfortunately, in the mind of Lt. Pearshape, the noise and

confusion triggered off painful and long repressed memories of the Whore House Charlie—Computer Death Duel, and, without a moment's hesitation, he threw his arms around the computer, as if by hugging it, he could protect it from whatever diabolical scheme Whore House Charlie was up to. He seemed determined that never again would a computer under his command suffer the humiliation of having a magnet and several apples (or anything else) shoved up its rear aperture.

Several days later, when the Thai guards and their reinforcements had finally been convinced that the attack was over, and Lt. Pearshape's arms had been pried from the computer, Corporal Napalm was demoted from buck sergeant to corporal and threatened with a court martial the next time he discharged his weapon out of the line of duty. Corporal Napalm was once again assigned to the guardshack where he found a completely unexpurgated and undamaged edition of *Flora Fleshes It Out* on his desk, as well as a rare first edition copy of *Little Known Sex Obsessions of the Pilgrims* on his shelf, and from that time on, he was constantly supplied wth salacious reading material upon request.

Patterson ambled back into the room as Butterball left, his gaunt face creased in consternation. "Hey, Hog, you better get outside. A very drunk Fat Eddy and a computer creep are about to have a fight outside the club."

Hogbody had finished typing his letters and had attempted to read a magazine article. Unfortunately, as the article had only text without pictures, he had fallen sound asleep. I got up and headed for the door. "Goddamn lazy Spec 6's. Roy, come on."

The two of us approached, and then pushed our way through a boisterous crowd of about thirty GIs in various stages of crapulence. Fat Eddy stood in front of the door to Club Victory facing a GI nearly a foot taller than he was.

Much to the delight of the crowd, Fat Eddy and his opponent were rapidly leaving the insult-hurling stage and entering the shoving stage. Fat Eddy spotted me and pointed toward his grinning antagonist. "These guys are making fun of my religion," he said.

His adversary spoke up. "Religion? Lutherans ain't got no fucking religion. They're as nutty as the fucking Mormons."

The GI and his buddy then gave a rundown on the Lutheran religion which, according to them, included regulations to the effect that, at Fat Eddy's church, worshippers have to leave their helmet liners at the door, participate in hand-to-hand training at nine o'clock sharp which finishes in time for bayonet practice at ten-thirty. It seemed that in the narrator's hometown, Lutherans were disliked because of the noise the half tracks make when they arrive after services to pick up the congregation.

Fat Eddy's adversary continued: "You know what Fat Eddy got for his sixth birthday? His mama took him to the grenade-throwing range out behind his church. He got to practice for three hours."

Fat Eddy drew back his fist and attempted to move toward the GI. I moved in behind him and held his arms. "Come on, Fat Eddy, no fighting in the court while I'm on duty, OK?"

Fat Eddy's opponent began again. "Hey, Fats, think how well off the world would be if Luther hadn't found a nail to hang his theses on. But I suppose he would have gone to the PX and bought some scotch tape."

Fat Eddy fumed. "They didn't have PX's back then, asshole."

The GI seemed genuinely astounded. "No PX! Then how did people get their jollies off?"

"They went around nailing ideas on doors," said Fat Eddy's tormentor's companion. "I wonder why he just didn't give his ideas to the *Army Times*. They publish all kinds of crap."

Fat Eddy redoubled his efforts to charge forward. Patterson stepped in between the two and glared at the GI. "Luther wasn't in the Army, asshole," Fat Eddy said, as he peered around Patterson to stare hatred at the blasphemous heretic.

The heretic's eyes widened and his grin lengthened. "I bet he would have been if they'd had PX's," he said. He raised his hand and addressed the crowd. "Everybody who thinks Martin Luther would have joined the Army for PX privileges raise his hand."

As nearly all the GIs present raised their hands and cheered, Fat Eddy shoved me to get me out of the way forcing me to give him a cross between a punch and a shove to stop him. He pushed back and finally after a brief wrestling match in which his elbow clipped my ear and poked my eye, amidst the roars of delight from the crowd, I slugged him.

Patterson and I at last steered him toward the orderly room. Patterson straddled a chair and carefully applied iodine to Fat Eddy's cheek. I held a compress over one eye and with the good eye glared at Fat Eddy. "You are without doubt the dumbest prick I've ever seen."

"I said I was sorry."

"Hold still," Patterson said.

"Do you realize I've got to write us up in this fucking logbook?" I asked. "And we'll be restricted to the court for 15 days, not to mention cutting grass for two hours a day for two weeks."

"I said I was sorry."

"Yeah, well, next time you want to fight a religious war, could you wait until I'm not on C.Q.?"

Butterball tilted his head in satisfaction at his designs for a pornographic puzzle. He turned to me. "Where's Rick? I want him to see this."

Hogbody continued typing as he spoke. "I saw him drinking in the club."

"I thought tonight was bingo night for the lifers and their leeches." Patterson said.

Hogbody growled as he typed over dozens of words. "It is. But we can still drink at the bar."

A minute later the door opened and Wat entered diffidently. "Hi, Wat," Butterball said, "what's up?"

Wat looked at Fat Eddy and then at me. "You have a fight?"

I held the compress at my eye. "Do I look like I've been in a fight!?"

"I think you better come Club Victory, Pineapple. Mr. Rick confuse bingo game. Every few minutes he yell 'bingo' and lifers no like. I tell him too many damn lifers around to cause trouble but he no listen. He say 'prediction celebration' no can wait. I no understand."

I jumped up and grabbed my hat. "Shit!"

Hogbody grabbed his hat and together we strode off toward the club. Everyone knew what Taylor's 'prediction celebrations' were all about. For as long as anyone could remember he kept track of the predictions visiting VIPs made about the war. Every writer or general or movie star who passed through Bangkok during the 1960s would be interviewed by the press and somewhere during the interview would make the statement that the war would be over in six months. Taylor kept track of all the predictions and dates on his calendar.

Six months before, one writer and two generals had come through Bangkok and made the predictable prediction. Their time was over, the war was not, and not bingo night nor any other force was going to keep Taylor from his 'prediction celebration.'

As we neared Club Victory, Hogbody shook his head. "Taylor's fucking crazy," he said.

I held the door open for him. "And every day in every way he's getting more fucking crazy."

The club was full of smoke and densely packed with sergeants in civilian dress and sergeants in uniform and wives in unfashionable outfits that looked like uniforms. A microphone had been placed at the far end of the room and a staff sergeant was reading out numbers. Almost every table was covered with beer bottles and bingo cards.

Taylor was sitting at the bar drinking and smiling, at his ebrious best. He was still dressed in fatigues, and one of his trouser legs remained inside his boot and one had very unmilitarily slipped outside his boot. His crumpled-up fatigue cap was stuffed into his pocket. He was very drunk. The man at the mike continued to call off the numbers. "I-29."

Taylor stabbed the air with a finger: "Bingo!"

The man at the mike paused momentarily then continued. "B-12."

Taylor again pointed a finger in the air: "Bingo!"

Just as Hogbody and I reached Taylor two hefty sergeants also approached him from the other side. Hogbody stood between Taylor and the sergeants. "We'll handle this," he said.

I put my hand on Taylor's shoulder. "Come on, Rick. Butterball wants you to check out his obscene picture puzzle in the Orderly Room."

The man at the mike continued calling out numbers. "B-3."

"Fucking bingo!" Taylor said, banging his fist on the counter.

As Hogbody and I physically escorted Taylor toward the door, an obese sergeant's obese wife in blouse and slacks looked up from a nearby table. As she glared at Taylor her eyes nearly disappeared within the puffy layer of surrounding fat and then suddenly reappeared, reminding me of a submarine on maneuvers. "Someone should teach you some manners!" she said.

Taylor broke away from us and pointed his finger at her. "Listen, leech, you think you got manners? Fat red-necked racists sitting around in an air-conditioned club playing bingo with other fat Americans? Yeah, B-12! And don't forget about the fucking *B-52s* blowing the shit out of Asians. Are those *your* manners? B-fucking-52! Bingo!"

Hogbody and I finally forced him out the door just as he made one last yell: "There's a war on, you bleached blonde bingo bitch!"

I sat again on my orderly room chair wondering what to write up in the logbook. *Unit goes berserk—read all about it—Sp. 4 Pineapple now serving ten years in stockade.*

I looked over at Taylor. He had sobered up considerably and was now working with Butterball on ways to improve the pornographic picture puzzle. "This must be the night of the lunatics," I said.

Taylor shrugged. "Anyway, it was fun," he said.

"If I don't report it some lifer type will and it's my ass. Do you realize how long I'll be cutting grass?"

The field phone rang again. I picked it up. "Orderly room. Specialist—"

Corporal Napalm's voice interrupted me. "Hey, Napalm, how's it going. . . . Don't mention it. . . . Sure, sure, we'll send some sex books out on the van. But keep your pecker in your pants. . . . Up yours too, Napalm. See you."

As I was about to hang up, I heard a distant voice crackle over the field phone. "This is Major Thompson, Udorn, Thailand. Come in, Bangkok."

I turned to Hogbody. "Hey, what gives? It's Udorn."

Hogbody looked up from his typing. "It's been happening a lot lately. Long distance phone calls going to the airport but we pick them up instead. Something to do with the atmosphere. Blinky's in Udorn for a few days."

Taylor pulled himself away from his erotic enterprise and walked over to the phone. "Let me see that. Can Blinky hear us?"

"I don't know," I said. "Maybe."

Taylor sat on the desk. "Let's find out." He spoke into the phone in a deep, official voice: "This is Good Pork Underground Control. Have you pinpointed unidentified aircraft over the city? . . . Outstation Charlie, this is Good Pork Underground Control. Repeat. Please repeat sector of enemy location."

After some static, Blinky spoke again. "Hello, Bangkok. What's going on there?"

Fat Eddy began laughing. "He really can hear him."

Taylor continued. "Sector Charlie, that puts them over the area of Lumpini Park. None of ours there. Will they identify? . . . Sector Charlie, give the plane a ten count to identify and inform them that Good Pork Underground Control construes their silence as an unfriendly act and will take all necessary measures."

A hint of panic entered Blinky's voice for the first time. "What's happening there, Bangkok? Do you read me, over?"

Taylor continued. "Sector Charlie, tell Squadron Leader to open fire!"

Blinky completely panicked. "What in hell is going on there? Hello!"

After a long pause Taylor gave an imitation of a machine-gun burst, and started banging on the desk with a paperweight. He then held a letter-opener as a baton and pointed to each of us in turn. Everyone followed his lead and within seconds the room was in an uproar as we made as much noise as possible, slamming drawers, kicking waste-baskets, clanging ashtrays, hammering walls, and rapidly and repeatedly pressing on staplers next to the phone, all directed by Taylor as guest conductor and accompanied by oral noises simulating machine-gun bursts, the whistles of falling bombs, and the screams of doomed combatants and helpless civilians. GIs from all over the compound crowded in to get a glimpse of the impromptu improvisation titled, "Deceptions in A. Major," Op. 1., *fortissimo, con fuoco, con spirito, con brio.*

After performing brilliantly as conductor, Taylor held up his hand, holding the letter-opener-cum-baton perfectly still. The battle-cum-*divertissement* ended as abruptly as it had begun. After several moments of total silence, he spoke into the phone: "You forgot to *what?!* Well, Sector Charlie, how did you expect him to answer if you didn't have your volume on? He must have been one of ours. . . . All right, Sector Charlie, don't panic. . . . Is there anybody there with you. . . . Good. Now listen carefully. You don't say anything, and I won't say anything. If anybody asks you, you don't know anything about it. But you have to promise . . . cross your heart and hope to die? . . . Oh, forget it, you can buy me a drink sometime."

Blinky was near tears. The static increased and his voice began wavering. "Has everybody on this phone gone crazy? What have you done?"

Taylor continued as if he couldn't hear him. "Damn it, Sector Charlie, I told you not to say 'over and out'. That's only in movies. 'Over' means that you're going to listen to me. 'Out' means that you're going off the air. . . . All right, forget it, This is Good Pork Underground Control signing off. Over and out."

Taylor hung up the phone and spoke with a great deal of

pride in his voice. "Good Pork Underground Control strikes again," he said. As the room erupted in cheers and tributes, it was clear that the concert, although judged a trifle heavy on the percussion, had been a huge success. Taylor bowed modestly and called to Freemen, his First Percussionist, to stand, then for the entire orchestra to rise. "Whore House Charlie would be proud of us all," he said.

26

A QUIET FAREWELL
5 December 1968

Taylor, Freeman and I went to Chulalongkorn Hospital to see Watana for the last time. Or rather what was left of her after clumps of cancer cells had traveled far enough in her blood stream to do the job God must have wanted them to do. On the third floor, a Thai nurse with a mouth full of teeth and the skin of a Hershey bar showed us the way.

We took our shoes off and entered the room. It was a small room and there were people everywhere. A middle-aged Thai woman sat sobbing next to the foot of the bed. The small, dark form of Mr. Jayasutra stood at the head of the bed. His face had the serene expression of a man reaching enlightenment. He saw us and smiled. We nodded.

Preyapan sat beside him in a small chair next to the bed. Her dress was the same pale brown color of Watana's skin. Her big beautiful eyes seemed to reflect all of the room's sadness but she too was facing the day's final sorrow with as much equanimity as she could muster.

There were cards and flowers all over the tables. It resembled an American hospital room except for the large, sitting Buddha on one of the tables near the bed and a religious-looking diagram with Sanscrit writing and drawings of

Buddha on the wall above her head. Watana was lying unconscious with her arms out of the covers. There was a tube attached to one of her nostrils which ran along the bed and into an oxygen container on the floor. The nurse kept feeling her face and checking the container. Her breathing was forced and heavy. Lying helplessly in bed gave her an even younger appearance than usual, and she looked like one of the kids at the School for the Blind. I had an urge to cradle her on my lap and tell her everything would be all right. She had been unconscious for hours so at least she wouldn't feel any more pain.

Some of the women sat in chairs and cried. A few times the emaciated form of what had once been a lovely and vivacious Thai woman sighed more than breathed, as if it were her last breath. Then the women would cry louder and more uncontrollably.

I stood near the window looking out over the crescent-shaped driveway. I could see a large picture of the King in a grassy area across the street. It was his birthday and his pictures were on buildings all over the city. The picture showed him in full regalia, with uniform and sword, and, although it had been reverently drawn, the painter excelled in bold color rather than in realistic likenesses, and as he looked up at the window the King's serious, almost mournful, expression seemed to ask:'Why?'

A school band sped by on a flatbed truck about a block away. The only music I recognized was the King's Anthem, more stately and more somber than the National Anthem. I was hoping no one thought I was too preoccupied to look at Watana as she breathed her last. The truth is I was trying not to bawl like an idiot.

After about ten minutes, Taylor nudged me and we took a last look at her, then went into the hall. Mr. Jayasutra followed us out. He thanked us for coming and, with Preyapan as interpreter, told us how often and how highly she had spoken of us. While he was talking, the nurse came out of the room and motioned for him to go in. We didn't know whether to go back in, leave, or stand there. But in a matter of seconds he came back out and said in English: "Not yet." We said goodbye and left.

I found out later from Preyapan that Watana died about four hours after we left. I asked her what the Buddhist paraphernalia on the wall of the hospital room had meant. She said it was about purity and release from suffering. And about following beliefs rather than rituals. It told about a man who had walked into a temple and spat on a statue of Buddha. The monks and attendants had run over to him to seize him, but he smiled and spoke softly. "Show me where Buddha is not and there will I spit." Then it ended with a reminder of how fortunate is the escape from suffering in this world and how death is not a time for mourning but for joy.

Maybe.

27

A GOD IN DISGRACE
23 December 1968

Although he was well-liked by enlisted men almost to the point of worship, Doc Spitz was always out of favor with Bangkok's chain of command. But with the exception of his preference for patients who had nothing wrong with them, there was not one thing he could be disciplined for. Yet, Blinky and Bumbles pooled, or rather, puddled, their imaginations and finally decided that, the town of Udorn, 170 miles to the north of Bangkok, needed a doctor of his caliber. In other words, for the heinous sin of being popular with *enlisted men,* Doc Spitz was being dicked away 'upcountry.'

Those of us at the court decided to throw a surprise farewell party for him at one of our favorite brothels. It was still early evening as a speeding and careering taxi crammed with Taylor, Freeman, Hogbody, Fat Eddy, Doc Spitz and I forced pedestrians and other traffic off the streets. The erratic nature of the journey was due less to the driver's lack of skill than to his insistent attempts to make additional income as a pimp. At least once a minute, he would turn to Freeman who was sitting next to him and hit his fist into the palm of his other hand. "Poom poom?" he asked. "You like? I know number one girl."

"Hey, man," Freeman said, "can't you recognize doctors when you see them? We're going to check these girls for V.D."

"Which you probably gave them," Taylor said.

"Bite my ass."

"Move your nose over."

The taxi pulled up inside the compound of a sprawling, dilapidated, rat-infested wooden hotel in the Chinatown district. As we got out and walked toward the stairs a plump girl in miniskirt and blouse ran down several steps at a time and hugged Freeman.

"See?" Freeman said. "My girls don't forget me." He whispered to the girl. "Kanika, where's Johnny? "

"Upstairs," Kanika said. "He listen to music and play with pussy."

Her lascivious laugh, which revealed one or two missing teeth, made it clear that she understood the *double entendre* and found it hilarious. Johnny did indeed play with pussy, but Kanika and her friends had nothing to worry about. Johnny was Bangkok's most distinguished ailurophile. His love for cats was matched only by his love for Beethoven. He had studied at the University of Hawaii for two years and had worked hard enough at his English so that when he returned to Bangkok he had become the city's most notable pimp.

As we entered the brightly-lit room, he was sitting behind a desk intently reading a book entitled: *The Common Sense Book of Kitten and Cat Care.* The only other occupants of the room were the girls who worked there and the cats which cavorted there. Two beautiful Siamese were curled up on a shelf, and at least a dozen others disported themselves on the desk, in chairs, on the floor, or in the laps of semi-nude prostitutes. A few of the girls were applying make-up or watching TV. The intellectuals were reading love stories and one was standing beside a record player attempting a go-go dance to the incredibly scratchy crescendo of Beethoven's Fifth in C Minor.

Johnny was about 35, of medium build and with nearly shoulder-length hair which he shaped so that by an enormous and obliging stretch of imagination, it somewhat resembled the mane of Beethoven. As soon as he saw Taylor and the rest of us he jumped up. Cats scampered from the desk and his lap and panicky blurs of fur made their way in all directions, like frightened fish in an aquarium. "Hey! Rick! Flat Eddy! Good to see you!"

"Hi, Johnny," Taylor said, shaking his hand. "Good to see you too, but it's not 'Flat Eddy,' it's 'Fat Eddy'."

"Oh, yeah sure," Johnny said. "Here, sit down."

The few cats which had been reluctant to vacate their chairs were unceremoniously removed. "Where you fellows been keeping yourselves?"

"Keeping busy keeping Thailand safe," Taylor said. Then he looked around quickly as if to insure he couldn't be overheard, and lowered his voice. "There is a war on you know, Johnny."

Johnny nodded solemnly to show that the arcane message was safe with him. Taylor continued. "Doc Spitz, this is Johnny." He then recounted to Doc the details of how Johnny had perfected his English and had become one of the greatest pimps in Bangkok's history.

Doc Spitz shook Johnny's hand. "There's a lot to be said for a good education."

"A great honor, Doctor," Johnny said. "I've never had anyone above the rank of sergeant in here before."

"The honor is all mine, Johnny," Doc Spitz said.

Johnny continued to expound on how it was the first time he had ever received a GI above an E-6 rank at his whorehouse. Taylor told Doc Spitz that he should feel as proud about this lupanarian encounter as Johnny. Doc Spitz again assured Taylor and Johnny that he was extremely honored. Johnny pointed toward a nearby door. "Excuse me, doctor, but I think there's something you would like a look at in the next room."

Doc Spitz' eyebrows raised in astonishment. "Me?"

"Yes, doctor."

Johnny walked Doc Spitz over to the door and motioned for him to go first. As Doc Spitz opened the door the light in the next room went on and bedlam broke loose. The room was crowded with GIs, bargirls, Thais from around the court and throughout the compound. Long rectangular cloth banners had been draped across the room with the words:

LAST CHANCE TO DICK AWAY DOC SPITZ IN BANGKOK PARTY

LAST CHANCE FOR DOC SPITZ TO CATCH THE CLAP IN BANGKOK

PARTY

Then we all began singing: "For he's a jolly good fellow, For he's a jolly good fellow, For he's a jolly good fellow, that nobody can deny."

Bargirls and prostitutes ran up to kiss him and GIs pumped his hands. He was both embarrassed and proud. "Son of a bitch!" he said. "I didn't even know you people knew I was leaving."

Johnny and Taylor broke out an enormous quantity of beer and after a few hours of Bacchanalian revelry, the room was full of drunken GIs, empty bottles, inebriated kittens, and sleeping bargirls. Brazen cockroaches scavenged the battlefield unmolested. One of Johnny's girls was sleeping on Doc Spitz's lap, her head against his chest. When she began snoring, he woke up and looked around. "Where's Taylor?" he asked.

"He went outside to the latrine but never returned," I said. "Missing in action—presumed drunk."

"Effective immediately," Hogbody growled, "no—repeat—*no* personnel will be allowed to remain sober."

Taylor entered and sat down. "Doc," he said sadly, you're leaving us. You're never coming back!"

"Of course I'm coming back, you shithead. If I'm going to be stationed up north, how the hell can I get out of the country without coming back to Bangkok?"

"What'd Blinky say when he heard you were leavin' us, Doc?" It was Patterson, who had just woken up.

"Heard I was leaving? Who do you think arranged to have me transferred? No more V.D. for *his* kid. Not on the records, anyway." Doc blinked rapidly in imitation of Blinky. "He said my leaving would create a 'big hole' in the unit. I think it's because of him this unit is in a big hole."

"That's all the wise man had to say?" Taylor asked.

"Him wise? He may have an officer's rank and an electric toothbrush but that doesn't make him wise." Doc Spitz took out his cigar. "Rick, give me a goddamn match for my cigar."

Wat was first with the match and lit it for him. Doc eyed Wat disapprovingly. "This idiot!" he said. "He thinks every goddamned star out there is really there."

Wat grinned. "I can see star. How can no be there?" Doc Spitz rose and grabbed him by the collar. "Goddamn it! I'm going to settle this once and for all before I go. Everybody out on the porch."

Everyone woke up everyone else and the party mood was re-established as we all moved to the porch. Doc Spitz continued to hold the sleeping girl with one arm. Out on the porch he pointed to a star. "You see that star?"

"Which one?" Wat asked.

There were hundreds of stars visible. Doc Spitz pointed to one as if it was the obvious one. "That one! Right there."

After a few moments Wat said, "I see."

Doc Spitz spoke with great resolve: "It's not there."

Wat's eyes followed Doc Spitz's finger as he determinedly

tried to pull out a hair on his chin by catching it between two one-baht coins. He seemed undecided as to whether he should pretend to see a star that wasn't there, or else pretend not to see a star that was there. "I see star," Wat said, "you see star?"

"Yes, I see the damn thing," Doc Spitz said. "But that doesn't mean it's there! I told you it burned up light-years ago. It ain't there now."

"Yeah," I said. "The communists got it."

"One idiot is enough," Doc Spitz said.

Wat grinned. "Yesterday I tell my mother what you say; some stars there, some stars not."

"So what'd she say?"

"She say you crazy old man been in Army too long."

Doc Spitz set the girl down and shoved Wat inside. "Christ! Get back in there, you clown."

As we started to enter, we heard Freeman and Fat Eddy pushing each other inside the room and arguing. Doc Spitz and others rushed in to separate them. "What kind of behavior is this at my farewell party?"

Freeman spoke heatedly and without lowering his fists. "Fat Eddy says 'murmuring' is the most beautiful word in the English language."

"So?"

"So he's full of shit. I say 'disembowel' is the most beautiful."

Everyone looked expectantly at Doc Spitz. He pondered for a moment while silently mouthing the words. Finally he spoke. "'Disembowel' all the way."

Everyone except Fat Eddy cheered. "Come on, Fat Eddy," Doc Spitz said, "no sulking allowed. Attitude check!"

"Fuck the army!" Fat Eddy said.

"Morale check!"

"Fuck the army!" Fat Eddy repeated.

Some of us sat on a bed and some sat in the chairs. The ceiling had a large fan which turned slowly and noisily with only a minuscule effect on the room's air currents. There was the usual sign on the wall giving rates for all night, or else for a 'casual stay,' the latter being the Asian euphemism for a short time. I pushed up the blind and looked out but there was only an alley outside. I turned to Doc and Johnny. "Johnny, you remember the last time we brought Fat Eddy here and he couldn't find any girl he liked. So he said?"

Johnny grew thoughtful. "Oh, yes, I remember Flat Eddy's problem well. His is a very complicated case."

"'Fat Eddy'," Fat Eddy corrected.

"Yes," continued Johnny, "Eddy's is a very serious case, but I think I may be able to effect a cure."

Taylor turned to Doc Spitz. "Fortunately for all of us, Johnny is descended from the great Greek philosopher Pornographies and if anybody can cure Fat Eddy's problem, Johnny can."

"Admirable!" said Doc."

"Fat Eddy's cherry," I said. "Nothing complicated about that."

Fat Eddy attempted to maintain his dignity while blushing from ear to ear. "I'm *choosy,* that's all."

Taylor began explaining to Doc Spitz the often crucial role Johnny played in our lives. As long as we had known him he was a kind of pimp-psychiatrist for GIs. Any GI who had a sex problem which was mainly mental rather than physical, Johnny would take care of him. His usual prescription was several hours of Beethoven's music which, according to him, would, in proper surroundings, cure even the most acute case of cherryitis. Sex therapy through music involved the best of Beethoven with a brief but invaluable encounter with a young, experienced, voluptuous, lascivious, wanton, Thai beauty—Johnny the Pimp's remedy (patent pending). Indeed, Johnny's faith in bed-and-Beethoven as an infallible cure for almost anything was unshakable.

He began to study Fat Eddy so intensely that Fat Eddy began to squirm. Finally, he spoke. "Flat Eddy's is a very serious case, but I think I have just the treatment for his kind of problem. I call it my Beyond Beethoven cure." He then walked to a doorway and called out. "Tiamsiri! Tiamsiri!"

I overheard Taylor whispering to Doc Spitz: "Oh, my God. That used to be Whore House Charlie's girl here. She'll destroy Eddy!"

The door opened and an incredibly sexy-looking female of indeterminable age in short skirt and largely unbuttoned, largely transparent blouse walked in. Her eyes lingered on each of us in turn, like a fighter pilot searching out targets on a search-and-destroy mission.

Johnny pointed to Fat Eddy, now wide-eyed with both undisguised fear and unprincipled lust. She sat on Eddy's lap, kissed him hard on the lips, and applied pressure in his lap with one hand. She had both a sexy smile, and a hungry look that seemed to turn Fat Eddy on. Johnny turned to Doc Spitz as a student might seek approval from his teacher for an experiment in progress. "Tiamsiri is my specially recommended cure for acute cherryitis. Doctor Spitz, would you agree?"

Doc Spitz lit a cigar. "You're damn right I agree. Best medicine a man ever had."

Johnny was obviously very pleased. "Thank you, Doctor," he said beaming.

"Besides," Hogbody said, "in this case, opposites attract."

Everyone cheered as Eddy took Tiamsiri out of the room. Johnny looked around at the rest of us. "Now then, what can I do for the rest of you?"

"Something special for Doc," Taylor said.

"Thanks anyway, men. I think I'll just listen to Beethoven and wait for Eddy to finish. My wife is joining me so I've reached my PCOD."

Our PCOD, or Pussy Cut Off Date, was that regrettable but inevitable ritual we had to observe when we would temporarily abstain from sex. As Kissinger was later to describe a different kind of American withdrawal, it was our 'decent interval,' completely void of sex before we reunited with our loved ones. During this interval, not only would we be in no danger of contracting any new venereal diseases, but should we have contracted any before, this was the time they would make themselves known—or so it was hoped. PCOD was, of course, an occasion observed only by those who had families and loved ones they did not want to pass on venereal diseases to. Most of us seldom observed PCOD as we had no 'loved ones.'

Johnny nodded thoughtfully. "I see," he said. "Well, Doctor, it doesn't have to be all night. We have special rates for casual stays and group therapy rates of two girls for only fifty percent more. And I can assure you they are as clean as a whistle."

Doc Spitz smiled and shook his head. Taylor stared absentmindedly at a cat he was petting. "I'm just afraid we'll create a monster in Fat Eddy," he said. "After a night with Whore House Charlie's girl, he might become the next Whore House Charlie, freckle face and all."

Johnny laughed and shook his head.."Whore House Charlie. He always used to say he was getting more ass than a toilet seat."

We stared at each other in astonishment. Freeman finally spoke. "You *remember* Whore House Charlie, Johnny?"

"You mean there really *was* a Whore House Charlie?" Hogbody asked.

"Of course!" Johnny said. "Of course! He was one of my best customers."

Taylor was all smiles "There! You see! Now you doubting fucking Thomases can pay some respect."

Johnny stroked a cat thoughtfully. "I do wish I could have cured his problem though. I tried everything I could."

"Problem, Johnny?" Hogbody asked.

Taylor became nervous immediately, smug I-told-you-so smiles instantly replaced by anxious please-don't-say-anymore expressions. "Johnny's just—"

"Shut up!" Hogbody interjected. "What was Whore House Charlie's *problem*, Johnny?"

Despite his innocuous intentions, Johnny the pimp-psychiatrist was about to become the mythoclast who would seal Whore House Charlie's fate forever. "Well, it was the strangest thing. He couldn't seem to get an erection unless he was paying the girl for the screw."

Hogbody was again incredulous. "What!? You mean the great Whore House Charlie was *impotent?"*

Taylor panicked. "It isn't true, goddamn it! Charlie may have had a little problem but—"

Hogbody turned to him and spoke ominously. "You been lying to the boys," he said.

Freeman grabbed Taylor's collar. "A disciple of the great Whore House Charlie, huh?"

In the melee that ensued, several GIs, prostitutes and cats were sent staggering before Taylor was finally subdued. Johnny was to say later that it was the most violent commotion he had at his brothel since a large brown rat scampered across the room during Beethoven's Overture to Prometheus. Fortunately, the only record broken before Taylor was captured was Beethoven's concerto No. 5 in E. Flat Major for piano and Orchestra ('Emperor') of which Johnny had a second copy.

Taylor sat sullenly in the center of the room petting a satiated brown-and-white kitten. Hogbody, Butterball and others
positioned themselves in easy reach of striking distance
should violent measures of restraint become necessary. The
trial of Taylor VS. Bangkok Warriors was about to begin.
Without looking up, Taylor mumbled, "It isn't true!"

Sitting behind the desk which was now placed in a more
central location, Freeman looked up from his notes with
more than a trace of a frown on his face. "This court will tolerate no further outbursts from the defendant." He glanced at
all of us to ensure that all was ready for the trial. Only one of
the spectators, namely Fat Eddy, had to be encouraged to pay
more attention and not to play with Tiamsiri's tits while court
was in session. Fat Eddy reluctantly complied and Tiamsiri indignantly buttoned her blouse and turned toward the TV
screen. The trial was momentarily delayed when I remembered that Lincoln's picture was back at the court, but after
much discussion, it was decided that Doc Spitz could sit in as
a friend of the court. Doc Spitz announced his consent and
sat quietly to one side with two playful kittens on his lap.

Freeman placed his hands on the desk, sat up straight, and
began. "Hearye, hearye, hearye, the 18th session of the Tennis
Elbow Club is now in session. Rick Taylor, Specialist 4th
Class, United States Army, known participator in PX privileges, debauched devotee of Happy Hour, frequenter of
fornicatoriums, builder of brothels, black market wheeler-
dealer, college-graduate and collector of ant-infested stuffed
birds, mongeese, snakes and rabbits, the charge against you is
one of the most serious ever brought before this court."

As each description of his activities had been stated, Taylor
had slumped farther and farther down in his chair. He now
looked up from an almost horizontal position. He spoke with
the wavering voice of a man who knows he is condemned. "It

isn't true. Whore House Charlie got more ass than a toilet seat."

He was about to say more, but stopped when he felt the hands of Hogbody and Butterball gripping his shoulders. Freeman referred to his notes and continued. "You are charged with deliberately, elaborately, deceptively, intentionally, premeditatedly, and knowingly creating a monstrous myth thereby attributing to said ordinary individual—one Whore House Charlie—powers, abilities and gifts which he did not in fact possess." Taylor sat up slightly but hung his head still farther forward as if baring his neck for the guillotine. "You are also charged with deliberately, elaborately, deceptively, intentionally, premeditatedly and knowingly using said monstrous myth of said ordinary individual to enhance your own position, which you do not in fact deserve. Said myth is monstrous in that it has created over the years a body of thought and a way of action based completely on the belief that the myth was true." For a moment, Freeman paused, as if himself overwhelmed by the enormity of the charge and the turpitude of the defendant in the dock. "Specialist Taylor, how do you plead?"

Taylor continued to look at the floor in repentance. "If . . . if it please the court."

Freeman leaned forward in expectation of the lachrymose confession and abject plea for mercy. "Yes?"

Taylor was on his feet and moving toward the door even before the cat on his lap realized he was falling through the air. It isn't clear whether Taylor would have made a successful escape or not, because, as it was, his feet became entangled in Tiamsiri's bra lying on the floor, which was held fast by one strap caught under her chair. In the uproar which followed— the crashing of chairs, the smashing of records, the screaming of cats, the shouts of GIs—it was not clear if Taylor appreciated the irony of being recaptured because of the bra into

which snuggled the breasts of the girl who had once belonged to Whore House Charlie. Taylor, with one arm held
tightly behind his back, was once again invited by the bailiffs,
Butterball and Hogbody, to resume his seat. Freeman again
presided over the court-martial, and solemnity and dignity
were again restored. He turned to Wat. "Wat, you are this
man's legal representative. Do you have any witnesses to call?"

Wat shook his head to indicate a 'yes.'

"Will these witnesses aid in dicking away the accused?"

Wat shook his head to indicate a 'no.'

"Fine. In that case, their testimony would be irrelevant
and immaterial. Therefore, the prosecution calls prostitute
Tiamsiri Chaisuwan to the stand."

Taylor was incensed. "You're the judge, for Christ's sake.
You can't act as the prosecution."

Freeman first drank from his half-empty Mekhong whiskey bottle and then employed it as his gavel to bang on the
desk. "A judge acting as prosecutor saves the people money in
taxes, asshole. And I'm warning you for the last time that this
court won't tolerate any further bullshit from you." Shouts of
approval filled the air. As Taylor attempted to continue, Freeman made a sign to the bailiffs.

"No prosecution can rely on prostitution as evidence.
You—"

Hogbody and Butterball again encouraged the defendant
to cooperate.

Tiamsiri took the stand by sitting in a chair from which
she could cast glances at the television set. Her mouth moved
almost continuously in its attempt to finish off some hard
candy. Her constant attempts to see the television screen cast
some doubt as to her interest in the proceedings. Nevertheless, Freeman continued. "Wat, would you swear in the witness?"

Wat turned to Tiamsiri and pointed his finger at her. "You goddamn whore; you fucking bitch; you—"

Freeman banged his Mekhong whiskey gavel on the desk. "Wat, for Christ's sake, I said 'swear *in* the witness', not 'swear *at* the witness!' Learn to distinguish your fucking prepositions!" Taylor rolled his eyes and leaned back to stare at the ceiling with the resigned expression of a man who is aware that everyone in the room except himself is mad.

Wat hung his head. "Sorry."

"Never mind," Freeman replied. "I think this court is already cognizant of the witness's name and occupation; so let us begin with the important questions. Would you kindly ask Tiamsiri if she knows or ever knew a person by the name of Whore House Charlie?"

Wat complied. At the mention of Whore House Charlie Tiamsiri delivered a long, nearly hysterical outburst. When she had finished, Wat replied: "Yes, she know him before."

Freeman continued: "And did she have coitus with him?"

"What you say?"

"I mean, did she screw him?"

"She already tell me she done lot more than that. She—"

Taylor seemed about to explode with anger. "Objection!"

Freeman spoke calmly. "A defendant cannot object to the proceeding of his own defense unless his defense is not proceeding objectively. Objection overruled. You may proceed, counselor."

Wat's face lit up in a smile. "She say Whore House Charlie like to strip her and—"

Taylor suddenly spoke rapidly to Tiamsiri in Thai. "He say she no speak he pay one thousand baht," Wat shouted.

Taylor struggled unsuccessfully to rise as Freeman again banged the desk. "You dare to attempt to bribe a witness in this court to stop her from testifying? This court finds you guilty of attempting to harass a harlot and attempting to pervert the cause of justice. Sentence will be passed later." He again turned to the counsel for the defense. "Wat, does the witness have anything to say on Whore House Charlie's behalf? Please ask her to think carefully and to attempt to recall any time in which Whore House Charlie got it up without money passing hands."

Wat complied. Tiamsiri stopped chewing and grew thoughtful. As she spoke, Taylor apparently thought his chances of being found innocent had improved, as his face grew brighter. Wat turned to Freeman. "She say one time him no have money; he give her six appen; one no good. While she eat appen Whore House Charlie watch; get big erection. He like her to spit seeds at him."

Freeman paused to consider this and then spoke again to Wat. "Counsel for the Defense!"

"Appen same-same money. Him guilty!"

Freeman smiled sweetly at Wat. "Thank you counsel. Will you now see if the jury is ready to return the verdict?"

Wat walked to the door leading to the first of innumerable bedrooms and opened it. He said something in Thai. As he held it open, the bargirls and prostitutes who were previously in the room walked solemnly in single file and filed into two rows of empty chairs arranged for them.

Taylor was again incensed. "The fucking jury wasn't even in the room when the witness was giving testimony, for Christ sakes!"

Freeman was unperturbed. "It is the opinion of this court that the testimony of witnesses only serves to confuse a jury. In any case, this is no candy-ass civilian trial; this is military justice. And you show me anything in the Uniform Code of Military Justice that says the jury has to be in the room when a witness is giving testimony. Objection overruled!"

As Taylor slumped back into his chair, the girls sat down without a word. Most were in blouse and skirt, two had only skirt and bra, and one was occupied during the entire proceedings with putting on make-up. Several were eating fried rice out of banana leaves which had been supplied for them by Doc Spitz. Kanika was allowed to keep her kitten but was ordered to turn off her radio. The trial was momentarily delayed until she finished brushing her teeth.

Freeman smiled pleasantly at Wat. "May I have the closing argument for the defense?"

"Him guilty!"

"Any rebuttal on the part of the prosecution?"

Several GIs spoke at once. "Him guilty!"

"Thank you gentlemen." Freeman then turned to the girls. "Has the jury reached a verdict?"

Kanika, in skirt and bra, put down her fried rice and handed Wat a slip of paper. "Mee, *kha,*" she said.

Freeman asked Wat for assistance. "Would you be good enough to translate and freely interpret the verdict for us, counselor?"

Wat studied the paper. "Jury say him guilty. Say him no can have sex for one month." Everyone began cheering and racing toward the jury to embrace its members.

Taylor began screaming without attempting to rise even though he was now free to do so. "You wanted to believe it you bastards! It's your own fucking fault! You wanted to believe!"

It was left to Freeman to officially close the court. "Going once! Going twice! Sold! Guilty as charged! Free beer for everyone back in the club for one month on Specialist 4th Class, Rick Taylor. For his contempt of court and harassment of a harlot, he shall have no sex for one month, shall be required to replace the valuable record collection which he caused to be destroyed, and shall supply every one of Johnny's girls with apples for one month. This court wishes to thank the members of the jury for their patient deliberation and just verdict. This court will now personally thank the jury. Dismissed."

Amidst *double-entendre* cries of "All rise!" Freeman then joined the others in picking up members of the jury and laying them down on couches or taking them into various bedrooms. Only Rick remained seated, mumbling despondently to the few cats prepared to listen to him that "they wanted to believe."

28

BUTTERBALL'S VICTORY
25 December 1968

This was the day a completely inconsolable Butterball was to leave for the Land of the Big PX. It was also the day that a sensational rumor swept the entire length and breadth of Court Countdown. As the rumor was completely unfounded, unlikely and unsupported by any evidence, it was readily accepted as being completely true.

No one ever discovered who started it but its message was electrifying. According to the rumor, none other than Noy the Laundry Girl had actually been Whore House Charlie's girlfriend! She was in fact the girl who had been with him at the time the soothsayer had examined his ominously short lifeline. Except for saying, "I told you bastards!" (which he had not), Taylor had little to say and would neither confirm nor deny the hearsay.

So it was that Freeman was chosen to represent all of us by confronting Noy, as tactfully as possible, with the question. In an attempt to avoid looking suspicious, and to give Noy no cause for alarm, Freeman tore off one button from a shirt-sleeve and waited patiently in line with the houseboys until it was his turn. As he handed the shirt to Noy, Freeman phrased the question as delicately as he could: "Hey, Noy, some of the guys been saying that you actually made it with Whore House Charlie, that right?" Whereupon Noy raised one hand to her face in an attempt to hide her giggle and promptly sewed Freeman's button on the wrong sleeve.

As Butterball's 18 month tour-of-duty was nearing an end, he had put in a request for an extension-of-stay. After Blinky had turned him down, Butterball began drinking even more heavily. One morning he dashed out of the bathroom, bare-chested, his beady, bloodshot eyes peering wildly through layers of shaving cream covering his face and neck like a beard. He ran down the stairs and out into the lawn shooting his underarm deodorant can toward the sky and shouting obscenities.

He later said that he had hoped that the fluorocarbon in his aerosol spray would destroy Bangkok's atmosphere so that no plane could ever fly him out of Thailand. Although Butterball's vain attempt to destroy the sky was much appreciated and fervently applauded by Thai neighbors on all sides of the court, Bumbles happened to be passing by at the time and brought charges against Butterball for allowing fluorocarbons to "irreparably destroy a non-maligned (sic) ally's natural protection against dangerous and insidious ultraviolet rays from the sun." Fortunately, Blinky was having one of his more rational days at the time, and summarily dismissed the charges. The night of Butterball's departure finally arrived. Several of us were at the Military Airport trying to get him safely on his plane bound for the Land of the Big PX. We guided him to the ramp of the plane but he had great difficulty in heading for the steps. A few American Air force maintenance men were also milling around, sneering and laughing.

"Come on, Butterball," Freeman said. "If you miss the flight you'll be in a world of hurt; court-martial kind of hurt."

"Oh, oh." Patterson pointed toward the ramshackle office

building. "Here comes an Air Force Superlifer out of his lair."

The Superlifer was all military: "All right, let that man go. Regulations say ever' man has got to be able to git aboard the plane under his own power. If he don't make it, he don' go. He's got three and-a-half minutes to git aboard that aircraft."

As we released him, Butterball began staggering in the general direction of the ramp steps weaving like a bowling pin which may or may not stay upright.

The Air Force Maintenance men stood around with I-like-to-watch-GIs-get-dicked-over grins. "He'll never make it," one of them said.

"I got five dollars says he'll make it, Zoomie." Freeman thrust the hundred baht bill practically in his face.

The maintenance man checked his watch. "You're on."

Everyone began calling out sums of money and in about fifteen seconds Patterson had nearly sixty dollars of Air Force money and sixty dollars of Army money. One of the Thai mechanics walked over and gave him 20 baht. "I been around GIs long time," he said. "Twenty baht say he make it, OK?"

An Air Force maintenance man put up another U.S. dollar. "I'll take funny money as well as American."

By this time Butterball was sweating profusely and had gone in the general direction of the steps, gone beyond, returned, and made it to the bottom step. One of the maintenance men said, "One minute, thirty seconds."

"Butterball, you got to get up those stairs," Fat Eddy screamed, "or else we all got to walk home."

"And they'll try to hang you for missing your plane," Taylor said. "They'll dick you away and throw away the dick!"

Butterball reached up and caught hold of the side of the ramp and swung himself up a step. He continued forward but still seemed about to pass out. Hogbody moved near him and spoke in his best military voice. "Soldier, you're a Bangkok

Warrior! And that means you can hold your liquor. Now you get up those stairs, boy."

Butterball pushed himself away from the side of the ramp and used the momentum to go up a stair. But that seemed to be as far as he was going to get. He turned toward us, sat down on the steps of the ramp, and closed his eyes.

I motioned for Patterson to hand them their money. He dug it out of his pocket and started to hand it over, eliciting cheers of triumph from Air Force personnel.

"Now I know how the Japanese felt on the Midway," Freeman said.

Suddenly, a deep, booming voice shot through the cries of despair and triumph like an incoming mortar round. The voice came from the top of the ramp in the doorway of the plane, and bellowed out words in perfect cadence, more like a song then spoken words. "Your left, your left, your left, right, left! Your left, your left, your left, right, left! Your left, your left, your left, right, left!" The figure's dark skin looked even darker in contrast to the light from the doorway which seemed almost attempting to avoid him as it shot out of the plane around him. To the Airmen, he must have appeared as a powerful and terrifying behemoth conjured up in an exorcist's dream or recently escaped from a Conradian nightmare. Our cheers erupted into the stunned silence.

Sgt. Jigaboo stared at—or rather into—Butterball. "You better *mooove,* boy!"

Butterball rose slowly, turned unsteadily toward the plane, and marched in time to Sgt. Jigaboo's cadence. "Your left, your left, your left, right, left! If I die in a combat zone, box me up and ship me home; If I die on the Russian front, bury me with a Russian cunt; sound off, one, two; sound off, three, four; sound off, bring it on down—one, two; three, four!"

Butterball fell once but pushed himself up. He then

marched into the doorway of the plane and some of those who had been watching from the windows came over to congratulate him. Sgt. Jigaboo shook his hand. Everyone quieted down. Then Butterball held up the victory sign and shouted: "Bangkok Warriors!"

We all returned his cry, and toasted him and Sgt. Jigaboo long into the night.

29

A VISION
26 December 1968

The combination of marijuana supplied by friendly taxi drivers in exchange for messhall apples, and Mekhong, Thailand's powerful distilled rice liquor, supplied by Corporal Comatose also in exchange for messhall apples, had produced some of my most vivid and, occasionally, most terrifying dreams.

About 2 o'clock on a Sunday morning, as lightning and thunder ushered in a storm, I lay in my underwear on my bedsheet somewhere between a conscious and semi-conscious state. Every time I moved my head images blurred and colors deepened, faded or merged; so I lay still, facing the nearby wall just a few feet from my head. I watched a line of ants move slowly but purposefully from one large crack to another. Their relaxed movements had an exaggerated, surrealistic languor, but like Gulliver, my vision could distinguish even the slowest movements, and I perceived each step as it perfectly, effortlessly and inevitably fell into place like the arms of a swimming champion filmed in slow motion. They were carrying nothing and what their mission might have been I had no idea.

But at some point, as my consciousness began surrendering to sleep, the line of ants was suddenly replaced by figures struggling along a jungle trail in wind and rain. I could see an unarmed American soldier in jungle fatigues and, behind him, as far as my eye could see, were beautiful Vietnamese-girl bearers carrying barrels of apples. Just as the figure turned toward me, tracers streamed across the sky, lightning flashed, and, despite the heavy rain, I recognized Taylor. It looked as if he was about to say something but behind him another soldier in fatigues emerged from the jungle, took an apple from one of the baskets, reached back as with a grenade, and threw it at Taylor.

I tried to call out but, as in the worst of our nightmares, was completely unable to speak or to move. The apple exploded as a grenade and Taylor fell. The Vietnamese girls began to fade from view. As Taylor lay dying, he turned on his side to look at his assailant. The assailant's face was partly covered by his fatigue cap and by the heavy rain but his name tag clearly read: 'Whore House Charlie.' Taylor spoke into the rain: "Why, Charlie. Why?"

As Charlie began to speak I could hear music as well as the sounds of war and of the storm. It was the 'Battle Hymn of the Republic,' with long rolls of drums blending with thunder and with the sound of mortar fire.

Charlie's voice was that of a young man but of one who has seen a great deal more than ordinary men, as only those in dreams can. As he spoke he moved closer to Taylor: "Civil wars always take the best with them, Rick. And we are met on a great battlefield of the wrong war. So we're leaving. It is altogether fitting and proper that we should do this."

His features became slightly clearer as he spoke, but I felt, rather than saw, a young, freckle-faced all-American young man as young American men would never be again. But as he spoke into the storm, his visage changed and, within seconds, in both features and dress, Whore House Charlie had become

Abraham Lincoln. Taylor fell backward in death and Lincoln picked him up in his arms, the rain mixing with his tears.

I struggled to scream or to move but couldn't until lightning and thunder—real or in the dream, I never understood—woke me up. Sweat covered my body and soaked the bed sheet. The ants had disappeared.

30

JACK'S OFF BAR
31 December 1968

Thais who received the dubious benefits of contact with Westerners celebrated our New Year as we did. Those with money joined local *farang* residents and GIs in Western-styled, Christmas tree-decorated bars on such notorious centers of nocturnal activity as Sukhumvit, Petchaburi, Gaysorn and Patpong Roads, while those without money headed for one of the less rambunctious and less boisterous Thai-style festivals within the city. As we were foreigners without money we were unique. For awhile, it looked like we'd be attending a Thai festival, but after pooling our resources and fabricating sudden dire emergencies for the benefit of maudlin messhall waitresses and Noy the Laundry Girl, we came up with enough to get down town, and even enough for a few rounds of drinks.

Although no one said anything openly, it was also something of a sentimental occasion as several of us were either leaving the Army and returning to face life in the 'Real World,' or else being transferred to another station. As Udorn claimed they were understaffed, and as it had been discovered that several of their finance clerks owned a string of middle-class hotels in Bangkok, Fat Eddy was being sent to lend his

283

expertise to the deteriorating situation. Hogbody and I were about to return to the States and for several weeks Dang and other bargirls had been harassing us about returning to the Land of the Big PX and its eight-lane highways, vanilla-skinned, round-eyed women, TV dinners, IBM machines and credit cards. Wat was also getting his discharge from the Thai Army and had solemnly informed Taylor that he was going into the Northeast of Thailand to be a farmer. He had also told Dang that he was going to join a temple in Bangkok and become a monk. Patterson had overheard him telling Noy the Laundry Girl that he had decided to become a bartender for itinerant guerilla bands in the South.

We were also celebrating because Preyapan had been sent to an eye specialist who had concluded that her condition was actually a rare type of cataract known as 'congenital cataract' and one which could be treated. After an operation in which her lenses would be removed, she would be fitted with glasses or contact lenses, and her sight would be practically normal. We had already pledged more than enough for the operation which was scheduled for the end of January. Dang and the girls at Jack's Off bar had also pledged 25 per cent of all 'short time' earnings for the next three months to Preyapan's operation and hospital expenses.

Taylor was, of course, subjected to insinuations and admonitions that once the Taylor Preyapan dimly perceived in gradations of light and darkness was viewed in clear light, with normal vision, the romance would be over, and that it might be best if he only met with her inside Jack's Off bar, where the perpetual and nearly complete darkness could continue to hide the disgusting ugliness of his loathsome face. Taylor responded to such comments and suggestions with his usual equanimity and admirable self-control by attempting to smash everyone in the face with anything that was handy.

Christmas decorations were still up in Jack's Off Bar including small Christmas trees, Santa-and-sleigh, papier-mache angels and, just beside the bar, facing the men's room, three plastic Wise Men rode slightly chipped camels on their way to a Nativity scene encircled by beer glasses and overflowing ashtrays.

A Christmas tree about four feet high spread its branches near our table. Among its decorations was a Calvary in the form of a wooden statue of Jesus on a beer-stained cross. With great reverence, the bargirls had, so they believed, added to the pious quality of Christ's face by using lipstick to widen his eyes, to extend his eyelashes, and to place a smile on his now-upturned lips. But the same beer which had stained the cross had also caused the lipstick to smear and the most honest assessment of Christ's emotions would be to say that confusion and astonishment struggled for supremacy. The girls had also hoped that the lipstick would add a touch of gaiety to his otherwise somber face as, according to Dang, "it be his own birthday, so why he no look happy?"

Every few minutes, a firecracker would crack loudly, sending squads of cockroaches literally and figuratively up the walls. Under cover of semi-darkness, other GIs and their girlfriends were engaged in public displays of affection bordering closely on wanton displays of lust.

GIs in various stages of inebriation crowded around the bar singing every song ever written during the second half of the 1950s. Bumbles and two other NCOs were sitting at another table. They were drinking beer steadily but were far less boisterous than most other revelers. The quietest booth was that occupied by two female American military dependents who were sitting facing our table, talking softly, laughing properly, and occasionally favoring us with quick glances of disgust.

Dang walked by with drinks for another table. Taylor began the usual greeting. "Hey, Dang, where's Jack—"

"Off, " Dang said.

"I love you, Dang," I said.

"You full of shit."

"I crave your body, Dang. You make me explode."

"Yeah, you big noise Hawaiian firecracker with three inch fuse," Dang said, as she sat on my lap.

An inebriated Thai with shoulder-length hair and a greasy face came up to our table and smiled broadly. "Hello!"

"Hi," Patterson said.

Taylor's shirt was open and the Thai spotted his chest hair. He reached over and felt it. "Oh! Very good!"

"You like that, huh?" Taylor said. "James Bond, that's me."

The Thai laughed. "James Bond. You number one!" He then returned to his own table.

"You handled that pretty well," Freeman said.

During our rapidly approaching altercation with the American military dependents at the next booth, Bumbles would be thrown into a state of confusion so complete that he was helpless to comment much less act. On the one hand, the idea that his men were being criticized and threatened made him livid with anger. But, on the other hand, the idea that his men were being disrespectful to "ladies" consumed him with male, chauvinist rage. It was without doubt a traumatic and shameful experience for a military man like Bumbles to come across a battle and not to be able to join either side in attacking and annihilating the other, like a once-potent Casanova now reduced to voyeurism.

When it came to a man actually touching another man's body hair, however, his vision was clear and his emotions were instinctive. No one who had sat through countless hours of American television's golden 'adult western' years could fail to understand how to respond. And, as there had unfortunately been no war on at that time, Bumbles had devoured every episode of the adventures of Wyatt Earp, Bat Masterson, Lawman, Cheyenne, Bronco Lane, Texas Rangers, Arizona Rangers, The Lone Ranger, Gunsmoke, Maverick, Tombstone Territory, John Ringo, John Yuma, and Texas John Slaughter. Indeed, liberal that he was, he had even watched some episodes of characters in whom he did not have full confidence, such as Sugarfoot (who was a bit too "candy-assed"), and the Cisco Kid and Zorro, who although "foreigners," did seem able to "handle themselves like men." And, as long as they sided with the hero or else lost in the end, Bumbles even admired the courage and fighting spirit of TV Indians, although regarding the protests and demonstrations of real-life Indians he was heard to remark that "a few communist stupeedos have infiltrated the tribes and turned them against their natural allies," their allies in his view apparently being those who had taken their land and placed them on reservations.

Bumbles sat up straight in his seat and spoke firmly to Taylor. "You should have slugged him," he said. The other sergeants nodded in confirmation.

Taylor smiled slightly and shrugged helplessly. "Sergeant, if I slugged a Thai every time one felt the hair on my arms, legs or chest, I'd be in a fight a week."

Dang got up to return to the bar. "And," said Dang, "if I slug number ten GI every time one feel my tits, I no got time for nothing else."

Fat Eddy and Hogbody began collecting balloons from the few tables that weren't occupied and from some that were. They brought back about eight balloons, and while Fat Eddy held the little plastic cup with our bar bill in it, Hogbody tied the balloons to it. It was still too heavy and a hospitable Thai bartender gave them more balloons. Finally the cup was suspended in the air by the balloons and began rising slowly and stately. "We need something light to weight it down," Fat Eddy said.

Hogbody took out his wallet. "I've got just the thing." He placed a packet of contraceptives in the cup. "That should do it."

The cup was now suspended in the air at head level. Fat Eddy then took it up to the bar and gave it a good shove toward the table. It grazed the heads of customers—both western and Thai—but made it to Taylor's table. Freeman stood up and lifted the cup with the balloons above his head and was about to throw it toward Patterson standing near the door when a piercing female voice raised itself above the music. "Why don't you fellows act your age?"

Everyone at the table turned toward the two young American females, each about 23 years old, sitting at the booth. It was the bleached blond military dependent who had spoken to us.

"Excuse me," Freeman said. "Did you address me?"

"Yes, I did. I said: 'Why don't you act your age?' "

Freeman turned again to our table, still holding the cup with the balloons above his head ready to throw. He spoke as if no one else heard the girl. "Excuse me, a minute, fellows, but a young lady over at that booth has offered the suggestion that we act our age."

Taylor spoke in a mock-serious manner. "Does she mean our respective, individual ages or our collective age?"

"Why I don't know," Freeman said.

"Perchance you should ask," Taylor said.

"Perchance I shall." Freeman turned again to the girl as if she hadn't heard. "Miss, my friends suggest—"

"Buddies," Hogbody corrected.

"Right. Sorry. Miss, my buddies suggest—"

"Listen," the bleached blond said angrily, "I suppose

you're all *enlisted men,* but you can still act like human beings overseas."

"I tell you what," Taylor said, "we'll add up all of our ages and somehow try to figure our average age so that she can ask us to act one specific age. That way, it should be easier for us *enlisted men* to understand the direction."

As he held the cup with balloons attached in his right hand over his shoulder, Freeman bore a definite resemblance to the Statue of Liberty. "Madam," he began, "my colleagues concur in your suggestion, however—"

"If you were a little better-educated or better-mannered," said the bleached blond, emitting a slight burp, you wouldn't have to be told how to act in public."

Freeman turned again to our table. "The, uh, *ladies* to my right suggest that our poor manners may be due to our low educational level."

Finally the bleached blond's fat companion spoke up. "If she writes a letter to her father, you'll wish you were better mannered."

"From where did that angelic voice come?" I asked. "Or was it a samlor backfiring?"

Hogbody had been working frantically with pen and paper. "I've got it!" he said, "our average age is 86."

"A damn nice try, Hog," Taylor said, "but you've probably misplaced a period, which, truth to tell, could also be their problem as well."

The bleached blond's fat companion took a long drink from her glass. "All right," she said, "since you're so used to being with whores and have forgotten how to act in front of ladies, I won't act like one. I'll tell you right out that her father is Colonel Mawley in charge of all GIs on R&R in Bangkok. And if I find out your names and what unit you're from you'll all be up shit's creek without a paddle!"

"The *ladies*," Freeman said, "suggest that since we don't know how to act in front of *ladies*, they will drop all pretensions to being such, and that furthermore and henceforth, if they can establish our nomenclature, we will be up a well known estuary without a tangible means of propulsion."

The bleached blond's fat companion spoke again. "Isn't it something how some people get killed in the war and how some cowards manage to get out of fighting?"

"I think," said Hogbody, scratching his head, "they're having a self-criticism session over there."

The two ladies got up in a huff and left just as the Mamasan yelled: "Midnight! Happy New Year, everybody!' " Everyone began singing Auld Lang Sine along with a jukebox recording.

When most of the noise had abated, several GIs, obviously on R&R from Vietnam, walked to the microphone which had just been set up for the off-key Thai band. I say "obviously on R&R from Vietnam," but am ill-prepared to define how we always knew. But in the room full of people deeply immersed in Bacchanalian revelry, they appeared as candidates for the Masque of the Red Death. In the 1980s, Kurt Vonnegut would grapple with the question by asking, "What makes the Vietnam veterans so somehow spooky? We could describe them as being 'unwholesomely mature.'"

Four "unwholesomely mature" veterans of jungle combat began singing in voices that made us realize that they weren't amateurs. All other sounds in the room stopped. Their song was to the tune of "Hush, Hush, Sweet Charlotte":

"Hush, hush, sweet Vietnam, Vietnam, don't you cry
Hush, hush, sweet Vietnam, We'll bomb you 'til you die
You had to fight the French and Japanese,
Now you fight the Americans too

When will your land be left in peace,
When will all your sorrow be through?
Oh, hush now,
Hush, hush, sweet Vietnam, Vietnam, don't you cry
Hush, Hush, sweet Vietnam, We'll bomb you 'til you die.
You hold your still baby in your arms,
Its blood and tears have all been wept
But hush sweet Vietnam don't you cry.
America's commitments will be kept!
Oh, hush now,
Hush, hush, Sweet Vietnam, Vietnam, don't you cry
Hush, hush, sweet Vietnam, We'll bomb you til you die.
Oh, hush now,
Hush, hush, sweet Vietnam, Vietnam, don't you cry
Hush, hush, sweet Vietnam, We'll bomb you 'til . . . you . . . die."

During the song, Bumbles and several other NCOs at various tables had been obviously incensed by the lack of patriotism in the verses. An NCO at a table near the microphone stood up and shouted something at one of the singers. At the same moment, the same inebriated Thai returned from the men's room and this time stopped at Bumble's table. He saw Bumbles' chest hair through his open shirt and reached to touch it. "Oh, you have much," he said. "Very good."

I saw the scuffle break out as the singer attacked the NCO doing the taunting. Just as tables overturned at the front of the room, Bumbles was on his feet slugging the Thai on the jaw. The Thai went back about three feet and then went down, his eyes and mouth opened wide in shock. One of his friends at his table stood and threw a Singha beer bottle which smashed against the wall near our table. Two other Thais got up and started toward Bumbles but were suddenly enveloped in the fighting which had begun at the front of the room and was spreading like a contagious disease. In a matter of seconds, the entire bar had become involved in a brawl.

As Taylor tried to say something to one of the Thais, he was kicked on the hip by a Thai boxing kick. Taylor ignored the blow but continued to try to stop the melee. The veterans were fighting with anyone who wasn't with them, which meant most of the bar. I saw one of them exchange blows with Bumbles just as a beer mug smashed into a painting above my head. It hit the left breast of a naked Thai girl on a water buffalo and sent the wanton tableau spinning to the floor. Within seconds, several Thais and several GIs on R&R had knives or broken bottles in their hands. As my main interest in such a situation was defense, my only active contribution was the aiming of a chair at the back of a well-built, knife-wielding Thai who, unfortunately, moved just as I let go. The chair gave Hogbody a stunning blow.

The general fighting became confusing as well as dangerous. Taylor let out a yell and fell into the Christmas tree. The Calvary was sent flying across the floor against the wall. Hogbody and I rushed over to him. The fighting was stopping and Thais and GIs were running out the door. At first we thought he had just had the wind knocked out of him. As I helped turn him over from his prone position I felt the viscous warmth of the blood. Hogbody's fingers touched the handle of the knife sticking out of his stomach like a dirty joke.

31

A THAI KISS
2 January 1969

It wasn't until the following night that an American nurse in the military hospital allowed us a few minutes with him. The group consisted of Preyapan, Mr. Jayasutra, Dang, Good Pork Betty, Doc Spitz, Wat, Fat Eddy, Freeman, Hogbody, Patterson and myself. As we approached the bed the nurse remained near the door. Only Taylor's left arm was out of the covers. The tube and bottle were attached to it. His face was pallid and his eyes were closed. Freeman and I led Preyapan over to a chair next to the bed. We sat her down and put her hand on Taylor's. Taylor opened his eyes and looked at her. He spoke in a soft, disembodied voice. "Hello, Preyapan."

"Hello, Rick."

After a few moments of silence in which Rick seemed to be fading, Wat spoke. "Hey, Rick, you better get better. Bumbles say now have fucking war on."

"Yeah, Rick," Freeman said. "The lifers are making up for lost time since you've been away. They been dickin' people away right and left."

"Preyapan was asking me where that nut with the mustache was," Hogbody said.

"That's right," I said. "She says she kind of loves him."

Taylor's eyes remained on Preyapan. He spoke laboriously and obviously with pain. "Pineapple."

I moved closer. "Right here."

"Take . . . take care of her."

"You know I will," And then I quickly added, "until you're well."

"Freeze?"

"Right here." Taylor motioned for him to lean forward. He placed his ear close to Taylor's mouth. I couldn't quite make out what Taylor said. Freeman straightened up slowly. "Move your nose over," he said.

After a few moments, Taylor spoke again. "Don't let the . . . Jesus, it's cold."

The nurse moved to the bed and put her hand on Taylor's forehead. Then she pressed the call button. "I'm sorry, but you'll have to leave now," she spoke to us but her eyes were on Taylor. *I'm sorry but you'll have to leave now.*

As we left, Preyapan lingered behind, while Mr. Jayasutra waited near the door. I saw Preyapan lean forward to sniff Taylor's cheek in a Thai-style kiss. Her black eyes first brimmed and then flooded with tears. As she stared at Taylor she tilted her head in such a way that it seemed impossible to believe she could not actually see him. She spoke in English. "I love you, Rick."

Taylor kissed her hands and her face. "I'll never . . . leave you," he said.

Doc Spitz re-entered the room with another doctor and walked quickly to the bed. Mr. Jayasutra took Preyapan out.

32

NOTICES
3 January 1969

The next morning just before mail call we crowded around the bulletin board near the mail room. The usual pictures of those in the chain of command from Johnson down to Blinky were above the board. But everyone's attention was focused on the notices. The first one read:

> MEMORIAL SERVICES FOR SPECIALIST 4TH-CLASS RICHARD TAYLOR WILL BE HELD AT 4 O'CLOCK FRIDAY AFTERNOON.

Slightly to the right of that was another notice:

> ATTENTION:
>
> JACK'S OFF BAR IN PATPONG ROAD IS OFF LIMITS TO ALL MEMBERS OF THIS UNIT UNTIL FURTHER NOTICE.
> (SIGNED)
> MAJOR THOMPSON

And slightly below that was the third notice:

> ATTENTION:
>
> NO—REPEAT—NO MEMBERS OF THIS COMMAND

WILL CARRY BOXES THROUGH THE COURT AREA UN-
LESS REQUIRED TO DO SO IN PERFORMANCE OF
THEIR DUTIES. VIOLATORS WILL BE PUNISHED.
(SIGNED)
MAJOR THOMPSON.

As we moved away, I heard two voices, but I couldn't see who spoke. "Life is shitty," said the first voice.

"Life is all right, it's just people who are shitty."

33

THE VERDICT
5 January 1969

Two days later, many of the Bangkok Warriors had left for the Land of the Big PX. Even Blinky's tour was nearly over. His replacement had arrived at the court about a week before and had let it be known that as soon as he took command, he intended to "put this unit back in the army." Patterson, Hogbody, Freeman and I and several other GIs were sitting silently around tables and drinking in the club.

None of us knew who had plunged the knife into Taylor. Fixing the blame really didn't interest us anyway. Had he been killed because of the depth of American passion over the Vietnam War or by the different attitudes toward masculinity that exist between American Southerners and Thai Buddhists? Or simply because, as Preyapan said, it was his *karma*. Whatever the reason, his death had knocked the wind out of us more than anything Blinky could have done. And I knew we had to do something to regain our strength and spirit.

Patterson suddenly crushed a beer can and threw it across the room. "Damn! I wish to hell it had been me." He placed his hands carefully on the table and stared at them. Then he spoke again. "Why the hell couldn't it have been me?"

I looked up and stared at him intently for several seconds.

Then I spoke with an incredulous tone of voice. "You! . . . You! Why couldn't it have been you? Because you're a goddamn minor character that's why! Rick told you that a hundred times. His fucking body isn't even cold and you start beggin' to be a major fucking character!"

Other GIs joined in the attack. "That's right!" Hogbody said. "You're just a goddamn foil!"

"Yeah," Freeman said bitterly. "You know goddamn well it had to happen to Rick, not you, you greedy bastard."

Wat pointed at Patterson, "Him guilty!"

Patterson was confused. "Wait a minute! I only said   "

I stood and pointed a hand with a beer can in it at Patterson. "Meeting of the Tennis Elbow Club!"

"No, goddamn it!" Patterson yelled. "I'm not—"

But the room came to life with angry voices of accusation and denunciation and the sounds of moving tables and chairs. Patterson's table was separated from the rest and two GIs moved his chair into the center of the room with him in it.

"Fuck you bastards. I didn't do anything and I'm not guilty. You pricks just want somebody to dick over. Well, get your jollies off somewhere else. There isn't any goddamn reason for a fucking trial and you goddamn well know it. Leave me the fuck alone!"

Wat slipped the black book on the bar for me to pick up, Freeman affixed Lincoln to the wall in his place of honor, and the trial began. In the sudden silence, I spoke slowly and deliberately. "Hear ye, hear ye, hear ye, the 19th session of the Tennis Elbow Club is about to begin. Specialist 4th Class Roy Patterson, GI, high school graduate, all-round general fuckup, minor character and foil, you are hereby accused of trying to impersonate a major character in this fucking outfit. How do you plead?"

The verdict was never in doubt.

ABOUT THE AUTHOR

Dean Barrett first arrived in Thailand as a Chinese linguist with the Army Security Agency during the Vietnam War and was stationed with the 83rd Radio Research and Special Operations Unit. He later returned to Asia and lived for 17 years in Hong Kong and Bangkok. His writing and photography on Thailand have won several awards. His other novels set in Asia are *Kingdom of Make-Believe - A Novel of Thailand* and *Hangman's Point - A Novel of Hong Kong*.

This first American edition of *Memoirs of a Bangkok Warrior* was printed for Village East Books in 1999 by Bang Printing. Typeface is Monotype Bembo, a 1929 design supervised by Stanley Morison and based on typefaces cut by Francesco Griffo in 1495. Designed, composed and set by John Taylor-Convery at JTC Imagineering.